THE CAVES

A NOVEL

iBooks
Habent Sua Fata Libelli

iBooks
1230 Park Avenue
New York, New York 10128
Tel: 212-427-7139
bricktower@aol.com • www.ibooksinc.com

Library of Congress Cataloging-in-Publication Data

Taylor, John R.
The Caves, A Novel
p. cm.

1. Fiction—General 2. Fiction—Thriller 3. Fiction—Military
3. Fiction—Vietnamese War
Fiction, I. Title.

ISBN: 978-1-59687-977-5, Hardcover
978-1-59687-971-3, Trade Paper

September 2013

THE CAVES

A NOVEL

JOHN R. "RICK" TAYLOR

AUTHOR OF GRUNT AIR
and
A FEW BRAVE MEN

Author's Website:

http://www.afbm-blackbart.com/

Dedication

This is my third novel and in the two before this I always give tribute to great military leaders in the history of America and those exceptional people in my own personal life. Thanks to my wonderful parents I had the opportunity to go to St. Johns Military School in Salina, Kansas. The school transformed me from an academic underachiever and mildly rebellious kid with no focus into a disciplined young man with an excellent high school education. I had become a young leader with a vision and direction for the future. I owe the school a great deal as it was the turning point in my young life. The school has been blessed with a long line of outstanding leaders since 1887. In my lifetime there was Colonel Remy Clem, Keith Duckers, Russ Guernsey (whom my oldest son is named after) and more recently D. Dale Browning. Browning is also a St. Johns graduate that has become a laudable success in the banking and investment business. Several years ago the school fell victim to the economic downturn and less than stellar management. The school was suffering financially but not traditionally. Dale saw the problem and redirected a substantial portion of his life and business affairs to the salvation of the school. His dynamic personality combined with his exceptional business and leadership skills saved the school from closing and in the process totally rejuvenated the school. He used his powers of persuasion to raise millions for the renovation of the aging facilities and has created a state of the art educational facility staffed with the absolute cream of the crop classroom teachers. You haven't lived until that six foot six hulk of a man looks down on you smiling and saying, "I would like for you to…." You had rather check into GITMO before you said no to him. His efforts have resulted in new Hi-Tec classrooms and a dormitory that would make Hilton and West Point envious. Dale has not only saved the school but has elevated the academic quality back to the exceptional educational facility that I enjoyed.

Thank you Dale for saving our school! This book is dedicated to you for all that you have done for St. Johns.

SJMS Forever!

Chapter One

SONGBIRD INTERCEPT
Monday, 20 November 1972

Deep in the bowels of the National Security Agency building some ten miles north of the Capitol, Eddie Reeves listened to the North Vietnamese Army (NVA) High Command radio communications and decoded all transmissions regarding POWs (Codename "Songbird"). It was a little after one in the morning, Washington time, but it was just after two in the afternoon in Hanoi at the NVA High command. He started analyzing what was a longer than usual message from the Ministry of Public Security (MPS) to the General Political Directorate (GPD) for further transmission to the Enemy Proselytizing Department and Binh Tram commanders along the Ho Chi Minh Trail. Eddie could tell, after reading to whom this Top Secret message was addressed to, that this would be really important.

It was his duty to read and analyze all messages like this one that applied to American POWs since the NSA's legendary Jerry Mooney and Berkley Cook were not available. The full responsibility of getting the entire message accurately translated and analyzing its relevant meaning was his. As he read further he became cold and shaken causing him to spill some coffee on his desk and tan slacks without noticing it. "This is terrible," he thought. "They're getting ready to kill our prisoners." This time, the order came from the top, obviously at the direction of the Communist Party leadership.

His mind flashed back to previous execution orders that came from much lower commanders. He remembered the situation in April

1970 when two F4 pilots were shot down north of the DMZ. One was rescued but the other was captured and reportedly executed on order. The NSA intercepted a message that ordered the 238th Surface to Air Regiment to reposition across the Ban Karai Pass and take up position to shoot down the USAF U-2 spy planes (Codename: "Olympic Torch") as they flew down the Ho Chi Minh Trail. This intercept resulted in a B-52 "Arclight" strike on the unit before it could shoot down the U-2. Another incident was when the commander of the AAA unit guarding the 258th SAM Regiment was killed and the unit suffered very heavy damage by an airstrike on 5 April 70. The higher headquarters commander at the 367th Air Defense Division ordered that the next U.S. Pilot captured be executed in retaliation. This was not the last execution ordered. Eddie then remembered another event just after he was assigned to the Songbird team. They intercepted an execution message issued in retaliation of an F-4 pilot killing a senior officer of the 284th AAA regiment in another airstrike. Another execution intercept caused a "Flash" message to be sent out from the NSA to the headquarters of the Military Assistance Command-Vietnam ("MACV") on 6 July 72 advising them of the imminent execution of ten U.S. Pilots on 8 July near the South Vietnam border on Hill 310. The NVA unit was directed to relocate to another position near the Ho Chi Minh Trail. Selected personnel were to be left behind to kill the ten American POWs they had captured, complete the execution, and rejoin the unit, leaving no trace of the execution. This bothered Reeves deeply but not as much as the message before him.

He should have seen this coming two weeks before, since he got another major directive from the Ministry of Public Security directing that those American POWs selected for movement were to be moved to Hanoi and then to Russia and Romania for additional questioning. Those POWs were considered to be of high value, specifically very special officers such as Wild Weasel crews, Electronic Warfare Office, Navy Bombardier/Navigators, and advanced technology personnel. Those were the cream of U.S. secret technology and tactics. Talk about a brain drain on U.S. secrets! Wow! He read on with increasing anxiety.

The party headquarters reported that progress was being made in negotiation with the Americans. A satisfactory conclusion was expected by year-end or early 1973. The party directed that the MPS undertake certain preparations prior to the anticipated settlement, with the Americans:

1. All designated prisoners previously classified in MPS message, dated 6 November 1972, and were to be transported to their assigned accommodations in Hanoi and Vinh prior to 1 December 1972. Binh Tram commanders were directed to give elevated priority to the timely movement of the high value prisoners.

2. All other prisoners were to be relocated as directed by 15 December 1972 to camps in Laos identified by the Supreme Headquarters in San Neua area:

Ban Nakay Neua Complex
Ban Nakay Eune
Ban Nakay Teu
Ban Nakay Puem
Muong Soi Prison

3. The Enemy Proselytizing Department officers at each of the facilities identified above were, under the supervision of the General Political Directorate, to be prepared, upon direct order from headquarters, to execute all prisoners. All evidence and personal articles of their existence were to be destroyed. This action was to be completed within 24 hours after the direct order was given. General Political Directorate was charged with the confirmation to this headquarters that the executions were accomplished and that there was no evidence of the prisoners or their executions. The party considered the timely and efficient completion of this matter to be of the highest importance to the Revolution and the successful completion to the war.

All subordinate commanders were to acknowledge their receipt of this order.

Signed by ...

Reeves didn't care. He was sickened and emotionally drained by the message.

Eddie, realizing the critical importance of the message, snapped himself out of his mental stupor. He refocused on the accuracy of his translation and its specific meaning. This had to go to the top immediately. They only had 25 days to react to this impending slaughter of our prisoners. He needed to go to the bathroom but that had to wait until he completed his transmittal to his boss and the Command Authority and the President's personal attention. After reading and rereading his report he got up and took it to the senior duty officer.

The superior duty officer was visibly shaken. He immediately sent this message by Flash priority to the Head of the NSA, Director CIA, Chairman Joint Chiefs of Staff, Secretary of Defense, Secretary of State and White House. After the message went out, the duty officer looked at Reeves and said, "This could have enormous repercussion and consequences. I just hope the President doesn't let this happen. It'll be a tough call given the current political situation."

Fifteen minutes later, the bedside secure phone rang next to the Chairman of the Joint Chiefs of Staff. The Admiral looked at the clock and knew it had to be damned important for them to call him at this hour.

"Yes," the chairman said with some irritation. The metallic voice over the encrypted phone line told him of the Flash message.

"My God," he said, "Call the key staff and other Chiefs." I want a meeting on this at 0900 hours." The voice responded with an "Aye, aye, sir."

Chapter Two

RATS!

Air Force Captain Robert O. Felderhoff laid on his back looking up at the limestone ceiling of the Cave located near Ban Nakay Enue trying to get comfortable so sleep would come sooner than later. His wrists were tightly secured by the homemade handcuffs that were too small for a man of his size. They would be a good fit for a small Asian man but not a six foot three heavy set black man from the Langdon area of Northeast Washington, D.C. He and three of the eight Air Force officers in the cave were also handcuffed to the same floor anchor. This made movement of any kind very difficult and would adversely affect the others who shared his discomfort. The other four were also handcuffed, but to what the Dinks called a bed. The bed was three boards put together across two carpenter's sawhorses. The good news was it was off the cold damp floor of the cave. The bad news it was only a little over four feet long. That made sleeping almost impossible due the length of the body of the man attached with cuffs. Comfort was not one of the NVA's objectives. Bob Felderhoff knew that he would be in this position for at least ten to twelve hours. He had been accustomed to this routine since his shoot-down almost a year and a half ago. A lot had happened to him in that time and he would never forget any of it EVER! These were horrifying memories that he could never wipe from his mind. He looked at the newest member of their cave and hoped that he would survive the ordeal.

Felderhoff shut his eyes and went back to his capture after a NVA 57 millimeter gun crew got lucky and shot his F-105 "Wild Weasel" down near Vinh City in August 1971. At first the local farmers beat him with poles, sticks and anything else they could pick up. Then the NVA Regulars showed up and stopped the assault. He was taken to the POW camp known as "Portholes" due to its proximity to the Yellow Sea. There were at least a dozen others going through hell on earth. During his interrogation he kept to his prepared story that he was just an F-4 Phantom pilot. It was widely known that Wild Weasel crews were interrogated much more severely due to the secret technical aspects of their mission and equipment. This worked out fine in the first two interrogations but that came to an end when they brought in parts of his F-105 and his helmet bag that had his name embroidered on it. That's when his captors really got mad and started beating the hell out of him for lying to them. This abuse continued until he and Navy Lieutenant Ed Mattingly, along with six others who had been kept separate, were moved up the Ho Chi Minh Trail to the Sam Neua area last October. The other group had been made to build a set of wooden stocks to secure the POWs. They had taken a large wooden beam and split it down the middle. Then they cut out opposing half moon holes on each side of the beam. The guards were watching to make sure that the holes would be tight and not let someone squeeze out and escape. They smoothed the wood the best that they could with the primitive tools that were provided, but by no means was it smooth and splinter free.

It was just as the sun started up on the east horizon when the Gomers drove an old truck into the compound. It was obviously Chinese made and well worn. All vehicles used in the massive supply operation along the Ho Chi Minh Trail were moving wrecks. The Binh Tram troops that coordinated and operated the supply system had mechanics and scarce repair parts spotted along the trail to maintain the vehicles and keep them hauling was supplies to their troops in the South. Every truck, car, wagon, and even bicycles, were considered precious and of importance to the effort. They were lucky that they were riding in a north bound truck instead of walking the 250 miles to Sam Neua. That spoke to the value the prisoners represented to the North Vietnam government. The group of six brought the wooden stocks out of the mechanics shed and placed them in the rear of the truck. The top half was lifted up and put to the side per the direction of a NVA sergeant who didn't look like he was too thrilled to be assigned to the task. A couple of wooden boxes, five gallon buckets and gas cans were put in the truck as well. The group was instructed to sit down next to the truck. Five minutes had passed when a young and cocky NVA officer came out and directed the sergeant to load the group.

The group of six got into the back of the truck and lay down on their backs in opposing directions. The first set of wooden stock holes were filled with the ankles of a POW that had his head toward the front of the truck. The second sets of holes were filled by a POW whose head was closest to the rear. The next four positions were filled in the same manner. Those left two slots open. It was then that Mattingly and Felderhoff were surprised to find themselves being herded by the guards to the truck and the open stock positions. Once in position the sergeant and another guard lifted the heavy wooden top section of the beam into place and locked it down. The sergeant and officer got in the truck and started the drive north.

The steel floor was hard on the men as it bounced along the very rough road. The stock holes were rough and abrasive to the skin. This wore the skin down to where it would bleed and become infected. One day a gas can was thrown on its side and a small leak started. The gas spread across the floor of the truck bed and added to the skin irritation on the scalp, backs and thighs of the POWs. At the next fuel stop the sergeant righted the can but the damage had been done. After almost a week of traveling over the frequently bombed out road, the ankles had become badly infected and the majority had become incontinent with severe diarrhea and urine which further contaminated the festering skin abrasions. The guard would take a bucket of water and throw it into the back of the truck to wash out some of the urine, feces and infected puss. They would also feed the POWs some cold rice and fish once a day. This may have kept the POWs alive but it did contribute to the never ending diarrhea problem and to the POWs that was a problem.

In the beginning of the trip the eight POWs talked freely and shared personal information and experiences. Towards the end there was very little conversation as the pain of the burses on the back of their heads, their backs and from the bouncing on the rough road and fever from infections had taken away the will and ability to say much. The truck slowed as it came into a small town surrounded by high rugged hills and limestone karsts. To the POWs, it was just another town in the middle of nowhere but it was the end of the road for them. The officer got out and walked over to a small limestone and thatch building and reported to a NVA Colonel and three other officers. There were smiles and friendly comments between the group and the young officer. They walked over to the back of the truck to look at the POWs. The Colonel became outraged at the condition the prisoners were in. He started yelling at the officer about the high value that these POWs represented to the Central Government in Hanoi. He then instructed one of the other officers to get us out. Other soldiers came out running to assist. The Colonel directed instructions to another two officers who immediately grabbed the young officer and took him off behind the building. Two shots were heard coming from behind the building. That brought smiles to the filthy POW faces despite the pain and fever. They were removed from the truck and taken to a stream where we got to clean up from our trip. Two were so ill that they had to be carried by the others. The water was cool, invigorating and refreshing to the men who savored every moment in the water. After they were clean, the local NVA doctor tended to their illness and infections. The medicine was limited to sulfa powder but served their needs. They were then fed and then taken to their various cells in the local caves. Generally the NVA gave the POWs food and water twice a day. It wasn't much but the 600 grams was greatly appreciated. The group was taken over the steep hill behind the local headquarters building to the cave at Ban Nakay Enue. The cave was about fifteen foot wide and nine foot tall. It went back into the karst about ninety feet possibly more. It had a four foot high rock and cement blast deflector some twenty five feet in front of the cave. Of course there was the usual concertina barbed wire fence surrounding the front of the cave in a thirty foot arc. The cave had lights provided by a generator. The lights were used for the benefit of the guards, not the POWs. The cave also had a phone just outside that went to the local headquarters intelligence office. Twice a day the guards would take them out in front of the caves for about an hour to get some sunlight and exercise. Then back into the usually dark and damp caves. The fourth day came and with it the resumption of the interrogations. The NVA interrogators were much more professional than those in Vinh. That wasn't good news for them.

Night fall came early and they settled in for the night. Felderhoff was about to go to sleep when he felt something run across his legs.

"Shit," he exclaimed, "Rats!"

Chapter 3

WE HAVE MET THE ENEMY AND IT IS US

Newly promoted Brigadier General Morton J. Herbert stood at attention as the Chairman of the Joint Chiefs of Staff entered the secure conference room in the basement of the Pentagon. He motioned for the assembled group of the highest military officers of the nation to take their seats. Present were the Chiefs of Staff of each branch of the service, as well as a representative of the Central Intelligence Agency, the U.S. State Department, National Security Agency and other very senior officers like Herbert's boss Stewart Jackson Lee, the Joint Chief of Staff for Plans and Policy Directorate, more commonly referred to as "The J5."

"OK, gentlemen," started the Chairman. "You have the message text and the Situation Evaluation Summary from the CIA and NSA. What options do we have available for extraction? Start with the Army."

"Sir," the famous heavy frame Army Chief of Staff stated. "All of our SOG-OPS-80 Teams, Navy Seals, Air Force Green Hornets and Green Beret units capable of this type of mission have stood down or departed country. To organize a competent force, gather adequate Intelligence, train and deploy would take at least 6 to 8 weeks minimum. If we take shortcuts to reduce time, we endanger mission personnel and the POW's. We have almost no current or confirmed Intelligence on the area. We would need to get four or five recon teams in there to properly evaluate the situation and area. That's assuming we can even get them in there with out compromising the mission or losing the personnel. That is truly in the backyard of the North Vietnamese Army and Pathet Lao headquarters for all of Laos. Besides the lack of Intel and qualified personnel, we just don't have the time to do it right. Even if we cut corners and did meet the time schedule, the size and complexity of the force would be as big of an undertaking as the Son Tay Raid. They had months to prepare and we have less than a month," the general said in exasperation and frustration.

The Chairman looked over at Major General Lucius Sommer, the acting Joint Chief for Intelligence J-2, and Bob Langdon the Deputy Director of Central Intelligence Agency and pointed in the direction of the two men. "On a crash basis, can you get the Intel that the Army and Air Force are going to need to pull this off in time?"

Sommers looked over to the CIA rep to his left who slightly shook his head negatively, then looked back to the Chairman and stated in a clear and confident tone, "Not a chance, sir. I am very familiar with massive the Intel ramp up on the Son Tay Raid and we just can't do it in time. The lack of viable Intel could jeopardize the mission and possibly create a political nightmare for Kissinger. I see Kingston from the State Department over there shaking his head in agreement, sir."

"Gentlemen," he said with a slight note of anger, "you aren't being very helpful. I just can't let these guys be lined up and shot. I also can't risk the political fallout and deaths of our strike force by going in unprepared. Can anyone think of any reasonable possibility that can save these guys?"

"Sir," sounded off the barrel-chested J-5, Lieutenant General Stonewall Jackson "Jack" Lee, "with me today is Mo Herbert, who just arrived here from Headquarters, 7th Air Force, who thinks there may be an option open to us. Mo, brief the Chairman," the burly Marine Corps general said.

From the far side of the room, General Spike was overheard saying to the Air Force Chief of Staff, "Oh great, another Coroneos disciple in the Pentagon."

The Chairman looked at General Spike with a cold look, then back to Herbert. "At this point I'd listen to a plan from just about anyone, even George McGovern. What do you have?"

Herbert stood up and started to brief the Chairman. "Sir, General Coroneos had formed a crash site evaluation unit to cover the northeastern Laos area and ..."

General Spike interrupted in a hateful tone, "They were non-combatants and nothing more than an administrative evaluation team. It's just another one of Coroneos' Follies."

"Spike, dammit, I want to hear his idea!" the Chairman retorted. "OK, hold on, Mo. We aren't getting anywhere fast. Let's break at this point. All of you review one last time your assets and Intelligence. We will reconvene at 1300 and go over the options then. Gentlemen, I want options, not excuses. Any questions? OK, Mo, you, General Lee and Captain Bayouth stay behind."

Everyone stood and departed the meeting room except the Chairman, Herbert, Lee, and a heretofore unnoticed Navy Captain sitting quietly in the corner of the room. They moved toward the Chairman and listened as he spoke. "I can't stand that SOB! His petty hatred for Coroneos constantly gets in the way."

Then the Chairman looked directly at Herbert as he folded his arms across his chest. "OK, Mo, what's on your mind? Do you really have something?"

"Sir, can this be off the record?"

The Chairman replied as he nodded, "Sure."

"There is a possible option open to us. Actually, there is a unit that is experienced, trained, and very familiar with the Laos POW matter. General Spike is wrong! What he and others didn't know is that General Coroneos had set up a small tactical unit under the Crash Site Evaluation Program authorized by Ambassador Godley. They were substantially more than that. Do you remember the detailed Intelligence reports that came out at the very beginning of the NVA Dry Season offensive earlier this year? I think that you will agree that they were extremely detailed and accurate. Also, the prisoners that Vang Pao supposedly rescued were actually rescued by this unit."

"You mean Sister Jannette was not rescued by Vang Pao?" said the Chairman.

"No, sir." replied Herbert. It was done under great secrecy by this unit.

"Sister Jannette is a very close friend of my priest. She gave a seminar at the church last month. She never would talk about it, she just said that God's Angels from the Sky came and got them. I assume that she was referring to Vang Pao. How do you know this to be factual?" the Chairman questioned in a stern tone.

"The day of the raid Coroneos sent me up to observe the operation. Unexpectedly they were short a qualified copilot so I flew the mission with the Ops Officer as his copilot. Over the course of preceding three months I observed them set up every detail of the planning and I actually went on the mission. The CO of the unit is unorthodox and very competent. I understand that they have been planning several different scenarios to go back after the POWs in northeast Laos and in particular, The Caves. After the raid last December they were deployed from Udorn Royal Thai Airbase in Northern Thailand to Clark Air Force base in the Philippines when General Coroneos was relieved."

"This is incredible. This is far beyond belief, Mo," the Admiral said in a doubtful tone of voice.

"Sir, may I call General Mattox at Offutt Air Force Base and let him confirm what I just said? If he does confirm, will you call Major Roman to your office for a private briefing off the record?"

"Very well. Go ahead. This does sound like something Coroneos would cook up. Get Mattox on the horn."

Herbert activated the secure speaker phone and dialed a number from memory.

"Good Morning, sir. This is Mo Herbert. I am here at the Chairman's office and you are on a speaker phone. Sir, we have an extremely serious situation concerning the POWs in the caves. Some sixty or so prisoners are scheduled to be executed on order depending on the outcome of the Kissinger negotiations. There are less than thirty days to react. I would like to recommend to the Chairman ..."

Mattox interrupted, "Get Roman! Now! He's the only one who can do it."

"General Mattox, this is the Chairman. At Mo's request this is an off the record conversation. He has indicated that this unit you speak of has done some very amazing things and has kept it secret, including a POW rescue in Laos. Is there any truth to it?"

"Sir, I don't know what Mo has told you but I will say that if you want to save those poor devils, get Dan Roman. His Big Casino raid was an unqualified success. He can do it, period! Tell him the facts. If he says he can do it, he will succeed. He may also say no. If he does, then it's hopeless. He knows the area and is very experienced in this type of mission. He is very competent, loyal and obviously he can keep a secret. I hope that answers your question, sir."

"Thank you, General it does. Goodbye," the Chairman said as he disconnected the phone and looked at Herbert. "OK, Mo, start from the very beginning and leave out no details. What is the fairytale story about this Roman fella and his hot shot unit that I have never heard of? I assume that it will start off "Once Upon a Time ..."

Herbert smiled and took a deep breath and started recounting the history of the unit. "Sir, in July of 1971 we all saw the Vietnam peace talks in Paris going nowhere, especially when discussion turned to the POW issue. The North Vietnamese stalled those discussions because, with the American public heatedly divided about the Vietnam War, the POW issue was their ace-in-the-hole. Furthermore the U.S. Military 'draw down' in Vietnam had effectively ended most efforts to recover American POWs in Laos and Cambodia. The U.S. was eager for an end to the war and was afraid that continued rescue missions Might be construed as hostile acts, which Might slow down the peace talks. This frustrated General 'Pistol Pete' Coroneos, the Commanding General of the 7th Air Force in Southeast Asia.

"He wasn't going to let Washington force him to keep using outdated Rules of Engagement and leave downed pilots behind in the hands of the enemy. You know Coroneos and his loyalty to his men. He was a man with a need for a loophole. In this case, the loophole provided the Commanding General with a ruse to rescue pilots who had been shot down and were being held and tortured by the enemy in Laos and Cambodia.

"The U.S. Ambassador to Laos authorized small, lightly guarded military survey teams to go into American aircraft crash sites for crash site evaluations. The information we got from these evaluations were used for future pilot training. Washington didn't realize that by authorizing these evaluation teams, it opened a loophole for clandestine POW rescue operations.

"When Washington authorized these crash site teams, Coroneos put together an elite combined forces unit using the best ground reconnaissance and intelligence support personnel he could find, in direct support of combat veteran Army helicopter pilots. The unit was nicknamed "Grunt Air" by the Air Force boys. It was formed in late July 1971 and deployed to Udorn Royal Thai Air Force Base in Thailand. Officially, Grunt Air flew crash site missions while secretly locating downed pilots and POWs who were held in the northern part of Laos and the Plain of Jars. To avoid suspicion, Grunt Air flew back to Udorn each night, just as any non-combat, purely technical team would do.

"The original commander of Grunt Air was a by-the-book professional, good at administration but lousy at combat. The Commanding General soon replaced him with Dan Roman, a somewhat irreverent Army Captain flying combat assault missions with the 175th in the Mekong Delta. Previously, Roman had flown some off the books clandestine counterinsurgency missions for Major General Mattox, in Colombia some years before. His impressive history of flying clandestine and dangerous operations persuaded the General to transfer him to Grunt Air. Roman was a no-nonsense, get-it-done type leader, with zero tolerance for unrealistic regulations and naive, egotistical 'staffers.' His attitude often landed him in trouble. In short, Roman was the perfect man to lead clandestine rescue missions behind enemy lines.

"Not long after Roman took over Grunt Air, three POWs were located in a North Vietnamese prison camp called 'The Homestead.' The NVA had captured the officers - an American, an Australian and a South Vietnamese - and were holding them at a point along the route to Hanoi. Grunt Air sent news about the POWs to the Commanding General, who soon discovered that these three officers were regarded as high priority captives. The officers had knowledge of sensitive information that could under no circumstance reach enemy commanders in Hanoi and Moscow. Their fate was sealed: either Grunt Air rescue these men or a B-52 strike would be ordered to take care of them.

"Roman's obsession about leaving no man behind compelled him to track the three prisoners and spring a rescue when the time was right. The key to the operation was that nothing could compromise Grunt Air's secret mission. Its real objective had to remain a secret. Otherwise, staffers and Coroneos critics like General Spike would shut the unit down.

"Roman ordered his recon teams to search the Plain of Jars for other POWs while they kept track of the NVA's three high priority captives. Roman patiently devised a plan to rescue the officers before they checked in to the notorious Hanoi Hilton prison or blown into oblivion by B-52s.

"On December 17, 1971, the North Vietnamese Army started an all-out Dry Season Offensive to take over Laos. Grunt Air's deployed recon units in northern Laos were situated in strategic positions. Not only could the recon teams follow the transfer of the three high-priority POWs, but they were also able to monitor the advance of the NVA and provide real-time intelligence to Headquarters 7th Air Force, information that enabled the enemy thrust to be halted by tactical air strikes.

"Using intelligence obtained from these reconnaissance operations, Roman concocted a deception plan using fake documents to bait the NVA into moving the three POWs to Camp number 711, which was nicknamed the 'Big Casino.' The camp was near the NVA Headquarters for Laos at Sam Neua, just 22 miles from the North Vietnam border and 125 miles from Hanoi. Roman felt that the camp was so far into NVA held territory that it would be lightly guarded and vulnerable to a surprise attack. Roman's deception plan worked and the NVA took the bait. They moved the prisoners to the 'Big Casino,' thinking it was the safest place to hold the POWs before moving them to Hanoi. This was the decision Roman wanted the NVA to make; it was the decision that would make a surprise rescue mission possible. He clandestinely moved men and equipment into an abandoned USAF tactical radar site known as Site 85. You may remember the radar SKYSPOT site as the Heavy Green operation which used radar to assist bomb delivery in bad weather. Site 85 was on one of the very highest and inaccessible mountains in far northern Laos. It was a perfect location to execute the very dangerous rescue mission at the Big Casino.

"At great risk to his career, General Coroneos approved Roman's plan, giving Grunt Air the go-ahead to extract the POWs. On the night of January 19, 1972, within sight of the lights of Hanoi, Grunt Air launched their rescue operation. Flying low through the dark mountainous valleys out of sight and sound of the enemy as they went to the Big Casino. The Recon teams busted into the camp initially without a shot being fired. They had achieved the mission critical element of surprise. Unfortunately a phone was accidentally knocked over in a struggle alerting the local enemy military forces in nearby Sam Neua. The enemy arrived just as the Grunt Air attack force was ready to depart with the three high value prisoners as well as other military and civilian prisoners whose presence was not known until the raid was executed. This included a delirious American nun who had been repeatedly beaten and raped by the enemy captors. Yes, that was Sister Jannette. A violent gun battle occurred that destroyed a helicopter and killed Roman's best friend, Jan Toothman, the unit Operations Officer. I was his copilot when he bought the farm. We beat back the attack and flew to a Laotian airfield where Laotian General Vang Pao was waiting to take charge of the POWs and return them to the USA, without exposing Grunt Air and its critical ongoing mission.

"While the secret rescue mission was being executed, the President had relieved General Coroneos of command for violations of the Rules of Engagement covering air strikes in Cambodia. Without the support of Coroneos, Grunt Air had to suspend its operations in Laos and redeploy to the Philippines and wait for the call to return for the other POWs left behind. They have been gathering intelligence and training ever since for this very mission. Needless to say they are ready to go."

"Unfucking believable!" exclaimed the Chairman as he threw back his head and arms. "OK, where is Roman located?"

Sir, he's on leave in Oklahoma. I can have him here by noon tomorrow." answered Herbert.

"OK, my office 1400 hours tomorrow. Gentlemen, this remains between the three of us. The other Chiefs will blow up over it. They certainly won't believe it can be done much less by this unknown unit. There are also the usual Pentagon turf battles, but most of all we have to protect the boss. He has enough problems." The Chairman then said as he pointed with his thumb, "I want Captain Bayouth here to be directly involved with this. Maybe he can put some rational sense to this whole damned thing."

The Chairman got up and left the conference room.

Brigadier General Herbert reached into his pocket for a small address book, and then dialed a number.

Chapter 4

MEET THE ROMANS

Amy Riddell stubbed out her cigarette in the ashtray of her seat in the first class section of Braniff Airways flight BN501. She admired the spaciousness of the first class cabin of the big orange Boeing 747, affectionately called The Pumpkin. It was almost back in its Dallas, Texas home base from its daily flight to Hawaii and back. It was a world of difference in this plane and the usual cramped seating normally provided government employees and their dependents.

Amy had traveled the world over with her father in his many government assignments prior to his death a little over a year ago. In her 19 years she had lived in Moscow, Munich, Germany, Rome, London, Manila, and of course the obligatory assignments in the McLean, Virginia area. She liked the education and adventure that came with these overseas assignments but resented the lifestyle as she never could make and keep friends for any length of time. She would just be getting comfortable in a new place when they were transferred again and again and again.

After so many shattered friendships and loss of boyfriends, she became somewhat wild, rebellious and resentful, knowing that her father could come home any night and announce the next move. Accordingly, she didn't waste a lot of time playing the romance game with boys she cared about. If they showed any real interest in her, she had them bagged in the backseat of some embassy staff car.

Amy mentally snickered to herself as she reviewed her romantic past. It started in Moscow when she was barely fifteen. She was seeing the son of the U.S. Air Attaché to the U.S. Embassy in Moscow, who was eighteen. He was attracted to her blonde hair and big boobs. All he was interested in was sex. That was fine with Amy as that was all she wanted. There was no future for them as a romantic couple since there was the inevitable transfer looming for both families. She had resigned herself to emotionless sex spiced with a little pot or something stronger to take away the unpleasant realities of her life. She provided frequent sexual favors with other kids as well as guards or anyone who would provide her with the drugs she craved more and more. She suddenly closed her eyes and mentally rejected the memories of the two drug rehab centers that she had been sent to.

She told herself to get off the subject and think about something more pleasant. She looked over at her older sister Morgan who was looking out the window at the passing clouds.

"Hey, Sis, ya' getting nervous?" Amy said with a positive tone. "You've only got a couple more hours until you meet Dan's family. This isn't going to be a casual meeting. Dan's father didn't bring both of us halfway around the world first class just to say 'hello.' This is serious shit with you and Dan, and the family wants to meet you and your black-sheep sister."

"Cool it, Amy!" Morgan said with distain. "You are not a black-sheep. Maybe a little fucked up in the brain, but not a black-sheep." Morgan retorted with a big shit-eating grin and an elbow in her ribs. "Yeah, I guess that I am a little nervous, and I have some serious doubts as well," Morgan said in a clearly stated tone.

"Well, you should have some concerns and serious questions about this man." Amy said in an antagonistic tone. "Let me remind you that you had the hots for him in Germany and he dumped you for that slut, Cindy," Amy said, continuing the verbal attack. "And may I remind you that her murder was never solved. He was the obvious killer but they couldn't prove it."

"Amy, how could you make such an accusation?" Morgan replied with anger. "He was totally cleared by the police and Army CID. He was the Air Field Duty Officer that night and several other personnel saw him throughout the night. He couldn't have done it. Besides, he didn't really dump me. We only went out twice before he chose wild over mild. Cindy was a wild sex driven woman that came along in Dan's life when he needed someone like her. Unfortunately, her lifestyle and lack of character got her killed and destroyed Dan and his two kids. That was 6 years ago. The times and Dan have changed. That part of Dan's life doesn't bother me. It's his professional life that scares me. He is a Special Operations junkie. He thrives on danger and challenges.

"If ten percent of the things that I've heard about him in combat or working clandestine missions are true, he'll never be satisfied with conventional peacetime military life. He lives for that adrenaline rush of combat or Special Ops. I can't compete with that, nor can I live knowing that my husband is out there hanging his ass out big time in a hostile environment day after day. Each day that he leaves for work is a day that I will live in horror waiting for his return or the military staff car driving up to tell me he is dead. Those are the concerns that I must deal with before we can get married. I know for a fact that he has had at least four really good offers from the CIA to come work for them. Normal assignments that would greatly reduce his chances of being killed, but he said no. Grunt Air and his loyalty to General Maddox and Coroneos have him committed for now. He is safe here in the Philippines, but someday he will get the call from Coroneos to hang his ass out again. He'll be gone in a flash. He loves Special Ops because of its challenge and danger. It gives him a real adrenalin rush.

Amy looked on in amazement as her sister's usually bubbly and passionate demeanor was replaced by calm and dispassionate analysis of the relationship. Then Amy jovially responded, "Other than that, Mrs. Lincoln, how did you like the play?"

Morgan laughed then said, "How are you going to be staying off the shit for five days?"

"Not to worry, Sis. I have been pretty clean lately. Actually I haven't had anything other than booze for months. I will be on my best behavior just in case you actually decide to marry Dan. You two have been a hot item for over six months. That's a record for you by three months," she said, poking fun at her more reserved and conservative sister.

Amy fell silent as she compared herself to her sister. Morgan was 27 and was as calm and dignified as Amy was wild. She was a full three inches taller than her sisters petite five foot three frame. Both were blessed with the problem of keeping them in a C cup bra. While Amy had pure natural blonde hair, Morgan had a slight red tint to her blonde hair.

Amy thought of herself as the undisputed/unchallenged life of any party. If there wasn't a party going on when she arrived at any bar or group of people, she would create one. Amy loved to dance and be an extrovert in any crowd. Her slightly high toned voice could always be heard over the music or conversations. Far from her not to get on a bar or table top and imitate a go-go dancer. Her wild body gyrations and unique toss of her short hair would get the attention of any normal male present. Amy thought life should be one big party, unlike her mature and regimented sister who was the perfect example of a military version of June Cleaver.

Amy frequently told Morgan that she had missed out of so much in life by her less than exciting attitude. She had always been mission oriented, as her late dad always observed. Despite frequent moves, she always carried on her college education and business training. Even when their father had been killed in what they said was an unusual traffic accident; she only took a couple of days off from her training to be a shipping company operations manager.

They were back in the Washington area when he was killed. Morgan had completed her college degree and had accepted a job with Acacia Air Freight. It was an air freight and shipping company out of London. She was undergoing eight weeks of very concentrated training in the McLean, Virginia area at the time of her father's death. Her first Acacia assignment would take her back to the Philippines, where they had lived after the Rome assignment. Amy loved the wild life and all of the available military personnel there. Amy was glad that Morgan wanted her to go with her to Manila.

The Captain made the pre-landing announcement which got everyone's attention and habitual fastening of seatbelts and the other pre-landing tasks. "Morgan," said Amy, "do you want me to go change seats with Dan or stay here?"

"Please stay here," Morgan said in her smooth almost smoky voice, a voice that always commanded everyone's attention and interest.

Amy always respected her sister even though she frequently disagreed with her. She was always chiding Amy about her wild hippie clothes and attitude. Morgan could never stand her intelligent sister's rebellious and socially disrespectful attitude toward authority. She came from a fine family and had been exposed to many of the world's finer cultures. Yet, she chose the lifestyle of a pot smoking hippie that had barely finished high school despite having a 136 IQ. Morgan had excelled in school and college. She was always a favorite at Embassy social events. She really had the charm to play the diplomatic game. Apparently one of those pompous stuffed shirts, as Amy referred to them, got Morgan a great job with the shipping company. The fact that she spoke Russian, Chinese and enough German to order a beer and schnitzel didn't hurt her resume.

Dan Roman looked back from his seat one row ahead and to the left to see if the girls were OK and ready to land in Dallas. There they would be greeted by his Dad who would fly them to Oklahoma City in the company Lear Jet.

Morgan was apprehensive about the next few days and in particular the first meeting with Dan's parents. It was always hard to meet anyone's parents for the first time. The usual questions of will they like her and is she good enough for their son always bother people in this situation. Of course there was always the fear that Amy may say something completely off the wall and offend them. Oh well, we can only do what we can do, she thought to herself as the monstrous plane came to a halt at the gate. Morgan gently slapped Amy's leg and said, "Well, as Dan always says its show time."

Amy smiled and said in reply, "OK, do I do a bar strip here or once we get off?" Then she broke out laughing and said, "Not to worry, Sis."

The three disembarked the jumbo jet, walked down the long concourse of Dallas-Love Field, and entered the massive main terminal area. There were people walking briskly in all directions trying to catch a flight or meet arriving passengers like themselves. Morgan noticed the twenty foot statue of a famous Texas Ranger in the middle of the lobby. She quickly read the story behind the Ranger and was impressed. Dan came to a halt as he looked around the mass of humanity for his father.

Morgan was not sure what to expect. She knew that Dan Senior was ex-Navy pilot who flew for an airline for awhile after World War II until an eye problem grounded him. He went into the oil business with an old family friend in Illinois and then moved to Oklahoma in the early

50's. He had been very successful and had built up a very prosperous oil business.

Roman suddenly spotted the elder Roman and went over to him almost at a run. They shook hands and hugged, both beaming with happiness. Dan turned and motioned for Morgan and Amy to come over. As they approached, Morgan carefully looked the father over. He was a little taller than Dan and didn't look even close to being 64 years old. He wore a London Fog jacket over a navy blue polo shirt and khaki pants, a very casual and nondescript outfit for such a wealthy and prominent man in the oil industry. He wore his black and rapidly graying hair in a flat top. Morgan looked into his hazel blue eyes and suddenly felt totally at ease with him. Those kind eyes could disarm an army.

"Dad, I'd like for you to meet the lady that had brought so much joy to my life. This is Morgan Riddell," Dan said with warm pride.

Morgan extended her hand and said, "I am delighted to finally meet you, Mr. Roman."

"Please," said the elder Roman, "Just call me Roman. Lately it's become Old Roman." he said with mock sincerity.

Dan then turned to Amy and put his arm around her shoulders, catching Amy by some surprise. "And this," Dan said with warmth, "is Amy, who will be giving my sister a run for her money as top party animal."

Old Roman smiled and in a joking way said, "Good grief, two in one family. Oklahoma City will never be the same. You and Marty can team up once we get you home. There wasn't enough room in the Lear for everyone to come along. We'll get your bags and head over to the plane. It's just across the field waiting. Do you have jackets with you? It's a little cold outside," Old Roman said in a gentle tone.

Amy saw the warmth in his eyes and knew that she didn't have to put on any act for this man. She could be herself and that was very comforting to her.

Morgan was impressed on how smoothly Paul Maulqueenie, the Lear pilot, landed the corporate jet at Wiley Post Airport in west Oklahoma City. Maulqueenie had been in naval aviation since the late 30s and flew with the senior Roman in the Pacific Campaign during the war. He later flew jet fighters in the Korean War off the carrier Leyte Gulf before retiring from the Navy and going into corporate aviation.

A cold blast of Oklahoma winter hit Morgan as she stepped off the plane. She was glad that she had brought a heavy jacket. This was a far cry from the 80s she was accustomed to in the Philippines. Old Roman quickly brought his treasured old 57 Black Cadillac El Dorado convertible over to the door of the aircraft. It took no prompting to get the visitors into the warm car.

As they drove towards the city, Dan was commenting on the changes since he had been here last. They turned north on Pennsylvania, then back east once in the Nichols Hills suburb of Oklahoma City. Morgan and Amy looked at each other in silent comment as to the luxurious homes they were passing. This was not just the other side of the tracks; the people living here owned the tracks! They turned into a large gate that was the Roman estate.

"Wow! What a house!" Amy said quietly to her sister.

Before they could drive up to the front door, two young kids and a big white German shepherd came running across the lawn. It was Dan's kids, Beau and Mandy, along with Old Roman's dog, Baron, who braved the cold snowy weather to see their father - a reunion right out of Norman Rockwell.

Everyone quickly went into the house and out of the cold. Once inside they went into the den with its roaring fireplace.

Dan quickly introduced the group with an excitement and warmth that Morgan was pleased to see. "He is definitely family man material," she thought, "if he can ever give up special operations."

Old Roman brought a tray of brandy snifters with a liberal amount of Benedictine and Brandy. "This will take the chill out of you, "he said. "Please take a seat for a few moments. I know you are tired and want to clean up some, but I'd like to chat for a moment," he went on. "It's so nice to have you all here for Thanksgiving. Now, as I understand it, Amy needs to get some warmer clothes. Marty has volunteered to take you over to Penn Square shopping." Taking a sip then going on, "After you have a chance to clean up and a nap, I propose that we go to supper about 8:00 at the Beacon Club."

"Mother," Roman said, "are you going shopping or staying here?"

Sandy Roman looked at Marty and Amy and replied, "Those two barracuda don't need excess baggage. Besides I want to chat with Morgan and Dan."

"OK, then. We will meet here at 6:30 for cocktails before we go downtown," Old Roman said in a soft commanding voice.

Chapter 5

ROASTING DAN
Tuesday, 21 November 1972

It was almost 8:00 am when Morgan came downstairs for breakfast. She found Dan and Old Roman in the den drinking coffee. She could hear Sandy in the kitchen.

"Well, there she is," Old Roman said as he stood up. "What can I get you to drink - coffee or orange juice?"

"Orange juice would be great, sir," she said as she sat on the couch next to Dan. "How long have you two been talking?"

"A couple of hours," Dan said drinking his coffee. "He is still trying to get me to resign and come to work here. But I'd be bored to death."

Morgan started to comment when Old Roman came back into the room with a large glass of hand squeezed orange juice. She took the glass and immediately noticed that he had fresh hand squeezed the juice for her. "Thank you. Dan was telling me that you want him to join you in the oil business. I am not sure you are stressed for a Kamikaze oilman," she said with a sharp note in her voice.

Before he could comment, she continued, "Dan has an addiction problem. He can't give up the high risk life of Special Operations to be just a normal Army aviator or for any other normal job in the military. He could certainly not be a stable 9 to 5 businessman. But I will do everything possible to help you get him back here," she said with conviction. Looking at Old Roman she said, "I want for him to slow down and be a family man whether in the Army, CIA, or here as an oilman. Until he makes that change in his life, we will never be able to get married and build a family life with Beau and Mandy."

Dan sat stunned like a deer in the headlights. He was pinned down on both sides. He was about to respond when Old Roman said, "Damn, I like her! She tells it like it is. Absolutely refreshing, my dear! I have been telling him this for years. Keep beating on him, Morgan, you might actually get through that hard head of his."

"Well, for now I am going to go help Sandy with breakfast. Has anyone heard any life from the dynamic duo?" Morgan asked.

Dan recovering his composure said "Not since they came dragging in about 2:30 this morning."

Morgan shook her head. "Amy, how does she do it? I could hardly stay awake for supper. I certainly couldn't fly across the Pacific and party all night. I guess that I am just getting old," Morgan said as she left the room to help with breakfast.

"Dan, she's right! Whether you stay in the Army or come join me, you must stop taking chances. You've done your share of high risk assignments. The military has other people who can do some of these missions. She is a real keeper, Dan," he said with warmth. "You need to think about her and your kids. Beau and Mandy need a Dad, not a memory of a dead mother and father. Speaking of the kids, here they come."

Mandy and Beau came running down the stairs still rubbing the sleep out of their eyes. They immediately jumped on the couch with Dan, smiling as wide as their little faces would permit.

"Well, what do you want to do today?" he asked the kids.

"Let's go to Springlake Amusement Park," Beau said.

"Whoa," Dan said. "It's too cold and I think the park is closed for the winter. How about playing games at Wedgewood Park?"

Both agreed yelling and jumping.

From out of the kitchen, the voice of Sandy said, "Breakfast is ready."

It was just after 4:00 in the afternoon when Dan, Morgan, and the kids returned from playing games at the Amusement Park. They were greeted by Sandy Roman, who welcomed everyone back. As they came through the kitchen heading to the den, Sandy said, "Dan, a General

Herbert called for you. He will call again about 4:30. He sounded quite nice and cheerful. Is he a buddy of yours?"

"I wouldn't say that we are buddies, but we worked together in Saigon earlier this year. He has a job in Washington now," Roman replied. "Probably just wants to wish us a Happy Thanksgiving," Dan said, knowing that damned sure wasn't the case.

Morgan looked over at Dan with a lowered eyebrow and said, "Happy Thanksgiving, my ass," then looked at Old Roman. "Herbert was one of the key figures in Dan's Special Operations back in Vietnam."

"Well, Morgan," Old Roman said as he handed her a champagne cocktail. "Let's not prejudge General Herbert's motives just yet."

"That was very gracious of you, but you know that I am right," she said with a smile, then turned to see Amy and Marty coming down the stairs all dressed up and looking absolutely no worse for having been up till 2:30 in the morning.

"Well, ladies," said Dan. "It would appear that you dressed up for supper with us."

Marty was quick to respond, "Oh, thanks, but there is a party at the Capri and another one at the Chandelle Club. We are going just long enough to make a social appearance."

Everyone started laughing as the phone started ringing. Sandy picked it up then turned to Dan, extending the phone to him. "It's General Herbert."

"Dad, could I take the call in your study?" Dan asked as he went into the adjoining study.

"Major Roman, sir," Dan said with respect.

"Dan, I am sorry to interfere with your leave, but I need you in Washington tomorrow by 1000 hours. Meet me in room 2E676 of the Pentagon. That is the office of the Chairman of the Joint Chiefs of Staff. Be prepared to brief the Chairman on ROADSHOW."

"Yes, sir. I'll head over to Tinker and catch a hop or take an American, but I'll be there, sir." Roman replied.

"Dan, this is the real thing and not a drill," said Herbert with emphasis.

Dan tingled with excitement as he rejoined the family who were making idle talk while waiting his return.

"I have been summoned to Washington to brief the Chairman of the Joint Chiefs of Staff on our training of the Philippine Reaction Force and Grunt Air operation," he said, knowing that nobody would believe him.

Morgan quickly turned to Old Roman and strongly said, "You see what we are up against! He won't quit and they won't let him! All it takes is one phone call from them and he's like a kid in a candy store."

Dan responded with a firm commanding voice, "I am briefing the Chairman of the Joint Chiefs of Staff. The big dog himself! That's a fact. Dan said with a tone of anger in his voice. There are no Special Operations involved. You talk about Special Operations like it was a bunch of Lepers. This is a great opportunity for me to get into a good job at the Pentagon. That's what you have been wanting," he said with a look that clearly reflects disapproval of her comments. "Now, I have to get airline reservations to Washington and hopefully back tomorrow night. I am only going to be there long enough to brief the Chairman and then come home."

Morgan was silent as if in shock at the strong rebuke by Roman.

Old Roman thought, then said," The chances of getting a round trip to Washington on the day before Thanksgiving are remote. Take the Lear so you can be sure to get back. I'll call Maulqueenie. If you depart here at 5:00 am you will be there at Washington National by 9:30 or so. That will give you time to get there on time.

"Why don't Morgan, the kids, and I go with you? We can see the sights of the Capital while you do that thing that you do behind closed doors. The kids need to see the majesty of the Nation's Capitol. We might get lucky and have lunch with Senator Kerr."

Dan was delighted with the plan. He was about to say so when Morgan handed him a scotch on the rocks. She just looked into his eyes but said nothing. She didn't have to say anything. He wasn't going to get lucky tonight.

Chapter 6

STRICTLY A NEED TO KNOW

Roman was just finishing putting up maps of Laos, SW Pacific, and Philippines as the Chairman, his Aide and a Navy Captain entered.

"What have you got for me? I assume this is Roman," he said pointing to the obviously uneasy Dan Roman.

"Yes sir. General Coroneos anticipated the need to go back in the Cave area in northeastern Laos. So Grunt Air has developed several Op Plans for just such a situation."

"You're kidding. Even for a dire situation like this?"

"Yes sir. General Coroneos had us planning and training for Ops in the Cave area as well as in the area northwest of Hanoi, southern North Vietnam, and northeast Cambodia. We have focused on the caves as that seemed the most probable deployment area." We have been running training exercises once or twice a week for over six months on the ROADSHOW Op Plan and variations."

"You are training for Laos in the Philippines."

"Yes sir. The area east of Clark is very similar to Laos. There is a series of valley, rivers and mountains that are very similar to our route to the Cave area from LS59. We practice the mission at least three to five nights a week while there is a full or almost full moon. We use Baler as our stage field and it doubles as OASIS 1."

"What's OASIS 1?" the Captain asked.

"It is our Hot Refuel and rally point after we hit the caves. Well, sir, we navigate through the mountain valleys practicing recon team injections. Then come back after refuel and come in hot tactical to pickup the teams and practice POWs then fly to OASIS, Hot Refuel, then fly what could be our departure out of country, flying low over water to our pickup point."

The Captain says, "How close to the actual conditions are the route and other features?"

"Very close. We just don't have a carrier to practice landing on."

"Carrier!" exclaimed the Admiral.

"Yes, sir. For security reasons and element of surprise, we prefer the Navy take us clandestinely from 25-50 miles off the Philippines to 50 miles off Da Nang. Then pick us up 33 hours later 25 miles offshore just northeast of Vinh at recovery point called Crapshoot."

The Navy Captain looked hard at Roman, and asked, "If you run into problems and can't make the rendezvous with the carrier on time, how do you wave off the carrier? You have the carrier's ass exposed very close to enemy shore."

"Sir, we have our own internal flying Command and Control Center that will keep you informed of progress or problems."

"How big of a force would you use?"

"We would use our own C-47 Command and Control aircraft known as Arkangel. The strike force would consist of 8 UH-IH, 5 Recon teams and 5 Lao Recon teams. That totals 56 personnel on the strike force. I will also have a forward support team of maintenance; communications and Intelligence personnel deployed to LS59. They will return from LS59 to Clark with Arkangel as soon as we get feet wet. My other three recon teams will have our staging base at Baler secure and ready to receive the POWs. Sure can't let anyone see them while Kissinger is negotiating. It is secure and adequate for their short term support. We can fly those who need advance medical treatment to Clark and back. Once we are back we would have temporary operational control of the POWs until relieved. We would transition out of the program at that point."

"What about Intel?"

"Sir, Vang Pao is a great source of up to date Intel plus my Lao Scouts go snoop'n and poop'n in the cave area every month so we have a good handle on it. They are able to get within a few meters of the caves and prisoners as well as some of the locals who are full of good information. Plus the Air Force gives us everything they have and sometimes we bribe them for an occasional Olympic Torch (U-2) mission over our area."

"Why don't you use Air Force cargo planes instead of a carrier?"

"Sir, it is more difficult to airlift our birds. It would also attract too much attention or possible mission compromise. Grunt Air is well known to a lot of Air Force personnel. If we are seen it will start tongues wagging and the resident NV spooks will alert Hanoi. We burned them big time at the Big Casino. So they will be on the look out for us. I am sure they get regular reports on our activities in the Philippines. That's why total secrecy and element of surprise are critical to the plan."

The Captain looked somewhat amazed at what he had been told. He turned to the Chairman and said, "Sir, I think that I need to get some more details from Major Roman. If you would give us a couple of hours alone I think that we might have a plan for you to consider."

The slack jawed Admiral didn't respond to Bayouth but said, "So, Coroneos set this whole damned thing up. You actually executed the Big Casino raid, and he has you ready to go on this mission."

"Yes, sir. General Coroneos and General Mattox have been overseeing our program and plans development."

"OK, Major, you and Herbert sit down with Phil here and discuss this in detail. This stays totally in this room, understand?"

"Yes, sir," Roman replied, as did Herbert.

The Admiral and his Aide left the room.

"OK, Major Roman," said the Captain. Do you mind if I have a stenographer take all this down. It would be very helpful for me and the Chairman. I promise it will be kept in my possession and with "Chairman Eyes Only." It is totally off the record. "Let's start from the beginning of Grunt Air and come forward to your plan to go back. General Herbert, could you please stay and help fill in some of the details? It looks like we will be here for a while."

Herbert went through the complete historical background of how Grunt Air was conceived and created by Coroneos based upon his observations of the Son Tay Raid. The raid was extremely successful in every aspect except real time Intelligence. The personnel had been removed just prior to the raid. That failure had been compensated for by Coroneos through the use of recon teams and local Intelligence.

Roman went through his assumption of command, the dry season offensive and the raid on the Big Casino.

He described his mission as directed by Coroneos and continued by his friends after his departure. Roman went through each step of the Op Plan known as "ROADSHOW." Roman detailed his reasoning and logic for each of the events that would release the prisoners in the Caves.

After two hours of detailing the plan, Roman finally said, "Are there any questions for me or General Herbert, sir?"

"Not at this time, Major. I am still trying to mentally absorb what you have presented. You have definitely done your homework. If you would excuse me for a minute, I will let the Chairman know that we are finished. I'll be right back. He may have a few questions."

Captain Bayouth knocked on the door jam of the Chairman's office then went in when summoned.

"Well, Phil, it's been two hours. Did the kid have a plan, or were you guys playing poker?"

"Sir, let me make these observations: First, that kid is real. Should he survive the mission you will want him in your Ops Planning Office. Second, I believe he has a very viable plan that you should take to the President. Thirdly, I want to go as your personal observer. This ought to be one hell of an operation."

The Admiral silently got up, studying his long time friend whose advice and been flawless for over twenty years. He went out of his office and into the conference room where Roman and Herbert were waiting.

"OK, gentlemen, I will review the material with Captain Bayouth. If I feel it is a good plan, I will take it to the President. He must approve it especially with the political implications it could have on Kissinger's negotiations.

"If it is approved, I will personally advise both of you. Major Roman, like I said earlier, this must be kept strictly to a need to know basis. Brigadier Herbert apparently believes in the whole thing and is willing to play 'You Bet Your Stars' on you, Roman."

"If it is approved, Herbert, you will be detailed as overall Commander. Captain Bayouth will represent me directly and arrange any Navy or DOD support you may need. Again, it is strictly up to our President. We can't let the Boss down, gentlemen. That will be all," the Chairman said as he turned to leave.

Bayouth looked at Roman and smiled. He said in a soft but commanding tone, "You have a good plan, but the odds it will pass the political snuff test are slim. Keep up the good work in the Philippines." He shook Roman's hand, then Herbert's, and said, "By your leave, General," then departed behind the Chairman.

As they walked into the hall a Navy Chief Petty officer handed Roman a message from Senator Kerr's office.

"Well, Dan, I guess that you will try to get home for Thanksgiving dinner."

"Yes, sir. I came up in Dad's plane so I could at least try to be home in time."

"I'll be in touch," Herbert said as they went their respective ways.

As Roman left, Captain Bayouth grabbed Herbert's arm slightly and asked, "Could you spare a few more minutes for me?" "I have a couple of questions if you don't mind. Let's go into my office," he said nodding toward an office across the hallway.

Roman looked at the message. Dan, meet your family and me at The Rooftop Bar at the Washington Hotel at 6:00 pm. It was signed Bob Kerr. Roman knew that his dad and Morgan were bringing in the heavy artillery to get him out of Grunt Air and into some brain dead job. Now isn't the time for a job change with so many lives at stake. Morgan will just have to wait for Christmas. "Yes," Roman thought, "that would be a good Christmas present. She was right; it was time to get out of the high risk assignments but not before ROADSHOW."

Roman had barely walked into the hotel when Beau and Mandy ran up to him. After a hug, Beau said, "Follow us; we're at the bar," sounding like it was important. Roman's hand was taken by Mandy and they walked over to the corner table where Morgan, his dad, and Senator Kerr sat nursing cocktails. Mandy and Beau went to their seats and started drinking their Shirley Temples.

"Good evening, Senator. It is good to see you again, sir," Roman said as he shook his hand.

"Dan, it is great to see you. Congratulations on your promotion to Major. Ready to come to this Den of Despair and get it squared away?" the Senator said with the dignity of a true politician.

"That, sir is beyond my capability, unless I get nuclear release authority," Roman said with a certain resignation in his voice.

"Well said, young man," retorted the Oklahoma Senator. "How did your meeting at the Pentagon go?"

"Very well, sir," he said with a positive upbeat tone. "They asked a lot of questions on the training procedures we are using with the Philippine Light Reaction Company as well as our standard unit training. They are thinking about creating a battalion sized unit like Grunt Air." Roman said as if it were true. He did sound believable. "I might get a chance at the Operations and Training Officer Position if it is formed," he lied.

Old Roman chimed in, "That's great, son. Where will that unit be formed?"

"I got the drift it would be at Fort Rucker or Fort Campbell. My rotation date out of Grunt Air is in the spring, which is compatible with the unit formation," Roman said.

Morgan was obviously delighted and grabbed Dan's hand in excitement. Old Roman lifted his drink in salute. Senator Kerr smiled and looked Roman in the eyes knowing it was probably bullshit. If it were true it would be excellent career advancement however.

"Dan, sit down and have a drink. We are wheels up at 8:30," Old Roman said as he waved for the waiter. "We have time for a quick one before we go. We've got to stop by Bob's office to pickup his suitcase. He is flying back to Oklahoma City with us."

"Double Chivas on the rocks," Roman said to the young waiter. "How were the sights?" he asked the kids. They talked non stop at the same time in their recall of the day's events.

The waiter put the drink in front of Roman. He picked it up in salute and looked into the eyes of a wise old politician. Roman knew that his story didn't pass muster with him, or did it?

"To the flight back," Morgan said in a happy voice. "Dan would soon be out of Special Operations danger," she thought.

Chapter 7

WHO ARE THESE MASKED MEN?

Captain Bayouth motioned BG Herbert to a padded leather chair as he closed the door. "I can see the many reasons that this unit and its rather impressive accomplishments have been kept a deep dark secret. If anyone knew about you being on the mission, I am sure that you wouldn't be a new Brigadier General. Hell, they would have you flying cargo out of Hong Kong until your immanent retirement. Bayouth looked at his watch and then remarked to Herbert and said, "The sun is below the yardarm....somewhere. Could I interest you in a dose of medicinal liquid?" he asked as he pulled out an almost full bottle of single malt scotch.

"Well, I can't let it be said that the Air Force was not mannerly," Herbert said with a smile.

"You have an amazing unit here. It's exactly what we need for this mission. The professionalism is clearly shown in its comprehensive Operations Plan. That's a quality level of a plan usually found at Division or Corps level. It's very impressive, to say the least. How about giving me some details and background on this unit and the key people?" the Captain said as he poured a very liberal amount of the very fine scotch into the two Navy style glasses.

"Where do you want me to start?" Herbert asked.

"Let's start on organization then graduate into individuals and their background."

The overall concept of organization was one that General Coroneos developed after observing the Son Tay Raid from his position at PACAF Headquarters. He saw the good and bad aspects of the mission and created a hybrid unit that combined the best aspects into one unit. There was a need for a unit that combined internal aviation capability with reconnaissance. This was to be supported with its own internal support functions so it could operate clandestinely as one unit in an independent and hostile environment. The unit started off about the size of a small Army Aviation platoon with 6 UH-1H Hueys and one C-47 Command and Control aircraft that doubled as a logistical support bird. It now has eight Hueys. Initially Grunt Air had five Recon Teams consisting of highly skilled and experienced American members from the Army, Marines and Air Force recon and intelligence units. The teams were augmented with highly motivated and combat proven Laotian Scouts. General Vang Pao supplied the Scouts. He said these were the cream of the crop, and they were. The Big Casino raid showed certain short comings such as the need for additional Recon Teams. Now there are eight teams with one Recon team and one Laotian Scout for each Huey. Roman thinks it is best for the Recon Team and the Huey crew to work as a team. The Team Concept has provided more cohesive team work and confidence in the other unit members. It also provided a certain pride and competition between teams.

Captain Jake Best headed up the Recon Platoon. Captain Jason "Jake" Cornwall Best III had left the Cheese State for the somewhat warmer climate of Oklahoma after high school. Although he was bright in class, he wasn't the most worldly person you'd ever meet. Not much for school social life, he found more pleasure in solitary pursuits, and loves to hunt, fish and cross country ski alone.

His shyness was a disappointment to the girls because, by the time he left for college, he was 6'6" with blonde hair and deep blue eyes. It was a disappointment for him, too, because he could never bring himself to accept the invitations, no matter how boldly stated, to lose his virginity. Even so, he managed to get himself accepted to the most degenerate party fraternity on campus, which was where he first met Dan Roman, who, incidentally, led the fraternity in sexual home runs with the fewest strikeouts.

"There's a story floating around about those two," Herbert said as drank from the glass of scotch, and then continued. Once Best became comfortable around Dan and his friend Cort Fraley, he admitted he just couldn't seem to get himself laid. That was all Roman needed to hear. One of the fraternity's favorite party guests was a young lady named Mary Ann, who, much like Will Rogers, never met a man she didn't like. Roman arranged a date, but he briefed Mary Ann first about Best and what he and Fraley had cooked up. When Best picked up Mary Ann on the agreed-upon evening, he had to white-knuckle the steering wheel to keep from shaking. After picking up a six-pack of beer, they drove to an oil field miles from the campus and Jake, seeing the words "sure thing" swimming before his eyes, sneaked his arm up along the seat back and slid his hips closer to hers. All was quiet and going as planned. Suddenly, out of the underbrush, a screaming voice splits the night. "You son of a bitch, I'll teach you to screw my wife." It was Fraley, but his voice was disguised. Exactly on cue, Roman fired both barrels of a twelve gauge shotgun over the top of the car from right behind the trunk. Barely opening the door, Best soared out of the car and bolted into the darkness, scrambling through the thick scrub brush and thorny vines. He jumped over a five-foot high barbed wire fence like it was a low hurdle at a track meet and disappeared into the night. Fraley and Roman called for him to come back but he never did. Best ran the two miles back to the fraternity house through brush, brambles, undergrowth and who knows what else. When he dragged himself up the front stairs of the house, his clothes were in ribbons, he was bleeding from a mass of scratches, and he demanded Scotch. A few stiff shots later, Roman and Fraley drove up and filled him in on the little joke. He wasn't amused, stalked out of the house and disappeared completely until late the next day. When he returned, it was obvious that he had changed. Whatever emotional transformation took place, it allowed Jake Best to take his rightful place in the party animal pantheon, and he never had a problem around women again. He had become his own man and looked at life and his fraternity brothers accordingly. After graduation, Best joined the Marines, which was the same as volunteering for Vietnam. He pulled duty with the Force Recon Team at DaNang, and accomplished some things behind enemy lines that became the standard for other Recon Teams. He earned two Bronze Stars, one Silver Star and the Navy Cross for heroism. When Roman's path crossed his for the second time in their lives, he was the commander of the Recon platoon for Grunt Air, and Dan was glad of it. Best ran the unit in a very professional way. He had as his top NCO Army Command Sergeant Major Bradford Panfil.

Sergeant Major Panfil was an outstanding NCO with decades of experience. Panfil had been in the Army for over 28 years. He'd been on the second wave going ashore on Utah Beach invasion during World War II, at age 17. He'd been in combat in Korea with the 187th Regimental Combat Team called "The Rokkasons." He went ashore at Inchon in September 1950. He made a combat parachute drop at Sukchon-Sunchon and the famous airborne assault at Munson-Ni. Now, he was in Vietnam on his third and final tour before retirement. All of his tours had been in Special Forces or Ranger units and he'd garnered more awards for outstanding service and heroism than he could count. Roman looks upon him as the classic warrior, a man who embodied the true ideals of the military warrior. He was 45 years old and leading men half his age into every high risk mission he could get.

Also in the Recon Platoon, is Marine Gunnery Sergeant Roger Thornhill. Thornhill, is another of those who lied about their age and enlisted in the Marines in World War II. He went directly from Boot Camp training to Guadalcanal and was assigned to Chesty Puller's 3rd Marine Division Recon unit. After the war, he got out for a couple of years but hated civilian life so much that he pulled some strings to got back into the Marines about a year before the Korean War started, and was assigned to Chesty Puller's recon outfit again. He was with Puller at the Chosan Reservoir. He stayed in after the war and was with one of the first Marine units going into South Vietnam. He was on his third tour. When it came to Intelligence missions, he was the top of his profession.

Currently, all eight of the Recon Teams had one or more members that were on the Big Casino raid. Experience was not lacking in the Recon Platoon.

The Aviation Platoon Leader was Captain Eldon Barnes. All air and ground operations were directed by the Operations Officer, but aviation platoon was handled by Captain Eldon Barnes. He was another of Roman's hand picked members of the Grunt Air Team. He and Barnes had known each other a long time. They were together during TET 68.

Barnes always told the story about them while they were in the Advance Course at Fort Bliss. Roman and Barnes were both wild free-wheeling bachelors, running around as hard as they could with their "squeeze du jour." Once, they'd gone on a deer hunting expedition that neither of them would forget. Sands Missile Range covered thousands of square miles of desert and mountain areas making it ideal for missile testing and a haven for deer, which bred like crazy in the wild. The range commander, along with some fish and wildlife people, decided to let hunters into the area for three days to thin the herd. Just about everybody on the base was dying to go out and shoot some deer so they held a drawing for the precious few hunting permits that were available. Roman and Barnes put their names in just for the hell of it. They didn't care about the event one way or the other and knew they wouldn't win ... but they did. Of course, to turn down the highly coveted hunting permits would be sacrilege in the eyes of their buddies, and they weren't transferable, so they had to go.

Most of the diehard hunters had tents, but not Roman and Barnes. They rented a Winnebago the size of a semi trailer and equipped it with all the comforts, including a television for the big football weekend that was coming up. Big games were going to be on Saturday and Sunday. Then, they dealt with the food and beverage concerns. Barnes was dating four women at the time, each of whom gave him casseroles, pies, snacks and assorted morsels. The men each kicked in a few hundred dollars for beer and liquor and they were ready. They even bought a box of ammunition for their rifles. Not that they would use the ammo.

They hadn't counted on the fact that the other hunters, who would be sleeping in tents during the cold desert nights, would descend on their camper and make it party central for three full days. The first night, the liquor flowed heavily enough to float an ark, allowing Roman about three hours of sleep. At first light, they trooped off, heads throbbing, to their assigned hunting positions. Freezing their balls off, they trooped right back to the Winnebago within an hour. They'd spent the morning cooking steak and eggs, and then set themselves up in the Captain's chairs for an afternoon football orgy on a portable TV. If a deer came up and knocked on the door, they'd probably shoot it, but otherwise, they were determined to leave the deer overpopulation problem to the others.

Every one of the mad-dog hunters bagged a deer that weekend and couldn't understand why Barnes and Roman didn't. Barnes told them it wasn't their lucky day or maybe they were bad shots or maybe it was because they never left the camper. Besides, they didn't want to have to clean their rifles, much less a deer. Barnes was considered as a cool head under fire by the other pilots. They listened to him and followed him faithfully.

The Executive Officer was Air Force Captain Ancel Hammerschmidt better known as 'The Hammer." He was a one-tour veteran with a good combat record. Since he was new there was not a lot that known about him. He was a ladies man which got him into a little trouble from time to time. He was born in Landshut, Germany to a very important German rocket scientist that was brought over here at the end of the war to work on the U.S. rocket program. The father worked for NASA on the Mercury, Gemini and Apollo moon projects. He had a B.S. from Cornell and a Masters degree in aeronautical engineering from Emory. He flew the EC-121 electronic reconnaissance flights around Russia and North Korea. He had a couple of Intel assignments in Africa. He got bored with Intel work so he got a transition into Jolly Green helicopters and volunteered for Air Sea Rescue operations out of NKP for Heinie Adderholt. It was Adderholt that called Roman and got him his assignment. He was a very competent officer.

The Operations Officer is Sam Coltrane. Sam was the son of Brigadier General Bart Coltrane of "Black Bart Coltrane" fame in World War Two. Bart flew clandestine operations and support for the British Special Operations Executive prior to our getting into the war. Later, he and his British born wife Anabell started Acacia Air Freight after the war. It had grown into a major global air and sea shipping company. Unlike his father, Sam was a West Point graduate although you wouldn't know it to talk to him. He hated incompetent staff officers almost as much as Roman. His godfather is General Curtis Lemay a close friend of his father. Sam had been a Spook since he graduated from the Point and had been the man to go to when it came to Military Advisor Group Missions overseas. He had worked with the Indonesians, several governments in Africa, and Korea. He flew Special Ops with the 57th out Kontoum and later with the Pink Panthers. He was a workaholic and never took his ever-present unlit cigar out of his mouth. A habit he picked up from Lemay. He was a real character and was definitely a good match for the unit.

The Intelligence Officer was another pro. He, like many of the others, had been in the Army since WWII. Bill Abeel was better known as "The Sphinx" since he hardly ever spoke and then didn't say anything other than hard facts. He had been scheduled to retire and go to work for the CIA for the last year. Roman kept talking him out of retirement until the POWs were recovered. He couldn't say no to Roman. He was a legend in the Intel Community. When it came to Intel, he had a mind like a steel trap. He was incredible at what he did.

The Command and Control Operations was headed up by Doug Alberts. Chief Warrant Officer 4, Douglas Stanton Alberts, was young for a CW4. Heavy set and slightly over 5'11", he had sandy brown hair and eyes to match. While in school back in Oklahoma, he always appeared to be bored, because he was. Even though he always tested several levels above his assigned grade, his teachers wouldn't let him skip. He wanted to fly so desperately that he quit college after three years and entered the Army flight training program because only the Army would let you fly without a college degree. He racked up more than a few exceptional job performance ratings, became a talented pilot, earned two merit promotions, and got himself recruited by the Intelligence community. After C-47 training, he was assigned to flying radio intercept duty over Cuba, Haiti and the Dominican Republic just before the Cuban missile crisis. Later he flew the OV-1 Mohawk reconnaissance aircraft for a time, then went to Phu Bai, South Vietnam, again impressing his superiors with his performance under fire. Between his first and second tours in Vietnam, he spent 13 months with the Korean Military Assistance Group (KMAG) Intelligence section. Later, Roman would find out that Alberts was on his third tour in Vietnam. He had been flying reconnaissance missions across the border into Laos and Cambodia when his CO "volunteered" him for Grunt Air in hopes that the assignment would be less dangerous and would save him from himself.

As Arkangel, he flew an aging but dependable C-47 at 10,000 feet above the danger, controlling the aircraft and Recon Teams in Laos. His every command had life and death consequences, and he knew it.

Arkangel had two missions. First, the aircraft and its configuration of radio and weather radar equipment were the Command and Control Center for Grunt Air, acting like any other air traffic or mission control center. Off the ground at first light, they flew north to check the en route weather for the helicopters, reporting back to Operations, which would then launch the missions or stand them down for weather.

Arkangel also kept track of the flight plans for the day, mission objectives, Intel summaries, and just about everything else. After the unit's aircraft were released by the Udorn tower, they would check in with Arkangel and receive flight following services. Arkangel's only responsibility was Grunt Air, and the C-47 operated day and night, whenever required. The aircraft's radios had double and triple redundancy, monitoring other air control facilities, the airborne ones, and ground-based operations like Air America, Long Tieng tower, and the private frequencies of some of America's allies, like the troops under the command of General Vang Pao. "Just in case he gets some information or Intelligence he forgets to pass on," Alberts told me.

Equipped with two bilingual radio operators and a half ton of radio communications equipment, Arkangel was the first aircraft off the ground in the morning and the last to land at night, after orbiting most of the day at 10,000 to 15,000 feet for the widest area of radio reception. They flew far enough North to pick up transmissions from South China which had proved to be very interesting to HQ 7th Air Force Intel Section.

As if they didn't have enough to do, Arkangel's other mission was to provide logistical support to Grunt Air, flying a few times a week to take classified reports to the head shed and pick up parts and supplies.

Herbert took another long drink of scotch and started to go on when Bayouth interrupted him, "That's very helpful and most informative. What about Roman, Toothman and Reichert? They seem to be the real core of the unit."

"As you know, Toothman was killed on the Big Casino raid. I was with him when it happened. He was very close to Roman. It really tore Roman up to lose him. Filling Toothman's shoes has been a real challenge for Coltrane but he's already got Roman's confidence.

Dan Roman was a stocky 5'8" in his GI socks, thick through the chest from his addiction to any exercise that had the word "up" in the description. Chin-ups, pull-ups, push-ups. He did them obsessively because it helped him shut out all the smoke, fire and carnage he saw on his missions during the day and in his dreams at night. In spite of the "up" exercises, he teetered on the edge of the maximum weight authorized for his height as an Army Aviator. He had the kind of dark brown hair that made people think he was some sort of Indian – which he wasn't – and penetrating hazel eyes. Dan was within a few months of his 28th birthday, which makes him an old man compared to most of the other pilots in Grunt Air.

Daniel James Roman's DD-201 personnel file would reflect a 10-year career. It would also reflect that he had been a battalion S-2 or Intelligence Officer, then an S-3 Operations Officer with the Hawk Battalion, also a Brigade Level Operational Readiness Evaluator Team Chief in Korea and Germany, and he even had some time as an Assistant Adjutant. It was not a job he likes to remember. Not a lot of staff time, but some, and he hated incompetent or self-serving staff officers. He had two tours in Vietnam. He was in the Delta during TET 68 and again at the beginning of this overseas deployment. In almost every case, Toothman and Reichert were with him or stationed close by. They had always been of mutual support and created exemplarily units when jointly assigned. They were or should I say are a dynamic trio."

The other part of that trio was Tom Reichert, who lived for one thing: aviation maintenance. An excellent pilot under fire, his true calling was elsewhere. He had grown up in an aircraft hanger watching his father work on private aircraft and the passenger planes of Trans Texas Airlines. He'd absorbed everything he could about how to keep inert metal in the air. Six feet tall, reddish brown hair, persistent grease stains on his arms and in his hair because he refused to wear a hat when he was working.

Reichert was on his second tour and was headed straight for civilian life when this hitch was up, joining his wife and their three children. Last fall, he had married a woman named Carrie Blackburn, the widow of Larry Blackburn, a pilot who had bought the farm in a combat assault up in I Corps three years before. Carrie was a dedicated camp follower but Reichert knew she deserved to have a husband who stood at least a chance of coming home at night. That was not possible as long as he was with Roman.

Reichert wanted to tell Roman he was leaving the service and had, in fact, wrestled for months with how to break the news. He'd put it off four or five times. He knew Dan would be happy for him because he'd once had his own wife and children, a family life that had ended tragically. Roman was delighted when he was told as predicted.

Recently, Reichert has worried more and more about Roman. Maybe the shock of what had happened was getting to him. One of Reichert's tasks was to patch the bullet holes in Roman's chopper. Lately, their number had increased dramatically. Tom told me that he thought that Roman was taking too many chances. As long as they were together at Grunt Air, Reichert could keep an eye on him. There were three months left to his tour and he wouldn't let his good friend down. "Perhaps this is a point that he should consider after the ROADSHOW mission completed," Herbert said as he motioned for Bayouth to fill his glass again.

"Reichert's concerns were not unjustified." Herbert said in a soft lament. "Like many military pilots, especially chopper jock, Roman has been driven by forces he barely understands and could never put into words. Down low, where the tracers reached up for him and his machine, above the trees where the fear really kicked in until you could pull your straining helicopter up above the kill zone, the fear kept him going. But afterwards, when he was safely back on the ramp at Udorn or Tan Son Nhut, or wherever his service took him, the fear was replaced by … something else.

Aviation pretty much ran in Dan Roman's family. His father was a Navy aviator during World War II, and didn't bother to look for a flying job in the States like his fellow veterans did. Instead, he found work flying DC-4's and 6's for an airline in South America. After a tragic crash in bad weather, he moved to another airline flying between San Francisco and Hawaii, and made the long trip over open water until a problem with his vision put him out of the flying business. That took him back to Oklahoma where an old family friend got him into the oil business. The timing was perfect since the post war boom put at least one car in every garage. "He became quite wealthy," he said in a matter of fact tone.

Roman had two older brothers and a younger sister. The oldest brother died in a South American plane crash and the other went into missionary work in Central America. He became very well respected throughout the Central American region as a man of God and a defender of personal liberties. He fought the leaders of several corrupt governments for the human rights and liberties for all of the people. None of the other family members had any interest in or aptitude for the oil business. His father's long absences and the death of his oldest brother made him a bit hard to handle in his early teens, so his mother shipped him off to St. John's Military School in Salina, Kansas. His father wasn't too happy about it, but the tight discipline and high academic standards did turn him around. He loved the military environment and showed a real aptitude for the structure and regimentation. After completing his high school years at St. John's, Roman went to college and did another complete turnaround. The lack of discipline was disastrous and, when a few seemingly innocent fraternity pranks went awry, the Dean of Men reported him to the draft board for "poor scholastic attitude." They drafted him in a heartbeat and sent him to the infantry. From there, he volunteered for drill sergeant school hoping to stay out of Vietnam, but the plan backfired."

It didn't take long for Roman to realize that he'd be better off as a commissioned officer, and his military school background got him into Officer Candidate School fairly quickly. He had a natural ability to play the system and he maneuvered into the Air Defense Branch which had no assets in Vietnam at the time and then to flight school. Somehow, he was picked up by Military Intelligence and sent to Intelligence school but they left him in the Air Defense branch as a cover. His skills caught the attention of the resident CIA instructor, who recruited him for advanced training with the Company.

He did so well learning his tradecraft at the CIA "Charm School" in Virginia that he was sent to Germany for an advanced tradecraft course, and was turned into a European specialist. It didn't take long for the CIA to come calling with all sorts of recruitment offers, but he was more at home in the military life. And besides, while he was taking his advanced tradecraft courses in Germany, he met Cindy, an administrative assistant in one of the base offices, and they were married in practically no time at all. Instead of going to Vietnam, he accepted a CIA offer to fly "The Courier Run" for the U S Embassy from Bogota, Colombia to Caracas, Venezuela. His boss there was then "Colonel" Mattix, the Air Attaché. These dangerous clandestine missions excited Roman but, after six months, he elected not to continue in favor of a more normal family life. After all, he was a husband and a father. This career decision was rewarded by immediate assignment to Vietnam. Needless to say he is not a cheerleader for the CIA.

Back in the States after his first tour in Vietnam, things started taking several turns for the worse. By the time he was assigned to the Southeast Asia Tactics Development Department at Fort Rucker, he and Cindy had two small children, a boy and a girl. It was there that Cindy met Vic, a smooth talking, good-looking Italian from Brooklyn. Somehow, she managed to take a quick trip with him to a beachfront motel in Panama City Beach, Florida, a favorite resort for the Ft. Rucker pilots and not that long a drive from the base. She knew that her husband, as Air Field Duty Officer, was not allowed to leave the airfield and so she thought she'd be safe for the day.

The maid found the couple the next morning, Cindy and Vic, lying in a bloody bed with their throats cut. The police said there were no signs of a struggle or break-in. The detectives bore down hard on Dan because Vic's testicles had somehow become detached from his body and placed in Cindy's mouth. It was definitely a job done by a military professional. It's the kind of cultural thing that would have been done in Vietnam. Given the military connection, Dan Roman was the first person they questioned. The first session lasted over fourteen hours but that was a stroll in the park to someone who had survived The Charm School. Dan was eliminated from the list of suspects when they confirmed that he was on duty at the time of the murders.

The NCO on duty and three others swore to the police that Roman had never left the airfield that night. They checked him out in every direction. Had he stolen a Huey and flown down there, murdered his wife and her lover, then flown back? After all, Tyndall Air Force base was just east of Panama City, and he could have landed there. But, there was no record of any such landing or takeoff. It was decided that he could not have done it.

Cindy's father was dead and her mother was an alcoholic, which put the two children with Roman's parents and sister during his overseas tour. He wrote to them faithfully every time he had the chance. To shut out the bloody tragedy of Panama City, Roman pursued women wherever he found them. His in-theater R&R leaves from Vietnam are always to Bangkok for two-day blurs of drinking and womanizing. He came to know the city's notorious Patpong district like his tongue knew the inside of his mouth. On the outside, he was quiet, decorous, the very model of an officer and a gentleman. Inside, away from the base and away from people who knew him, he was just short of being a Mr. Hyde. It was frequently said that he was the man that mothers warned their daughters to stay away from.

His father, former military man that he was, tried more than once to bring his son into the oil business that he'd built so well, but, on some deep level, Roman realized that he not only loved the structure and regimentation of the military, but actually needed it. He often thought back on his days in military school and how much trouble he had when exposed to the complete freedom of college. He was smart enough or cunning enough, to understand that the nature of the military gave him all the structure that he needed as well as the opportunity to succeed. That's why he stayed in the Army instead of going back to Oklahoma and becoming wealthy.

Herbert became very quiet and subdued. Bayouth studied this newly commissioned Brigadier General and had a very comforting feeling come over him. He knew that the POWs in the Caves had a real chance of surviving the executioner's firing squad and his friend of 22 years had the best possible team going into harms way. "Yes," Bayouth thought, "The Chairman and President had the right team and the right plan with Grunt Air and the risk of failure greatly reduced to an acceptable level. He would strongly recommend approval."

Chapter 8

INTO THE LIGHT

"Life in a cave isn't all that bad," Felderhoff thought with tongue in cheek. "You don't have to decorate or fret over whether the furniture would match the wall paint." He was sitting on the floor with his back against the wall just inside the cave. His left arm was resting in one of the four-inch square holes in the rusty cage like bars at the cave entrance. There was a door in the middle that was always chained and locked at all times. He looked in detail at the cave as he had done hundreds of times out of boredom.

Boredom was often offset by their daily routine which included the twice daily feedings such as they were and the twice daily exercise periods. Of course there was the obligatory latrine duty that rotated among all of the inhabitants. That consisted of carefully picking up the five-gallon bucket that was in the back of the cave which served as the toilet. The bucket was brought to the cell door and the guard would open the door and let the prisoner out with his "Honey Bucket." The guard would escort him to a place some forty feet south of the cave where there was a natural hole in the ground. Nobody knew how deep it was but it never filled up. After disposing of the continents they went to the stream and washed the bucket out. This was also an opportunity to drop into the water and clean body and clothes. The guards generally had no problem with this as it helped the overall odor of the area. After the quick dip the POW would fill it with water and returned to the cave. He would throw the water on the floor at the back of the cave. This was repeated at least three more times. Meanwhile the other prisoners took thatch brooms and swept the water, dirt, shit, urine and other debris out the front. This definitely helped with the odor as well as sanitation. It kept down some of the diseases that often collected in damp caves with sick men living in the close quarters with each other. As punishment, the NVA would cut off the cleaning for a week. The buildup of urine and feces beyond the Honey Bucket was enough to make you throw up. It was really bad on the Thai women whose normal area was the closest to the Honey Bucket and overflow. It would often cause the POWs to get sick. Pneumonia and Dysentery were very common in these caves as were other tropical diseases that probably hadn't been seen or even named back in the civilized world. The guards really didn't like doing this form of punishment as it endangered their valuable negotiation pawns, the POWs. The guards especially didn't like it because when clean-up time came, all of the feces and urine had to be swept and washed out. In the hot and humid atmosphere of Laos, the nasty odor was repugnant and lasted for days.

Another aspect of life in the caves was the never-ending discussions about escape. Obviously they couldn't accumulate and hide picks, shovels, knives and other normal escape material. There was no place to hide it even if you were lucky enough to get something useful. Everything in the cave was hard limestone. Another major subject of endless speculation was WHERE WERE THEY? Everyone knew where they were captured, but nobody knew where they had been taken. The Dinks made sure of that when they moved them. A couple of the pilots had flown air strikes in this area of Laos and thought it might be somewhere in the northern part of Laos or even on the border with North Vietnam. They could not be sure and that was a major requirement to any escape plan. No maps, no compass and no information as to where they were made escape planning an effort in futility and endless frustration.

As a way to kill time and occupy their minds, the POWs would spend hours telling each other their life's story, albeit somewhat embellished. This and other distractions were important to keep one's sanity and take their mind off the inevitable torture dished out at next interrogation session. The thought about the torture was almost unbearable. Everyone had secret information that the NVA wanted. They would do whatever it took to break the POWs, and most of the time it took a lot of cruel torture to get them to break. But at the end of the day almost everyone breaks. Then it becomes an effort to give them some information about what they were interested in but not the real core of the secret data. This was done very successfully by the POWs much to the chagrin of the NVA. They had got the man to break and he gave them useful information but they knew that there had to be more. Most of the time, the POW's were successful in keeping the core secret from the interrogator. Some died keeping that secret and keeping faith with their fellow POWs. The bond between the POWs was forged in a faith much stronger than steel and flesh.

It was late morning when the Chief Intelligence Officer for the NVA Headquarters in Sam Neua came to visit the Cave and its residents. He was tall for a Vietnamese man. He had to be 5'11" or higher. He was often referred to as "Colonel Clam Shell," due to the shape of his head. He looked like a clam with two big eyes on top. He had two big bulging eyes with very hairy eyebrows. Normally he was all business and but not openly mean. He could stay above the nasty aspects of the torture conducted by his nasty subordinates. The Duty Officer called the prisoners to the front of the cave. Then he pointed to Lt. Mattingly and indicated that he was to come forward and out of the cave. He was immediately handcuffed with rusty iron handcuffs and a hobble around his ankles. Two guards took him off towards the path leading back to the Headquarters over the hill.

Colonel Clam Shell stepped forward and spoke to the POWs in fairly good English. "Lt. Mattingly will not be returning here. He has been selected to participate in high level technical talks with our Russian and Romanian comrades. He was the last to be selected for such a high honor. The rest of you will remain here until your government realizes that our cause is just and our victory eminent. Once they have agreed to surrender terms, you will be turned over to your government, and not until then. Some of you still have important information that you will share with us before you will be released. I can only hope that you see the realities of the situation and answer the questions without unpleasant assistance. Your lives will be only as pleasant as your cooperation is fruitful. Remember, there is a phone at the duty officer's station and he will call me anytime that you have desire to cooperate. Until then, you will be treated like the criminals that you are. Lastly, you will have four new residents to your cave." He motioned to the far side out of the prisoner's sight. The guards pushed three oriental women wearing Thai jungle fatigues. They were halted directly in front of the flat iron bars that formed the door and outside wall to the cave. The Colonel continued as he pointed to the women with his swagger stick, "These women were in an Air America aircraft that was shot down by our wonderful Pathet Lao allies. They were the only survivors of the downed aircraft. They will be staying with you in this cave. You will not talk to them. You will not touch them. Should anyone violate this policy, he will be shot! They too have information that we would like for them to share with us ... one way or the other. Now go about your business," he said as he quickly turned and left the area. The guards indicated with their bayonets that they wanted us to move back from the door as they shoved the three Thai women into the cave.

Felderhoff noticed there were only three newcomers when Clam Shell said four. The other must be a fourth arriving soon. The Thai women quickly walked by Felderhoff and the others towards the rear of the cave. They found a place that they liked and put the few personal items that they carried down and assumed a traditional squatting position often called a Kimshi Squat. They spoke to each other in very soft and quiet tones.

The guard then yelled some obscenities at them and motioned them to come outside into the open air into the heavily concertina fenced-in area that was guarded by two NCO guards and the Duty Officer. Felderhoff often wondered if those Hueys that he and Mattingly heard last January had anything to do with the always present Duty Officer. Before that night in January, there had not been an officer always present. He didn't know what the American Hueys did, but it sure got higher commands attention as they quickly put an officer in charge around the clock. As usual, the prisoners formed a circle and started to walk around the compound area always staying at least ten feet from the concertina wire. Often they heard the sound of an approaching aircraft. The POWs were quickly herded back into the cave so they could not be spotted from the air. After the aircraft had departed they walked for about thirty minutes to an hour before the guards motioned for them to go back into the cave. Once in, they put the lock and chain in place and went out to the guard shack to drink some tea.

Felderhoff stretched and sat down with the others. The walk tired him but it did feel good. The discussion between the prisoners focused around the sudden departure of Mattingly. Was he really going to Russia or Romania, or was he being taken out to be shot? Everyone agreed it could be either way these days. Then they shifted to the fact that Clam Shell said four but there were only three women brought in. They discussed the endless possibilities until the guards beat on the steel bars of the cave indicating it was time to eat. Everyone quickly got up and grabbed their two tin cups and went to the entrance and formed a line. The Thai women didn't take long to figure out the feeding formalities and joined the line. Despite his Air Force Academy manners, Felderhoff and the others did not offer the women cuts in line.

The food wasn't catered from Del Monaco's, to be sure, but it was eaten as quickly as if it had been. The meal was a little worse than recent meals. Why was the operable question, but nobody took the time to figure that one out. Felderhoff got to the bars and stuck his two tin cups through the four inch square openings in the rusty flat bars of the cave entrance. The guard put about six ounces of a pumpkin and fish soup into one cup and a two inch rice ball into the other cup. He carefully pulled the two cups back inside the cave so as not to spill a drop of soup or so much as a grain of rice. He savored every morsel of the rice and left nothing in the soup tin. It wasn't much but it was keeping them alive ... for now.

The sun went down and the hot steamy atmosphere of the day was replaced by the cool damp of the evening. The generator had been turned on so the two bare light bulbs hanging from the top of the cave could provide the guards with enough light to bring in the last prisoner. He had a black cloth around his head covering his eyes. Once in and the cuffs removed the guard removed the black cloth. The man immediately grabbed his eyes and screamed loudly. He buried his dead between his legs with his back to the nearest light bulb. He was obviously in great pain. Felderhoff and another man went over to him and asked what was wrong. He said that he had been in the isolation room for four months. There was absolute darkness in that room and his eyes had become sensitive to light.

One of the Thai women got up hurriedly and started toward the new man saying, "I am a nurse. His eyes will take days to readjust to light. It is painful and it will be a slow recovery." She was about four feet from him when she heard the loud metallic sound of an AK-47 rifle bolt slamming shut and ready to fire on her. The new guy held up his hand to stop all of the help before someone was shot by the guard. "Just give me time," he said. "I'll be fine in a few days, I hope. Just help me find the chow line in the morning."

The guards came in and cuffed everyone to the floor, beds and, in the case of the Thai women, to themselves back to back on the floor. Seeing that the POWs were secure for the night they left locking the door and turning off the generator. It was dark in the cave leaving the individual POWs to reflect on their life, family and their personal demons.

Felderhoff did not go to sleep right away. He pondered all that happened that day and, for that matter, the past few days. He mentally weighed the facts regarding his possible rescue before he was shot. "Yes," he thought, "we are not going to be repatriated." Those who were selected for Moscow had been taken away like Mattingly. Those who would go home were taken to North Vietnam. He and the others were on standby for the firing squad.

He looked over towards the Thai women and wondered what was going to be their fate? "Who the hell are they and how did they get here?" he thought. He heard one of the women move in the loose rocks on the cave floor. He looked over to the bars at the entrance and didn't see any guards. He thought that he would take a chance and talk to the Thai women.

"Hello, nurse," he whispered softly. "Thank you for trying to help our friend." There was silence then a slight sound of a body shifting on the rocks.

"You are welcome," came the very soft reply. "How long have you been here?"

"My name is Bob Felderhoff and I have no idea how long I have been here. I lost count months ago. I think it is November or December now and I got shot down a year ago in August. So it would be about fifteen months. When did you get shot down?"

Once again there was initial silence. Felderhoff looked at the cave entrance to see if there was a guard there. He assumed she was doing the same. Then she spoke to him in a low measured tone. "I am Nimu.

There is Farida right behind me and the one on the far side is Khem. We are from Bangkok. Actually we are from small towns near Bangkok. We were shot down just north of Sam Thong in late March. We were on our way to help Pop Buell with the wounded Laotian troops. They were fighting the NVA during their dry season offensive and had far more casualties than he could handle. After we were shot down we were hidden by some local village people until last week. There was so many NVA around us we could not take a chance on trying to slip through their lines to Vang Pao's side. Unfortunately a patrol came through and caught us. Now we are here."

"Are all of you nurses?" Felderhoff asked.

"No. We are actually doctors. We told the NVA that we were nurses so they would not force us to treat their troops. They have no respect for nurses and will treat us just like you. Please do not tell them that we are doctors or our lives will become very unpleasant."

"Your secret's good with me," Felderhoff said. "Have they tortured or abused you yet?"

"No, not yet. There has been no time or opportunity for them to do so but we know that will change soon." She lamented. "It is our hope that they will use us to get something from the Thai government. We are Trading Material as you GIs call it."

Felderhoff smiled at her Trading Material comment. He was about to say something when a guard came to the cave opening to check the lock securing the cell door. Both he and Nimu became silent and ended the conversation.

The next afternoon, four guards came and took the women away towards the Headquarters over the hill. One guard remained behind to drill three holes in the limestone cave floor with a sledgehammer and chisel. Once dug, he drove a long metal spikes into each of the holes. He added some cement into the annular space between the hole wall and spike to insure it would not come out. He then put a ring at the top of each spike so the women could be attached at night. He left, grumbling at the other prisoners. He was not a happy camper for some reason. His attitude toward the prisoners was not lost on Felderhoff. It was just another indicator that their time was limited. He looked out of the cave to the area where he saw the Scout. No joy for him as all he could see was vegetation. He went over to the others and joined them in the idle conversation about the situation.

There was still some ambient light just before darkness set in for the night when they brought the Thai women back. It was obvious even in limited light that they had been badly abused and beaten. The guards made the men go to their nighttime positions so they could be handcuffed for the night. Then the women came in were chained and cuffed to the new spike rings. The guards kicked the men as they left. "That was new," thought Felderhoff. He watched to entrance to see if the guards stayed or left to drink tea in the guard hut. The last guard watched the prisoners for a few minutes before he joined the others.

Felderhoff turned and quietly said, "Nimu, are you OK?"

"We will live. I don't know how much of this we can take but for now we are still alive," she responded in a pain accented voice. "Besides beating and embarrassing us by having us take our clothes off, they each had their way with us like we were B-Girls in the Patpong area of Bangkok. That was not the worst thing that happened. They told us that we would not be traded as we had no value. We would stay here with you until Hanoi directed that you are to be executed. One of them made it clear that that day was not far off."

Felderhoff turned his face away from her and had a sickening thought, "He was right. They were only waiting for the command to get rid of them. They would not see the States ever again." He almost cried at the revelation but chose to think positively. That Scout would bring a rescue team before they were killed. "God please help us!" he silently prayed before he went to sleep.

Chapter 9

SANPAN

The gathering of good quality intelligence for a mission like ROADSHOW was more than critical; it was the whole ball game. Without good Intel there was no chance of success. Roman reflected on what was happening in the field as they went about their preparations for the rescue attempt. SANPAN was the codename for Vang Pao's Hmong Scouts to physically go through the mountainous jungle and enemy lines to the caves and obtain every piece of information possible. Grunt Air had eight of the best Scouts that Vang Pao had assigned to the unit. They had been given the designation Lao Team One by the general himself. All eight of the Scouts considered the assignment to Lao Team One as a great honor. It also had the loan of the legendary Scout Sergeant Minh, assigned by Delta Team to assist with this critical operation. Normally SGT Minh stayed at Vang Pao's headquarters to oversee the activities of all the Vang Pao Scouts. He coordinated the flow of all POW intelligence to Captain U. Moung of the Royal Laotian Air Force who was assigned to Grunt Air as its direct liaison with the General. Captain Moung was a talented and courageous attack pilot. He had been pulled from combat as he was worn out and the general didn't want to lose a national hero. It would have a negative on the military morale. Moung also worked as a relief pilot in Arkangel and assisted with the collection of intelligence by the Scouts. He was a man that commanded respect from everyone especially the members of Grunt Air.

The Scouts were the product of the recruitment and training of the Hmong and other hill tribesmen by the legendary CIA Operative Tony Poe and Captain "Pappy" Hicks back in the early 60s. They set up a training base in the Nam Yu area of northwest Laos. They trained some very talented Scouts and fearsome warriors that were frequently referred to as "Carbine Soldiers." That name came from the weapon that they usually carried which was an old World War Two and Korea vintage M-1A1 carbine. They also trained some very successful spies as well. One of the best at his spy trade was a Tony Poe protégé Fouhin Sang Chao.

Today, the Scouts were working alone in the Sam Neua area where the caves were located. Each Scout had been assigned a cave or other intelligence gathering task. Five of them were crawling through the jungle getting as close to the caves as they could without discovery. They listened to conversations between the guards from concealed positions often less than a body-length away. The carefully examined the terrain and vegetation for possible use in hiding before the raid. During the hours of darkness they went up to the cave and closely examined the door and lock that would have to be removed to gain access to the POWs. This was very dangerous and required skilled techniques and stealth. If possible, they tried to get specific numbers of POWs and their health condition, all of the information that was needed to plan the raid and the equipment needed to achieve a successful mission. The other two Scouts were in civilian clothes posing as farming equipment vendors inside the headquarters area, talking to civilians and, in one case, a NVA Sergeant obtaining information on the local military strength and activities, as well as anything about the caves and POWs. It was amazing to Roman how much sensitive and critical information could come out of a conversation with the locals. The mission would continue for eighteen hours before they would return to Long Tieng for debriefing at the general's headquarters prior to the arrival of the Grunt Air team.

Corporal Pao was inside the concertina wire slowly crawling along the wall of the karst towards the cave opening. He was lucky that nobody had cut back some of the vines that hung down the face of the karst almost to the ground. The NVA left them alone most of the time as it hid the cave opening from prying eyes and over-flying aircraft looking for the caves. Tonight, they and some scrub bushes would hide him from the NVA guards in the guard shack who were looking outside of the area as they discussed matters of no importance just to stay awake. The blast wall angling from the right of the cave towards the left also gave him some help as the guards could not see him directly from the guard shack as he came in from the left side. It was not a factor by the time he got to the cave entrance. He finally got to the opening which had an iron bar wall restraining the POWs. The iron was a quarter inch thick and two inches wide. The bars were laid out in a square pattern every ten inches. The iron bars might be rusty and old but they were very effective. The three-foot by six-foot door was secured by an almost new chain and a French padlock. "This would require heavy duty bolt cutters," he thought as examined it. He then peered into the cave from the lower edge. He didn't want to be seen as they might say or do something to alert the guards. It was very dark but he could see the outlines of eleven bodies. That confirmed what the POW indicated earlier that day. He saw a man with a black piece of cloth over his eyes. He might require special attention when the recon team came for them. He felt comfortable with the completeness of his gathering mission and quietly departed the area. It was time to go back to join the others for the trip back to Vang Pao's headquarters with this information.

Chapter 10

THANKSGIVING

Dan woke up early, despite getting in late from Washington the previous night. He was concerned for the gruesome fate of many American servicemen held in Laos. They were doomed unless the President approved Operation ROADSHOW. That wasn't likely, given the protests and political pressure put on him by the Democrats.

"Good morning, early bird," said Amy as she came down to the den and took a seat at the end couch with Roman.

"What got you up so early?" Roman asked.

"Jet lag! Even the booze couldn't keep me asleep," she replied with resignation.

"You and Marty having a good time?"

"Yeah, we're having a ball. I'm learning a lot about you and your checkered past. I act normally around your family and nobody gets upset. I guess they're accustomed to that type of wild behavior after you and Marty," she said coyly. "You are or were one hell of a wild man in the past, I understand. Now I think I understand why you have never condemned my behavior or tried to change me. All of Sis's other boyfriends always gave me shit about everything," she said.

"Amy, yes, I was wild and still have a little of that in me today. But change you, no. That's ridiculous, if not impossible. Besides, you'll someday change yourself. That time will come when you find a reason to change. It may be a job, event or a special person that gives the need or reason to change. Until then, have a blast!" Roman completed his statement getting up and going to the fireplace.

"Thanks, Dan," she replied. "You said in twenty words or less the reality of my life and you're absolutely right. I know that day will come soon. But for now I have to do my best to top your impressive record of drunken debauchery with your college friend, what's his name, oh yeah, Robie the Cockroach. I can't believe some of the crazy things Marty has told me about you. Toga pool parties when your Dad and mom were out of town. It seems that you and Robie have been on more sorority pillows than a chocolate mint. Some have questioned how you and the Cockroach had a 3.8 grade point average when you slept through or ditched most of your classes. Ah, the list goes on. You and the Cockroach should be locked up."

"None of that was ever proven," Dan said. "It's only a figment of somebody's imagination."

"Yeah right! Is that why you weren't permitted into the Alfa Gamma Delta house after one of your Toga parties?" Marty said with a smug look.

"Oh my God, not another college story!" interjected Old Roman as he entered the room. "Dan's earlier years were a little nerve-racking for a father, not to mention expensive."

"It's now my challenge to enjoy life as much as Dan did before I find my reason to change," Amy said warmly, looking at Dan.

"OK, gang," said Sandy Roman. "We're only having Danish for breakfast. Morgan and I want you guys real hungry for Thanksgiving dinner. We eat at 12:00 o'clock, just in time to watch the Cowboys take on the San Francisco 49ers."

A little after 2:30, with the Thanksgiving dinner behind them everyone was in the den watching a very close football game on TV. The phone rang. Old Roman picked it up with his usual cheerful voice.

"Dan, it's for Major Roman," he offered.

Dan looked surprised that anyone would call him here on Thanksgiving.

"You'd better take it in the study. It's too noisy in here and this isn't some young lieutenant calling. He sounds as old as I am," Old Roman said as he put the call on hold.

"Major Roman, sir."

"Without saying who you think this is, do you recognize my voice?" the man on the phone said.

"Yes, sir. I absolutely do recognize your voice."

"I met with the Boss this morning about your plan. Given the critical situation and timing you're the only chance those poor devils have. Effective immediately, ROADSHOW is approved. You know the schedule and conflicts. You'll report directly to Brigadier Herbert, who reports directly to me. Captain Bayouth will be my direct representative and will get you whatever support you may need. Under no circumstances is the Boss ever to be brought into this operation. I'm as high as it goes. Agreed?"

"Yes, sir. Agreed." responded Roman.

"Security is paramount for your safety, the success of the mission. You can figure out the many political aspects of this mission. Strictly 'need to know.'

"Herbert and Bayouth will catch up with you at Clark on the 26th or 27th. A lot is riding on you, son, so don't fuck up. Are there any questions?" the Chairman asked in conclusion.

"No, sir. ROADSHOW commences immediately, and WHIPLASH will start in nineteen hours, sir," Roman said looking at his watch. "I'll do my best not to let you, the Boss, and the poor devils down."

"Very good, Major. Now go back to your family."

"Thank you, sir, goodbye," Roman said as he hung up the phone. He thought for a minute, then picked up the phone again and dialed for a long distance operator. "Operator, I want to call the Philippines." He gave the number.

The phone was answered on the third ring despite it being 4:30 in the morning in the Philippines. "Captain Hammerschmidt, sir."

"Hammer, this is Major Roman. Can you hear me clearly?" Roman said in his official sounding voice.

"Yes, sir, five by five."

"This is NOT a drill!" Roman said with strong emphasis. "This is a go order for ROADSHOW. Execute WHIPLASH in eighteen and one-half hours, per Op Plan. Trigger pull on the 18th. Deploy SANPAN. ROWBOAT Option. Accelerate SUNDAY STROLL. Strictly 'need to know' and I mean 'need to know.' Any questions?" Roman asked in a serious voice.

"No, sir, can do," replied a very alert and excited Captain Ancel Hammerschmidt, Grunt Air Executive Officer.

"Very good. I will be back on the 26th. Goodbye." Roman hung up. "Well," he thought, "here we go again on another unbelievable challenge with only a couple hundred lives at stake, and the political destruction of the peace negotiations at risk." Roman returned to the waiting group.

"It was the duty NCO at the Chairman's office wanting some information so travel orders could be cut covering the trip and when I am due for reassignment," Roman casually stated, as if it were not important.

"On Thanksgiving?" Morgan stated as if it were a tongue-in-cheek question.

"Ah, the Green Machine doesn't sleep or eat turkey," he replied jovially, then added, "I think I'll be seeing the Philippines in my rear view mirror very soon. This new unit has a lot of high priority with the Chairman. I'm very sure I'll get transfer orders by Christmas."

"Fantastic," said Morgan. But Old Roman knew his son and smelled bullshit. Roman noticed his father's silence and knew he hadn't fooled him.

"How about a drink?" Old Roman said as he got up to fix a very strong one for himself.

In a Clark AFB BOQ, seven thousand seventy two nautical miles from Roman, Paula Madison rolled over and asked, "Who was that, dear?" Paula was a curvaceous and ruthlessly ambitious reporter for CBS News who was once again Captain Ancel Hammerschmidt's overnight guest.

"It was the Staff Duty Officer. We just got alerted for a joint U.S./Philippine Air Ground exercise in mid December down in Mindanao. Now, you can't say anything about this. It isn't going to be released to the public until 4 December," he said with conviction. "It's been in the planning for a couple of months. We're supporting the Philippine Light Reaction Company. I may run down to Davos tomorrow and work out some of the details with Captain Mac and the local support unit." The Hammer, as he was better known, had recited the prearranged cover story. Not only was the mission Top Secret, but Madison was a very nosey reporter. "Bad combination," thought

Hammer. He had to stop seeing her before she destroyed his career, but she was so good in bed it would be very hard.

"But that's Saturday. We were going out to supper," she reminded him. "Why can't it be done Monday like other people?"

"First, I need to get things finalized before the coordinating meeting on Monday. Second, since when did the military ever constitute "other people?" he said mockingly. "Besides, I'll be back by 9:00 or 10:00 so we can meet for a late supper. Now, let's either get a couple of hours of sleep or get real sweaty. Today is a work day for me."

She answered his question by reaching between his legs.

Later that morning, Hammer stepped out of the shower to get a bar of soap off the sink. He heard Paula in the bedroom talking on the phone. Despite her attempt to be quiet, he could hear her tell the person on the other end that Grunt Air would be a part of a joint forces exercise in southern Mindanao in mid December. Hammer was angered by this breach of faith and security. "This isn't a big news item," he thought. "Yes, she's a reporter, but this, a routine joint exercise, didn't justify a call to her bureau chief at 6:30 on a Sunday morning. There was a problem here and he would have to let Roman and Abeel know about this ASAP. Meanwhile, he had a very important task to perform.

Chapter 11

WHIPLASH

Promptly at 0900 hours Sunday morning, Captain Hammer entered the Grunt Air briefing room. He turned to the First Sergeant and directed that he post a guard outside the door and allows no one to enter or disturb the briefing. Then he went over to the chalkboard and wrote down Operation ROADSHOW. Everyone gasped and shifted in their chairs.

"Gentlemen, Major Roman has given us a Go Mission. This is not a practice drill or test. This is for real," he said with authority. "WHIPLASH is to be executed at 2230 hours tonight. We will deploy and recover the mission on a carrier. All other aspects are exactly as set forth in the Operations Plan. Execution of the ANVIL Op Plan will be at 0200 hours 18 December 1972. You all have specific tasks and objectives to accomplish prior to WHIPLASH. You are to accomplish these tasks and report to me no later than 1700 hours to confirm completion. We will use the Mindinao Cover Story as planned. Those on WHIPLASH will be at Arkangel ready to depart no later than 2200. All pre-load cargo will be delivered to the Arkangel at 2100 hours.

"Now let's review some of the details to bring everyone up to speed mentally.

"Our cover story is our participation in the joint U.S./Philippine training exercise in Mindanao in mid December. Details are classified so you won't have to say anything to those who you are giving the cover story. Grunt Air will deploy all assets down there as far as anyone is concerned. We will be in support of the Philippine Light Reaction Company as usual. That should do it for now. Additional disinformation will be provided as we go along so the story will be believed. Now Arkangel will go over mission times with you," Hammer said as he stepped aside as Chief Albert, the command aircraft chief pilot, better known as Arkangel took the briefing podium.

The old veteran pilot started writing times and positions on the blackboard, then turned around to the group. "As the Captain said, all pre-loads are to be delivered to the plane at exactly 2100 hours to avoid unnecessary attention. The load will be refueling equipment, tents, generators, COMMO equipment, air mattresses, water blister, LRRP rations and booze for VP's wife. Nothing not on the load list, we're heavy so nothing else."

Lieutenant Jenner and Lieutenant Kellogg will fly the over water legs from Clark to DaNang and back on the return leg. They will stay in DaNang and sleep while Davis and I fly us to Long Thien (LS20A). We should arrive at 0700 and drop off Captain Hammer, Captain Coltrane, Chief Abeel and Captain Best. We'll depart no later than 0715 hours, arriving at LS 59 at 0755 hours. Passengers for that stop are Captain Dorsey, Captain Reichert, Sergeant Major Panfil, Staff Sergeant Campbell, Staff Sergeant Nelson, Sergeant Nolan and one mechanic. You'll have only one hour to accomplish your assigned tasks before we depart for Long Thien at 0900 hours. We'll arrive at LS20A at 0945. We'll have a 45 minute ground time to refuel and load up the team. We'll arrive at Da Nang at 1315 hours. We'll refuel and Jenner and Kellogg will take us back to Clark at 1400 hours. These times are hard gentlemen. You must accomplish your tasks consistent with that schedule. Any questions?" Alberts asked as he took his seat.

The Hammer moved back to the podium. "Sergeant Campbell?" asked Hammer.

"Yes, sir," replied the supply Sergeant as he stood up.

"Do you have all required support equipment ready to go?" asked Hammer, already knowing the answer.

"Yes, sir, all equipment is on hand, checked by serviceability within the last 15 days and on pallets ready for deployment. Even the booze is still there," he said with a smile on his face.

"Communications," Hammer said.

Sir, all equipment has been tested and serviced within the last fifteen days and is a part of the LS-59 pre-load. Code books and Signal Operating Instructions ("SOI") will be distributed for tonight's mission thirty minutes prior to departure and special ROADSHOW codes and one time authentication sheets for the Lao Scouts are ready to go.

Maintenance was the next called by Hammer.

Staff Sergeant Nolen stood up as did Capital Reichert. Before Nolen could say anything, Reichert said "We're ready, we've arranged to pickup Vang Pao's aircraft mechanic at 20A." Then he sat down, as did Nolen without a word being said.

"Sergeant Major," said Hammer, "are you ready?"

"Yes, sir. We'll pick up our Lao Scouts and two additional Lao Scout teams at LS20A as well. No problems here, sir."

"Captain Best and Chief Abeel are on the phone with the Chief of Staff for Vang Pao. They gave me a thumbs up as I came in," Hammer said, then he went over the time schedule for the mission again and the specific tasks that each person was to accomplish. Then he turned to Chief Gedeon and the First Sergeant. "You are cleared to start on the rehabilitation of the Bales facility to accommodate the POWs. If you can't get something you need, let me know. Secrecy is paramount but so is getting that place ready. Your cover story is that Baler is going to become a training base for an American Helicopter Unit deploying here from Vietnam. That'll explain the construction and the security fence.

Hammer looked around the room at the very attentive faces, then said "This is for real, let's do it right. Dismissed."

Everyone left the room excited and with a motivated stride in their walk. Hammer went into the office area and motioned to Best, Dorsey and Abeel to join him in his office.

"Ok, Abeel, how was your conversation with Vang Pao?"

"That is one sly general," Abeel said, "All I said was that we'd be arriving at 0700 hours tomorrow and he interrupted with "Tell Roman that he and his staff will be ready for anything he had in mind." I told him Roman was returning from the states and asked us to brief him on our plans." He seemed disappointed that Dan would not be there but would be ready anyway. I asked that our old Scouts and two Lao Scout teams be ready as well." He asked if we were going to roll craps again. I said no, but that was the area. He immediately figured out what our objective was but didn't say anything. He knows the score from his own sources. I suspect he'll deploy his sources to the caves before we get there. We should get a preliminary report from his sources when we get there."

Hammer then looked over to Captain Best. "Get Lieutenant Christian and the three teams not deploying started on physical security here and at Baler," he said. We'll bring in Captain Mac's unit in a few days to handle physical security. We need Mac to keep Baler secure and interact with the locals so we don't attract the wrong type of attention. He and his men are familiar with us and can bridge the gap due to the Status of Forces Agreement between our two countries. Let Roman handle that hot potato once he gets back. The problem is that Mac has two pretty green platoons tracking some of those radicals down in Mindoro Island. We may need to fly down and give him a hand training his men in this type of Recon mission. If it becomes a Search and Destroy mission he'll certainly use our help taking them through their first hostile combat operation. Then we can bring them back. Jake, can you work that out with Mac?"

"Yeah, I can do that. The political fallout will be incredible if we extract them while they are tracking the bad guys so close to Manila," Best said in a serious tone.

"What if we sent Golf and Hotel Teams down there tomorrow and help Mac train his men on how to set up an ambush to take the bad guys out? That would help Mac's unit's reputation and take out the threat freeing him up without controversy from Manila?"

Hammer said "Good idea. Check with Mac and get his approval to the whole plan. Barnes and Dodson can fly the mission."

"How much can we tell Mac about ROADSHOW?" asked Best.

"Nothing," Hammer said, then changing his mind he continued, "Just tell him that we've got a big operation that has the Pentagon directly involved. Roman needs his support and will tell him more as he has the need to know. He'll do it."

Coletrane came into the room and looked at Dorsey. "Better work up a training schedule for SUNDAY STROLL that follows our new scenario," he said, looking over at Best. OK with you to use your guys to update the specific camps starting tomorrow?"

"Sure, Sam. If Dorsey will fly them out to the area and find what looks like good sites in the morning. The ones we have been using are not quite what we need. We can get some U-2 photos from Abeel that will make it easy," Best said.

Abeel chimed in, "I'll get Mr. Touchdown to get it to you in about an hour. They may be a couple of weeks old, but should be adequate. I'll request new Olympic Torch missions be flown on a priority basis. I'm sure we can get needed support from above since this is an authorized mission.

"OK guys, let's do it. The boss will be back in three days wanting results," Hammer said as he motioned the group out the door.

It was almost 9:30 and the last of the supper dishes were being removed by the O Club waiter when Paula Madison started her typical correspondent questioning of Captain Hammerschmidt. "I don't see why you don't delay your departure for Mindanao until 9:00 or 10:00 so we can have a nice night together," she said taunting him. "What difference does four hours make on this type of mission?"

"Paula," Hammer said with irritation, "You know I can't do that. I have to be at the airfield by 0430. I'm tired now much less after a night in bed with you. Let's payout and head home to our separate quarters," he said with emphasis. "We can have a later supper and drinks tomorrow night. I'll be back by 9:00 or 9:30, OK?" I won't be under quite as much pressure then.

"OK, but I plan to work you over big time tomorrow night. So don't wear yourself out down in Mindanao," she said with a sexy tone in her voice.

Hammer walked Paula to her car and kissed her good night. She drove off. He quickly went to the BOQ and changed into his flight suit and went to the part of the flight line that Grunt Air parked its Hueys and C-47. When he arrived fifteen minutes early he was the last of the group going on the trip to arrive. He climbed into the C-47 and walked up to the cockpit where Albert was standing just behind the pilot Lieutenant Jenner.

"OK, we can go. I am apparently the last to arrive," Hammer said.

"Roger that, sir," Jenner said as he flipped on the master power switch to begin the startup procedure for the long flight ahead. Hammer and Abeel went back and strapped themselves into the web seats with their legs being obstructed from full extension by the equipment pallets in the center of the aisle. This was the beginning of a very big mission and everyone knew it. There was little talking, which was unusual.

Chapter 12

THE AMBUSH

Captain Mac put his radio down and looked at SFC Lujan and Staff Sergeant Ramerez, then nodded to the map in front of him. "First Platoon is within 100 meters of the 20 or so Baugsa Moro Army (BMA) rebels. They just crossed a shallow point in the river just west of the mountain village of Amnay. Amnay is their apparent objective. I suspect they'll take over the village and set up an operating base there," Capital Mac said as he described the situation as he saw it. "From there, they can conduct terrorist operations across the island and support or control terrorism attacks on Manila itself."

Captain Mac looked at the terrain around him and said quietly to SFC Lujan, "It's protected by a river on three sides and flanked by two deep valleys that are difficult to get across under fire. Perfect conditions for an ambush."

"Well," said SFC Lujan, "Let's not waste a good ambush site." You know we can't be seen or caught being involved in this action. We are only here to give you our observations on your tactics and execution of the mission" he said with a big shit-eating grin. Lujan looked up and over the dirt mound in front of him and continued, "Both our governments would go nuts if they knew that we were here. I might suggest that your Second Platoon take the ridgeline trail and get ahead of the BMA, which is taking the concealed route up the valley. It'll take them time to go up the valley. Have Second Platoon meet Sergeant Ramirez and his "Hotel Team" at the draw coming off the upper valley. They can set up an ambush striking from their left side. Your First

Platoon will remain silent and stay back about 200 meters until they get to a point two hundred meters west of the ambush point. They can take up a defensive position and wait for the BMA to come to them after Second Platoon execute the ambush. We can take up a position just uphill from the ambush so they can't go up a hill and we can shoot them off the south side of the valley wall if they try. First Platoon has to remain silent and maintain the element of surprise. Second Platoon will execute the ambush when the BMA gets across from them. Agreed?"

"That's a great plan, Sergeant Lujan. Let me get 'em on the horn and set it up," Captain Mac said with excitement.

An hour and a half later the Second Platoon met up with Sergeant Rameriz and his team. They set each soldier up in a line of deadly interlocking and overlapping fire covering a fifty meter kill zone of automatic and semi-automatic weapons. The trap was set. As anticipated the ragtag BMA soldiers walked up the valley completely unaware of the presence of the Philippine force.

The point man for the BMA force was walking slowly due to the humid and oppressing heat in the windless valley. He looked up the valley and saw an incline in the valley along with some trees. A good place for an ambush, thought the point man. "Yes," he thought, "this was a great ambush position." Lucky for them nobody knew their force of liberation was even on this island much less here. He wiped the ever-present sweat from his forehead and started to walk towards the rise ahead when he felt the terrible sting below his left shoulder. Then he heard the noise associated with a bullet. His vision became blurred and he felt weak. He had to lie down and rest before he returned fire from the enemy. His vision and everything around him went black before his knee hit the ground.

The ambush fire from the Second Platoon was so accurate and intense that only a few survived the first salvo. The soldier directly behind the point man dropped to his knees and crawled away from the fire and attempted to escape up the steep south wall of the valley. His efforts were short-lived as the Second Platoon fire quickly caught him. The four at the rear turned back towards the west and back down the valley. By this time the BMA was in full panic, and ran towards the waiting First Platoon. Observing from the high ground up the valley, SFC Lujan and Captain Mac were pleased. SFC Lujan leaned over to the Philippine Captain and said "Call your headquarters and tell them you're in hot contact with a hostile force and you need immediate air support." The Captain smiled and complied. As expected, his headquarters had no support available. He then called for any available aircraft to come to their aid. "This is Blackjack 6 calling, any armed aircraft in the Mindoro area request fire suppression support." Blackjack is in hot contact."

"Roger Blackjack 6, this is Grunt Air 88 with you 10 miles to the northeast of Manburao, can we be of help?" replied the voice on the radio.

Roger that Grunt Air 88, we have been in contact with a much larger force in a valley to the south and west of Amnay. The fire-fight seems to be over but just in case can you fly over and advise as to what we're up against?"

"Roger, Blackjack, can do. On site in five minutes," Barnes reported with a big shit-eating grin.

The remaining four BMA had reached the kill zone of the First Platoon. They were immediately cut down, with the exception of one soldier allowed to survive to tell the tale of the terrible ambush to his fellow BMA rebels. It was a bitter lesson and a shocker to the BMA leadership who had thought their Intelligence and valiant crusaders were superior to the godless soldiers of the Philippines.

Captain Mac gave a clear and detailed report to the now-circling Grunt Air 88 and Grunt Air 22, knowing full well every word was being monitored by his headquarters. His Light Reconnaissance Company now had respect and the confidence that can only come from deadly combat. He then radioed, "Grunt Air 88, can you extract our force and take us to Cavity?"

"Roger that, Blackjack, proud to help. We have a visual body count of 20 BMA. Is that what you have for a count?"

"Roger that, 88, we're ready for pickup. Popping smoke now."

Chapter 13

RETURN TO THE PHILIPPINES

The hot humid air of the Philippines hit Dan in the face hard as he climbed down the stairs from the airliner back onto Philippine soil. Even being tired from the long trip across the Pacific, he was excited to be back and ready to get ROADSHOW going. It didn't take long to go through Customs and Immigrations, but it took forever for the bags to be offloaded and placed on the baggage carousel.

"Sky Cap! Anyone needs a Sky Cap?" came the familiar voice of Ancel Hammerschmidt, his Executive Officer, approaching from the rear with a baggage cart.

"Not if you drive that cart like you fly," Roman popped back with a big smile.

"I thought I'd meet you and save you a taxi bill second only to the Philippine National Debt," the Hammer said as he shook Dan's hand. "What do you say I drop you off so you can get cleaned up and rest a little? Then you join Paula, Coltrane and myself for supper at 2000 hours."

Noting the serious look in his face, Roman knew that he needed to speak to him urgently. "Sure," Roman replied. "I can make it. How about you, Morgan?"

"Well, since jet lag won't let me go to sleep right away, that sounds good. Will Paula be joining us or have you scared her off while we were gone?"

"Scare Paula?" Hammer responded. "Nothing scares or embarrasses that woman. She's the one who scares people. Hell, the

Devil himself quakes in his cloven feet when she's near. I guess that's a good trait if you're a news reporter for a major network."

"I don't see how you can date that woman," Roman remarked with a slight show of distain. "She is undoubtedly the Angel of Career Deaths. You are going to slip up and say something classified to her and we'll see you on the six o'clock news just prior to your court martial."

"Dan," he said, almost out of Morgan's hearing, "she's absolutely dynamite in bed. I don't have time to talk when I'm with her." Then he looked Roman in the eyes and said, "Although it could have happened."

Morgan responded in a chiding voice, "I heard that. You're talking about my friend. So watch what you say, Buster." Then she looked over at Hammer and smiled.

Roman had a cold chill go down his back. There had already been a compromise. Roman pulled Hammer behind the car and asked how bad the compromise.

"She was with me when you gave me the execute order. She asked what it was about. I told her the cover story about a joint exercise in the southern Philippines. She bought it, OK. When I was getting out of the shower I heard her on the phone with someone telling them about the secret exercise at 6:30 in the morning. A training exercise doesn't rise to a level of news worthy to call her bureau chief at that hour. I passed it on to Abeel. He's discretely talking to the Air Force Counter Intelligence boys and Abeel got Captain Mac to have the Philippine military security people to check out her phone records just in case.

"Good work," Roman said. "Let's keep up the charade with her for time being. There may be more to this than a news story. I'm glad we came up with that cover story for this situation. Now, let's get going. Could you stop by that roadside store just outside the gate? I sure could use a cold San Miguel beer right now."

It was just before 2000 hours when Hammer and Paula Madison walked up to Sam Coltrane who was standing at the Clark Officer's Club bar trying to order a drink. Paula put her hand on Sam's shoulder gently pulling him back and saying, "Stand back and let the power of the Fourth Estate get our drinks." She then put her elbows on the bar and leaned forward accenting the cleavage in her well developed chest. The bartender was there in seconds, and no one else standing at the bar objected. "Hi, I need a double Chivas on the rocks, two vodka martinis, and a San Miguel," she said to the smiling bartender.

They worked their way through the crowded bar to the dining room where they were seated one row away from the bandstand. Once seated, Coltrane started to comment on the stunning low cut black dress being worn by Paula, when Roman and Morgan came in looking over the crowd for their party. Paula's raised hand was immediately spotted by Morgan who pulled Roman's arm in the direction of the table.

"Welcome back," Coltrane said to Morgan. "We've missed your beauty and brains at our evening Attitude Adjustment periods."

"Thanks, but it was hard for me to leave the land of the Big PX for the Hinterland," she said in a jovial tone. "The weather is much better here, but it was great to see the States again."

Paula immediately joined in and asked, "Did you get to meet Dan's family?"

"Oh, my, yes," Morgan said. "They are down to earth except his sister who is just like Amy."

"Oh my god, there's two of them? Please tell me there's hope for the sister," Paula said in mocking tone. "How did you get along with his parents?"

"Fantastic! They are on my side when it comes to getting Major Disaster here out of Special Operations and into something safer. His father even offered Dan a civilian job in his oil company. Naturally, "Kamikaze Dan" wouldn't have a thing to do with it. Dan did find out that he may be transferred to a stateside job in the spring."

Hammer immediately asked, "Really? What's the position?"

"I'm being considered for an Ops job at a startup unit at Campbell. Still 'iffy' but I could have orders by Christmas," Roman replied with a cautious wink of the eye. Both Hammer and Coltrane caught the wink and knew what he meant. Bullshit, but it was a logical cover story.

Paula then chimed in with her correspondent's tone of voice, "Dan, does that mean you won't be going to Mindanao with Grunt Air on the joint exercise in December?"

Roman was caught off guard by the question, which was classified. "Actually, Paula, the exercise will be over before I even expect orders. Another thing," he said in a low and very stern professional voice, "That exercise is classified and you can't report even the existence of the plan until it's officially released to the public on the 8th of December. No scoops, please. We keep you in our confidences with the understanding that you won't violate security. Agreed?"

"Of course," she said, slightly embarrassed at the direct tone of Roman. "I'm glad to know the release date so I can be the first story out with all the details. That helps me and thanks."

Roman smiled." I'll make sure you get all the details for your story."

"Dan, I do have a question for you. I am personally curious as to why Grunt Air is the only unit on Clark that can't be detailed for various outside duties and even staff duty officer," she said in a pleasant but curious tone. "Hell, all the big brass seems scared of you guys. Colonel Daniels almost goes apoplectic at the mention of Grunt Air. What's the deal?"

"Actually, I think it is a little over-reaction on his part. The matter actually stems from our initial arrival here. LTC Potts tried to split the unit up to various units until the Vice Commander called him directly and told him that our unit was to stay intact and ready for redeployment on short notice. He was told that if that order wasn't acceptable to him, his next paycheck would be received in Alaska." Everyone laughed and Roman went on, "I think the word got around and nobody has been willing to bet their career on trying to detail any of us."

She smiled and said, "Now that makes sense. How long do you think it will last before they try again?"

"It doesn't matter," Roman said. "I still have the direct number to the Vice Commander." Everyone laughed.

Paula laughed and looked over to Morgan who had been quiet. "Morgan, with the stateside assignment only a few months away, does that mean that you might go back with Dan?"

Morgan smiled and leaned back in her chair, looked up momentarily then back to Paula. "If it is not in special operations, and it's a typical stateside assignment, yes."

Before she continued Roman interjected, "Now that I'm a major, my assignments will be staff oriented and I'm long overdue to a stateside assignment. I also should be selected for the Command and General Staff College soon. In short, my Special Ops days are over. Consequently, Morgan and I have decided somewhere over the Pacific that we'll be married once we get back to the states."

Congratulations and well wishes were loudly extended by those at the table.

"Now, how about let's order supper. We need to get some sleep. Tomorrow is going to be a busy day for me after being gone for so long."

Coltrane stopped the waiter and ordered two bottles of Champagne and a couple of cigars.

After supper the group broke up to find their individual ways home. The trip had taken its toll on Roman and Morgan. Coltrane and Hammer went to their BOQ rooms to get needed sleep. Paula was the only one who didn't go to sleep as quickly as the others. She went to her nicely appointed apartment just off base. It was 3:31 am when her overseas call to Alaska finally got through. It was 10:31 in the morning in the far reaches of the Aleutian Islands where a terse voice answered, "Command Center."

"Hi. This will be short. Roman is going to southern part of Mindanao on a joint exercise with the Philippine Defense Forces. It's secret until it's released to the public on 8 Dec. It is a week-long exercise. What do you think?"

"There is more to it. I don't believe a thing Roman says. It's got to be bigger than a simple company level joint exercise. Dig deeper, much deeper; there is something big going on and we must find out what it is. Goodbye." There was a sudden dial tone in her ear.

Chapter 14

A SPY AMONG US? IT MUST BE PARANOIA!
Monday, 27 November 1972

It was less than two minutes to 9:00 am when Dan Roman entered the headquarters offices of Grunt Air. After telling the clerks to be at ease and return to their work, he proceeded down the hall to the briefing room. As he entered, everyone stood up at attention as the Commanding Officer came in.

"At ease, gentlemen," Roman said as he approached the three gentlemen who were strangers to him. Chief Bill Abeel, the Grunt Air Intelligence Officer (S-2), introduced the trio to Roman.

"Major Roman, this is Major Singlaube and Chief Master Sergeant King with the Air Force Counter Intelligence section here at Clark, and Mr. Marcos, the chief liaison officer from the Philippine National Security Agency (Special Intelligence Department). They've joined us in the security for our pending operations with special emphasis on the Paula Madison matter."

"Thank you so much for your help. I'm afraid that Chief Abeel is correct when he determined that the matter with Miss Madison was beyond our internal capabilities. She could compromise our planned operation in southern Mindanao with Captain Macario Vallamor's Light Reaction Company. As you know, both our governments and higher headquarters are most interested in this very ambitious joint operation going smoothly and in complete secrecy. What can you tell me about the problem as you see it, and what can we do about it?" Roman finished with a concerned expression.

Major Singlaube started, "Captain Hammerschmidt and Chief Abeel did the right thing by bringing us into the picture. This could be very serious on two levels. First, she is a credentialed correspondent with a major news network which creates its own set of problems and public consequences. Secondly, she seems to be passing on critical and classified information to persons not authorized. Surprisingly, she is giving your unit's training and operational activities to an unidentified individual located at the U.S. Air Force Station on the Aleutian Island of Shemya, which is only 310 miles from the Russian Intelligence facility on Ostrov Beringa. Since we were brought into the case, we have determined that she makes at least one call per week to Sheyma, for the last six months, which is when she arrived in the Philippines. The two recent calls which we electronically intercepted have been short and professional, and only cover Grunt Air and Major Roman's activities. We have not determined who she is talking to in Shemya and there are 473 personnel stationed on that frozen rock. They are mostly civilian contractors, support personnel, weathermen and signal Intelligence personnel listening in on the Russians. It's hard for us to understand why anyone on Shemya would have an interest or the need to know about your operations. We're working on the matter with the head of Counter Intelligence at Alaska Command headquarters in Elmendorf. Give us a few days and we should be able to identify this mystery man. Mr. Marcos is taking all appropriate action from the host country side which is necessary since Miss Madison has included the activities of Captain Mac's Philippine Light Reaction Company with Grunt Air. It's definitely a national security matter to the Philippine government. This is now far from being a legitimate news story. Chief Master Sergeant King will brief you on what we know about her."

"Thank you, sir," King said with unmistakable authority. "She was born August 9, 1945, at McGuire AFB to an Army Air Force couple. The father was an Army Air Force officer training at the time. He's still active duty somewhere in the PACAF region. We are still checking on that detail. Her childhood was normal for an Air Force camp follower. In 1963, she entered USC Berkeley and immediately became a "flower child". She majored in Journalism and Peace Rioting 101. She was arrested three times but the charges were always dropped. At an anti-war demonstration, she met and later married Todd Madison, a local

TV reporter. The marriage lasted less than a year. He divorced her when she was arrested and convicted of striking an FBI agent during one of the Berkley anti-war demonstrations. When she got out of jail after 90 days, she hooked up with a bunch of anti-war activists and drug pushers that were on the FBI Watch List. She was about to have her parole revoked when her ex-husband got her a job at a local TV station. She turned the corner and has been a very successful TV journalist since then. She was recently picked up by CBS and sent here as local network reporter. It appears as if she hasn't given up her anti-war activities.

"She has a reputation for being absolutely ruthless and tenacious. It's widely known that she sexually compromised another senior reporter who was married to get him out of the way so she could get this assignment. She's left a clear trail of career corpses in her past. Captain Hammerschmidt is her current victim-to-be. The good Captain was wise to advise our office of her actions and has been of great help to us. We are at a loss as to why she selected Grunt Air and Major Roman as her point of investigation. That concludes my briefing, sir. Are there any questions?"

Major Roman got up and shook the sergeant's hand. "This is first rate work in a short time. "TOP," Roman said with emphasis. "It's a real shame that she and the unidentified man in Alaska are committing treasonous actions like this especially since she came from a military family.

The Counter Intelligence major said, "I don't care who he is or what he is. If he's divulging classified information or acting against the best interest of Grunt Air or the U.S. Air Force he's going to Leavenworth."

The Philippine security officer was even more hostile towards both Madison and the Alaska contact. "They're acting against the military forces of the Philippines. She's within our jurisdiction, not yours, and she will be arrested!"

Roman put his hand up seeking an opportunity to speak. "Gentlemen, let's look at this in a different perspective. To date, they've done no damage and at the end of the day probably won't do something that can hurt our operations. Grunted, they've broken the law and need to be stopped. The guy in Alaska doesn't appear to be an enemy agent. At least he isn't intentionally passing on classified information to the enemy that we can tell. Both must be stopped and prevented from future disruptive actions. Most of all, we must insure that they don't compromise our secret operations and possibly passing secrets to the enemy.

"Consider this approach," he continued. "Let's keep the full scale monitoring and observation of both of them. Continue electronic monitoring of their communications and see if we can identify the man in Alaska. Keep a tight tail on Madison. Mr. Marcos can continue to wiretap her home and office. Major Singlaube can tap Captain Hammer's BOQ room phone as well. Hammer, please continue seeing her as you have. If you dropped her now it would send up a red flag. Besides, if you don't get laid often you are hell to be around. Think of it as fucking for Old Glory! Let's build up a clear and solid case against both of them while we're training for our mission. If they start doing or saying anything that can jeopardize the mission, we can always arrest them. I would suggest that our case against the man in Alaska be complete and ready to submit to the PACAF Commander 48 hours prior to the mission. They can arrest him and keep him on ice until we execute the training mission in Mindanao. After that, anything he says won't hurt us. At the same time they arrest him, Mr. Marcos can arrest Miss Madison. I would appreciate it, Mr. Marcos, if you could keep her absolutely incommunicado for eight days once you arrest her. CBS will obviously go nuts and do everything possible to get her out, more for the story than her welfare. You can leak the full story of her transgressions to the NBC and ABC reporters here in Manila. That will ruin her journalism career. Then kick her out of country. The two events will hurt her more than you can imagine. Your government really doesn't want to put her in jail. That would be more punishment to your guards than her," Roman said with a little laugh.

Mr. Marcos looked at Roman then said, "I can't promise she won't go to jail. You can count on the rest of the plan. What will happen to her contact?"

Mr. Abeel injected, "If he doesn't go to Leavenworth, he'll get a dishonorable discharge and no retirement benefits as a minimum."

Roman looked around the table and said, "Well, then, we're in agreement on our plan of action. I'll notify my higher command so we are covered. You can be assured that only those who have a need to know shall be advised. Gentlemen," Roman said with a smile, "Have a good day," then left the room.

A little after 1500 hours, the side door of an Air Force KC 135 tanker opened and the crew chief fully opened the door just as a portable stairs was wheeled into place. Then an Army Brigadier General and Navy Captain descended the stairs to be greeted by Major Roman.

"Good afternoon, sir," Roman said with appropriate pomp and a salute. "Welcome to Clark Field."

Captain Bayouth responded, "Cut the shit, Roman, and get me to a bar. That was a terrible flight. We skirted a typhoon most of the trip from Hickham. I felt like a ping pong ball in a boxcar."

BG Herbert looked at Roman smiling and said, "OK, Roman, you heard the man."

"OK, sir. Should we move the staff briefing back until tomorrow morning, then go to Baler?" Roman asked.

"Absolutely!" Herbert said. "Please apologize to your guys for the delay. I know they had worked hard to be ready today, but we can start at 0700 and go on from there, OK?"

"Can do, sir!" snapped Roman. "I regret that I don't have a staff car for you. I thought your rank and a staff car might attract too much attention. I do have a nice Jeep, a clean one owner."

Bayouth looked at Roman. "I don't care if it's a jackass as long as it gets me to the goddamned bar."

"Dan," Herbert said softly, "could you and Morgan join us for supper tonight? We'd like to meet her. She's obviously going to be a long term thing with you."

"Delighted, sir."

Roman and Morgan entered the O Club at precisely 2000 hours, as planned. They took a table in the far corner so that others could not easily hear their conversation. Herbert and Bayouth came into the dining room ten minutes later wearing civilian clothes as Roman requested, so as to not attract too much local attention.

As they approached, Roman leaned over to Morgan and said, "Be on your best behavior. The Navy Captain is the guy who will get me that position at Fort Campbell." Roman thought the fact just might keep her from going on the attack like a pit bull over the Special Operations issue.

"Good evening, sir. May I present my fiancé, Morgan Riddell. Morgan, this is General Herbert and Navy Captain Bayouth."

"Captain Bayouth, it is a pleasure." Morgan said with all the charm of a southern belle. Then she turned to BG Herbert, "Ah, General Herbert, a member of the Coroneos Rat Pack." Roman almost choked when he heard her, and a big grin came over Herbert's face. Bayouth started laughing out loud.

Riddell continued as she took her seat. "That fiancé title is conditioned on my ability to get Dan away from you and General Coroneos and into a job that doesn't make him a slow moving target for every NVA and freedom fighter in the world. In short, I want him out of Coroneos Special Operations Fraternity."

By this time Bayouth is trying unsuccessfully to stop laughing and Roman was wishing that he was back in Laos where it was safer.

Brigadier General Morton J. Herbert was seated directly across from Morgan, listening to a woman who was in love and was going to protect her man. "She definitely doesn't pull her punches," Herbert said. He went on, "Coroneos Rat Pack and Coroneos Special Operations Fraternity. Mrs. Roman-to-be, you have just bestowed a great honor on Dan and me with those two titles. I can hardly wait to pass them on to General Coroneos. It'll make his day. Dan, you have a real winner here." Then Bayouth turned his attention back to Morgan, "I think it's safe to say that Dan's days in Special Ops are numbered. He's done his share and should look forward to something new by the end of the year.

Captain Bayouth, now composed other than his red face from laughing, said, "Dan's up for reassignment in the spring. There're discussions going on as to where and what he'd be best suited for in his next assignment. I'd expect that the decision and his reassignment orders should be coming down before Christmas. In the meantime, he's here training with the Philippine forces in a non hostile environment. So, I'd focus on my wedding plans with all this in mind."

Herbert looked over at a stunned Roman and said, "Dan, for god's sake don't even have a precautionary landing in training between now and your transfer. I don't want to have to face Morgan again if you do." Everyone laughed as the waiter came up for drink orders.

Herbert was laughing again and asked Morgan, "Where did you come up with Rat Pack and the fraternity names?"

"I got it from one of the Air Force wives. General Spike is the one who named you and General Mattox, the Coroneos Rat Pack. I don't think he meant it as an endearing term. Spike doesn't seem to like Coroneos very much. Do you know why?"

Herbert replied, "Basically, Spike believes that all Air Force aircraft should be jet, even Special Operations aircraft. Coroneos agrees with Heinie Aderholt that Spec Ops need the low and slow flying propeller aircraft that can put a lot of firepower exactly where it is needed and be able to stay on location for longer support. Coroneos and Aderholt have been proven right in actual application in Laos and along the Ho Chi Minh Trail, much to the embarrassment of Spike. Now, did you get the Special Ops fraternity nickname from the Air Force wives, too?"

"No, that one is mine," she said proudly.

Bayouth and Roman knew what was behind Herbert's question, and they were relieved by the answer.

"Now that Peace Terms have been agreed to," Bayouth said, "Let's eat."

Chapter 15

TRAINING FOR THE BIG SHOW
Tuesday, 28 November 1972

Promptly at 0700 hours, BG Herbert and Captain Bayouth passed by the two of Lieutenant Christian's large recon team members standing guard outside the briefing room to insure secrecy. As they entered the room came to attention.

"At ease, gentlemen," Herbert commanded. "Take your seats."

Roman stood behind the podium, which was directly in front of a large wall map of Southeast Asia. On one side of the large map was a map of the Grunt Air operating area in Laos, and on the other side a blackboard. On the side walls were blackboards with details of the mission and other lists relating to the upcoming rescue of the condemned prisoners.

"Per General Herbert's request, today we will generally focus on mission training and post recovery care of the POWS," Roman said in a matter of fact tone. "Let's look at the training program first. Captain Coltrane will brief you on this part of the operation."

"Good morning, sir. I'm Sam Coltrane, the Grunt Air Operations Officer (S-3)" Coltrane said in a commanding voice. "As you know, we've been preparing for a mission of this nature for over six months. Only three copilots and I were not on the Big Casino raid, which gives us an edge on experience. Our route of flight for the Hueys is almost the same as the Big Casino raid, from LS-85 up to the release point where each aircraft will proceed to its specific pickup point. The MI 8 and AN-2 Colt will take a higher altitude route and fly to the south of Sam

Neua. They're much noisier and a familiar sound to the NVA. Hopefully, the familiar noise and the use of the mountain valley to the north will cover the sound of the larger Huey strike force. As before, timing and element of surprise are essential.

"For training purposes, we've identified a series of valleys 64 miles east of Clark that closely replicates the valley route in Laos." Coltrane pinned a map over the Laos map which showed the mountainous terrain of eastern Philippines. A red line marked the flight path of the training route. "As you can see, General, our flight path is similar to the one you flew in Laos." He then turned to the Laos map which had a line marked in yellow that ended at the release point. Then there were four separate lines going to each of the four caves and a fifth red line which marked the route the MI-8 and Colt would follow to the south.

"You'll note Baler Field here which is ten miles from the four cave training locations. We're using it as our rally and refuel point, code name "OASIS", for training purposes. Actual distance from the cave area to OASIS is 64 miles. We don't think the flight time for training is important. The fifth camp that we will be busting is Moung Soi. The Colt and MI-8 have been assigned to that effort, given the longer distance from LS59 and the larger number of prisoners. Once we've picked up the prisoners and recon teams, each aircraft will fly directly to OASIS. There we'll refuel then take off together in a flight formation with the MI-8 and Colt in the lead. Again, they're familiar to the NVA and hopefully they won't be alarmed by the trailing Hueys. Upon departure from OASIS, enroute Crapshoot we'll fly low level through similar terrain to a point here on the Philippine coast, then fly 50 miles offshore. Then we'll return to Baler for refuel and mission critique. Each morning, we'll deploy the recon teams to points three to five miles from the mock caves and Moung Soi camp. The trip over the hills builds up their physical condition for the real thing. At a pre-arranged time, Arkangel will give the "Execute Order" and the operation will be on. We'll fly the mission just as we plan to do in Laos. During the nights that we have a half-moon or greater, we'll do the mission at night, just as we will later. I believe Major Roman will be flying the training route for you later this morning. Are there any questions, sir?" Coltrane said as he concluded his briefing.

Captain Bayouth looked at Herbert, and then asked, "How many times have you flown this specific route in the day and night so far?"

Coltrane picked up his clipboard and looked at the date, then looked up at the naval officer. "Sir, 48 times in daytime and 27 at night."

"How high do you fly in these practice missions in the day and at night?" Bayouth asked.

" Sir, we fly at treetop at all times. If you get more than ten or twenty feet above the trees in Laos you're dead meat."

Bayouth then remarked, "How many accidents have you had so far?"

"None to date, sir. We have been extremely lucky. Statistically speaking, given the hours we've put on these birds, we should have had at least two fatal accidents or serious incidents. We've had none. We attribute that to our maintenance program. Captain Reichert keeps our birds in top shape."

"OK, on to post-recovery program," said Herbert.

Coltrane sat down and Captain Hammerschmidt stood up. "Sir, I'm Captain Ancel Hammerschmidt, call sign "Hammer", the Executive Officer. I'm responsible for the Baler facility, security, and POW medical treatment and rehabilitation program. Chief Gedeon, whom you may remember from the Big Casino raid, has clandestinely acquired a great deal of materials for the upgrading and modernization of the Baler facility to house the POWs. They'll be sequestered at Baler during the period that they must remain out of sight from the outside world until the Kissinger prisoner matter is resolved. Security is provided by Foxtrot, Golf and Hotel Recon teams and is augmented by elements of the Philippine Light Reaction Company. The facility is capable of handling 100 POWs. Each will have his own room and 24-hour access to a very well equipped game room, television, newspapers, film library which has over 100 newsreels covering what's been happening in the world over the past five years. We'll "liberate" the newsreels from the local Armed Forces TV station when time comes. We'll have a cook on duty at all times for meals. A complete field medical facility is almost in place and can handle most medical problems including some routine surgery. The Army Medical team will arrive on sight 24 hours prior to mission execution. They have been alerted for duty involving disaster victims as a cover story."

Catching his breath, Hammer looked at the two VIPs, and then he continued, "Upon arrival on the Kitty Hawk, the Navy medical personnel will examine each POW and categorize them into three groups. First is "Ambulatory," which is for those needing little or no medical attention. The second group is "Guarded," which covers most medical treatment including surgery. The third is "Evacuation." Those are prisoners requiring serious surgical procedures beyond the capabilities of the surgical staff on the carrier. Those will be evacuated to the Navy hospital at Subic Bay under a false identity. Current Intel reports indicate that there are no prisoners known to be in the Evacuation category.

"During the time with us, we'll be working with the prisoners on the general cover story for when they're released. Other areas of personal assistance will be in current events, intelligence debriefing, administrative paperwork, physical training and, most of all, helping to recover from the stressful treatment they've endured. Our goal is to have them ready to quietly be assimilated back into the military and/or civilian life without mission compromise. Sir, that concludes my briefing. Are there any questions?" Hammer asked.

Captain Bayouth looked over at Roman and said, "Impressive. What about downed aircraft? Do you have a plan for escape and evasion?"

Chief Abeel stood up. "Sir, we have a plan that focuses on downed pilots and prisoners floating down the Song Ma to a recovery point called Land's End. Here's a detailed plan for your review. A copy will be given to the Kitty Hawk Captain upon execution. They'll need the plan to help us get our guys out, if necessary."

Bayouth looked at the half inch thick plan with maps. "I don't suppose you have a plan to save the President's ass if this mission blows up on us, do you?"

Roman looked at the Captain, who was a personal friend and longtime advisor to the Chairman and said, "No, sir, but if you will give us a few days we'll see what we can develop." Then Roman smiled.

Bayouth looked at Herbert and said, "I bet he could, too."

"OK, Dan," said Herbert. "Let's go watch your guys fly the practice mission. Then I want to see the Baler facility. I need to be back at Clark operations by 1615 hours. We're flying to Pearl to brief CINCPAC of the mission and arrange for the naval support."

"Yes, sir, can do. Do you want to observe the practice mission with the team or observe from above?" Roman asked.

Bayouth quickly injected, "From above please! Not from fucking treetop. I'm Navy and I'm not suicidal."

Chapter 16

THE MARGIN OF ERROR

The Grunt Air flight of eight Hueys in a tight, right-echelon formation was headed to the town of Carranglan, which was the start point of the training exercise known as SUNDAY STROLL. Arkangel was orbiting above the flight at 6,000 feet as the Command and Control Aircraft. B.G. Herbert was flying as observer with Roman while Captain Bayouth flew in Arkangel. Bayouth flew in the copilot seat next to Chief Alberts so he could see both the activities of the Command and Control ship and the low flying Hueys below.

Earlier that morning, Captain Best, the commander of the reconnaissance platoon, had created a training scenario for this mission. He and Arkangel changed the variables with each training exercise, so when the real mission was executed, the combined air and ground teams could adapt quickly to any changes or problems. Today, Alberts and Best would advise the approaching flight that the Ban Nakay Teu Camp, know as Tulip, would have eight POWs instead of the four that intelligence reported to have at that location. That would require Roman flying the reserve aircraft to accompany Grunt Air 77, piloted by Chief Dodson, to Tulip to pickup the additional POWs and SFC Anderson's Foxtrot recon team.

This last minute shift in aircraft assignments was a good exercise in preparation for what could be a very dangerous and complex extraction in Laos. After developing today's scenario, the five recon teams were flown out to a point 3.5 miles from the mockup of each POW camp. The teams would travel across the mountains and streams to points near the mockup camps. Each camp in the eastern Philippine mountains had been made to look like the real camp down to the physical terrain that would be encountered. There, they would conduct detailed observations of the camps, caves, and surrounding area. This information would be reported back to Arkangel who would then advise the inbound flight commander. Adjustments would be made prior to the start of the exercise which was always less than one minute from the Carranglan start point. This caused decisions to be made quickly and the formation to be configured to accomplish the mission.

Today, Lieutenant Ditton and Chief Donovan would be flying to the simulated Ban Nakay Neua complex, code name Rose. The strike force going flying to Ban Na Eune was Chief Warrant Officer Waldo and Chief Redding. Captain Tripp and Captain Barnes would be going to Nam Hang Long, known as Lilly. Roman could see the start point three miles ahead and knew that Arkangel would be springing the latest changes on him.

"SUNDAY STROLL, this is Arkangel. Tulip has eight bugs," came the voice of Doug Alberts. "BUGS was the codename for POWs" told Bayouth.

Roman immediately replied by triggering his radio transmitter twice. This was done to reply without compromising security.

"SUNDAY STROLL, execute trail with 6 trailing 77. Ready, execute!" Roman commanded. At that point the helicopters moved into a single file formation with Roman pulling out of the lead and moving to a position in the line of helicopters just behind Dorsey, Grunt Air 77. Roman was the only bird that had not been assigned a specific cave or POW site. His purpose was to be available in case there were more POWs at one location than expected or other complication. He also could provide assault fire from his two M-60 machine guns if necessary. Each aircraft had a specific POW camp or cave it had been assigned to. It worked with a specific recon team which observed the site prior to assaulting the facility to recover the POWs and get them to the rendezvous point for extraction.

The sequence in line was determined by the distance from the release point to the cave or camp. Ban Hang Long, (Lilly), was the farthest, so Captain Barns in 88 and Captain Tripp in 55 would be the lead birds. Behind them came Dorsey and Redding who were assigned to Gardenia. The third camp was Ban Nakay Teu which was Chief Dodson's assignment in Grunt Air 77. Roman would follow Dodson in today's training exercise. Bringing up the rear, so to speak, was the Rose, which was the complex at Ban Nakay Neua. Ditton in Grunt Air 11 and Donavan in Grunt Air 22 would pickup the estimated 14 POWs along with Captain Best's Alpha Recon Team. The Maung Soi (Cactus) team was being supported by Alberts, the AN-2 Colt, and Coltrane and Dorsey in the Mi-8 helicopter, which was already at LS 59. Thornhill's Bravo Team did the same type of training on a mock camp but was pulled out by the unused bird in training. This whole plan could change with the next intelligence report.

When the sequence was announced, Eldon Barnes realized that he had the lead in this mission, which he hated. He hated the comments from the other guys after the exercise about his airspeed and altitude above the tree tops. No one was ever satisfied with him. They'd say, "You were too fast" or "too slow" or "too high" or "too low," never "just right." He knew that they were just nervous about the mission. His altitude and airspeed was dead on and everyone knew it. The thoughts of flying combat missions that far behind enemy lines always made everyone nervous.

The next thing Barnes realized was the command from Arkangel, "Execute, Execute!" Barnes pushed the nose of his Huey down and headed for the tree tops in the bottom of the valley that connected to another valley near the town of Abaca. It was critical that he kept an even airspeed and low altitude so the eight-ship strike force would stay close together and not get too high above the trees so as to become an easy target for the NVA gunners. Barnes moved his ship and it's tailing companions up and down through the tree tops and valleys. The frequently changing terrain below him made him change his altitude every few seconds. From above Captain Bayouth commented that it looked like a bunch of bobbing corks on a pond.

As they reached the hill mass at Abaca, the formation rose up and cleared the mountainous obstruction then back down into another valley.

High above, Captain Bayouth looked out of the cockpit side window at the Hueys below. He asked Alberts without taking his eyes off the aircraft, "What's the difference in a daytime practice like this compared to a night time flight?"

"Only the Pucker Factor," Alberts calmly replied.

Bayouth shook his head and said, "The Navy was never like this. I can't believe there've been no training accidents."

"It's a credit to those pilots, Alberts said. "Normally, there would have been at least two accidents. We've been damned lucky."

Barnes spotted his next check point, which was the town of Gadeng. His eyes swiftly glanced at the clock on the instrument panel. He mentally calculated his time and where he should be at this point. "Damn!" he thought. He was almost a half mile behind schedule. He would slowly increase his airspeed to compensate and hoped that he didn't stretch out the formation behind him.

Barnes was checking the clock again to see if he'd made up the time just as he flew over Bazal, the release point. "Break," he commanded over the radio. Each Huey then turned to a direct heading for the landing zone where they would pickup the POWs and recon teams.

Barnes made his hard right hand turn towards Ban Hang Long, "the Lilly." He looked quickly over to the right to see if Tripp in Grunt Air 55 was still with him. The Lilly had one major problem that bothered Barnes. It was the closest to the main NVA headquarters in Laos. He had to fly 8 nautical miles back to the west from the planned release point at Ban Nam Hao on the real mission. "Granted," he thought, "it gives me the greatest noise suppression thanks to the mountain valley as well as the element of surprise." The "Dinks" won't be focusing on inbound flights from the east. Suddenly, his eye caught the LZ and his mental focus was back to this mission. "The real one could be considered later," he thought.

Meanwhile, Waldo in Grunt Air 66 was cresting the hillside that overlooked the simulated Ban Nakay Eune or Gardenia Camp below in a very narrow valley. Waldo had seen U-2 photos of the valley that the real Gardenia was located in. It would be very tight and difficult for him and the second Huey assigned piloted by Chief Redding. They only had a very small open space next to the small river flowing down the valley to land in. At night, it would be even more difficult.

The practice site that Sam Coltrane and Jake Best had selected was perfect. It was well-situated between two high tree lined cliffs, with only enough clearing for the two Hueys to safely land in during the darkness. If that wasn't enough, there had been unconfirmed reports of a Chinese anti-aircraft gun emplacement just above the POW cave and 100 meters from the clearing. The "Big Plan" was for SFC Richardson's recon team to take it out concurrently with the attack on the camp below. Waldo thought to himself, "if they didn't neutralize that 37 millimeter killer, I'll be the first to know."

From above, Captain Bayouth continued to observe the exercise. From altitude, the Hueys looked like toys darting across the hills and valleys. His attention was attracted to the almost invisible LZ that Waldo and Redding were landing in. "How can they squeeze into that small clearing?" he asked himself. "These guys are all pro," he said to Alberts. Alberts said nothing but did nod slightly. Bayouth was also impressed at how fast the recon teams loaded up and the Hueys departed.

It was then that Alberts and Bayouth heard for the first time radio traffic from the strike force. "Tulip clear with eight bugs," Dodson reported as he steered his aircraft south to the mock refueling point at Baler. Then came Ditton's report, then that of Barnes and finally that of Waldo. Roman had moved over a half mile to the Moung Soi prison mockup to pickup Thornhill's Bravo Team.

All birds flew independently to Baler. Captain Hammer and the three non-deployed Recon Teams had eight refueling points located along the north side of the runway which was a mock up of the OASIS refueling point on the mission. Laos Scouts would do this job in the real mission. Each bird would fly to the farthest open refuel point. The crew chief and door gunner jumped out of the Huey and closed the right side cargo door so they could open the fuel cap. There were two barrels of JP4 fuel and a hand pump at each refueling point. The crew chief and door gunner took turns pumping the fuel as quickly as possible into the still running Huey. This was known as a "hot refuel." Meanwhile, the aircraft commander got out and went to the center of the refueling area to report his aircraft status and get any late updates or instructions from Roman.

During the actual mission, they would all fly together to the awaiting Kitty Hawk, cruising 35 to 50 miles off shore. Alberts, who would be flying the AN-2 Colt on the mission, would be primarily responsible for navigation. As a precautionary measure, Roman and Alberts set up a separate navigation problem for each aircraft during training missions like this one to sharpen their skills. Upon departure from the Baler training OASIS, each aircraft was to follow an initial course over water and out of sight of any land reference. At the end of that fixed leg the aircraft crew had to navigate to a point some fifty miles off shore, then turning to another specific point on the shore line prior to returning to Clark AFB. Arkangel would fly high above the off shore point that each Huey would fly over. The Huey would report reaching the point over water before turning towards the shore line point. Arkangel would note the time each bird called in. If they had navigated correctly, they would be arriving at a specific calculated time. Sooner or later, arrival time would mean they had made a navigational error. Such an error could be fatal if they got separated during the mission and had to fly solo to the Kitty Hawk.

Bayouth listened to the reports as they came in and noted the time Alberts put on his navigation exercise clipboard. So far, Bayouth noticed only one aircraft was off by more than thirty seconds either way. Grunt Air 11, Captain Ditton, was out of tolerance. That would be reported to Roman who would not be pleasant about the matter.

"Well, that's one crew that won't be going to town tonight," Alberts said, pointing to Grunt Air 11 time.

"That's still not a bad time when you consider that at 100 knots that's only about a mile and a half off. You can certainly see the carrier that far off," Bayouth remarked.

Alberts looked over at the naval Captain and said, "Sir, you don't know Major Roman. That's unacceptable to him. In bad or marginal weather, you could totally miss the carrier and loose the crew, prisoners and the helicopter at sea."

"I see your point, Chief," Bayouth said softly. "Roman had this unit fine-tuned and ready for any contingency," he thought. The mission probability for success just keeps getting better.

When the C-47 had returned to Clark, Bayouth could see Roman chewing out Captain Ditton and his crew for the screw up. The crew chief was refueling the Huey to go back out.

"What's the deal with Roman and Ditton?" he asked Alberts.

"Roman has a real tough navigation problem that he keeps ready for situations like this. He sends them back out after they refuel and take a piss. They will fly the course instead of going for a beer. In the beginning, we usually had two or three screw up per navigation exercise. Having to fly for another hour and a half on a very demanding course has really got people's attention. Now this is the first screw up that we've had in the last sixteen exercises," Alberts explained. "When it comes to details, and especially life or death details, Roman is tough as nails."

"Got it!" Bayouth said. "Do we have to go back out or can we go get a beer or two? I'll buy."

Alberts smiled and said, "I can smell the hops now."

Roman had just dismissed Captain Ditton and his very disappointed crew to fly a navigational proficiency course when Herbert, Captain Bayouth, Alberts, and Coltrane walked up. Roman saluted the senior officers.

Bayouth began, "I'm buying Chief Alberts a beer for a most informative mission. Anyone care to join us?"

"That's a good idea," Herbert said. "We've got a couple of hours before we depart for Pearl to see CINCPAC. But let's talk for a minute. We can't talk at the club." He paused a minute then looked at Bayouth. "Captain, do you have any comments or changes to the plan that we need to discuss?"

"No, sir," said Bayouth. "The plans and training are fine. It's basically down to the usual unpredictable elements of combat."

"OK, Dan, we are still a go on your schedule and ANVIL Op Plan. I'm concerned about mission compromise regarding that Paula Madison thing. Stay on it. Don't be afraid to pull the plug on her. It would be best if we could find out who she's working with in Alaska."

"I'll have an update either tonight or in the morning. Hammer and I are having supper with her and Morgan. We'll let something slip out about where in Mindanao we are going. She'll undoubtedly call Alaska. The Philippine Counter Intelligence people are monitoring. Hopefully, the Alaska Command Counter Intel people have got their undercover man on Shemya by now. We're getting close. We'll keep it in control until we're ready to arrest them. We can't do it too early without attracting attention," Roman stated in a confident voice. Roman hoped that he sounded more confident than he really felt. "There's a big problem here," Roman thought, "and I just can't figure out why."

"Now, Arkangel, about that beer," General Herbert said with renewed spirit.

Chapter 17

AMY THE BAR FIGHTER
Wednesday, 29 November 1972

It was almost 2100 hours before Roman could get Herbert and Bayouth off to Pearl Harbor, check in with the First Sergeant on urgent paper work, pick up Morgan, and drag his tired ass to the O Club for supper. Hammer, Paula, and Coltrane were already there enjoying their second, or was it their third, round of drinks. Roman was not going to be left behind tonight. He ordered a double Chivas on the rocks. Morgan looked at him and ordered a glass of white wine.

Roman looked across the table at the others and said, "This has been one hell of a day!"

Everyone chimed in. Then the discussion went to the constant delays and foot dragging by the North Vietnamese Peace Negotiations. Paula gave the group all that CBS had learned about the situation.

Paula looked over to Roman on the other side of Hammer and asked if the training exercise would prevent the group from taking a weekend trip to the resort area of Bohol.

Dan looked at Morgan, then Coltrane, and said, "Sounds great to me. What do you think, Sam?"

"I think our training is up to speed and our birds need some maintenance down time," Coltrane responded. "We still have about two weeks until we deploy to Davos."

"Davos,", thought Paula. "That's news."

Hammer looked over at Paula. "Looks like we're a go! Can you get us some decent prices on rooms?" he asked.

"Sure," Madison said. "CBS won't pay for the rooms but we can use the company discount. Down on the 1st and back on the 3rd," she added. "Two nights in heaven!"

Morgan leaned across the table to talk to Paula about the hotels there and what great restaurants were available. Hammer took the opportunity to lean over to Roman and say, "The BMA rebels operating near Pikit is what they want to attack." He made sure that he appeared to be talking confidentially but loud enough for Paula to hear if she was listening, and she was!

"Good," said Roman. "I'm glad they made the decision to take the rebels out instead of the planned training exercise. Actual combat will do them some good, too."

Paula leaned back thinking about what she had just heard and still keeping up with Morgan's conversation. She thought, "Operating out of Davos and a joint combat strike against the rebels near Pikit. That's going to be great news to Alaska, and my bureau chief will love the detailed scoop when they do strike. What a story. This might get me out of this cesspool and to a real bureau like Tokyo, Hong Kong or Moscow."

Sam finished his drink and asked, "Am I the only one who's hungry?"

Morgan responded quickly, "OK. Someone throw Sam some red meat before he gets violent! Waiter, I think we're ready to order."

Four hours had passed since Paula had finished supper. She was now waiting in her apartment off base for the overseas operator to complete her call to Sheyma, Alaska. The phone rang and she picked it up on the first ring. "Hello," she answered.

"We are ready to put through your call now," said the Philippino operator.

The phone rang 3,400 miles away. A muffled man's voice answered, "Command Center."

"Hi. I've got some great news for you," Paula started the conversation with. "They're on a combat strike against the Baugsa Muno Army rebels near Pikit. It's not a training exercise," she continued in an excited but subdued voice. "They'll be operating out of Davos."

"Great! I knew that son of a bitch was up to something more than a training exercise. I'll make some calls to people I know in the Davos area and see if they'll help screw up his operation." We've got to make him look really bad if not incompetent.

Seventeen miles from Paula's apartment was the office of the Philippine Security Counter Intelligence Unit. The on-duty monitoring technician was shocked to hear that someone was going to work in conjunction with Paula Madison to interfere with a Philippine and American joint forces strike against those damned BMA rebels. This must be reported to his superior and Captain Mac immediately. He continued to listen and take notes of the taped conversation.

"Anything new on your request for reassignment?" she asked.

"Not a thing. I'm stuck here for now," said the bitter voice in Alaska. "I'd better get off this line. Bye."

The phone went to dial-tone in Paula's ear, but the tape recorder went on for another ten seconds before the technician turned it off with a big smile. "I've got 'em," he said as he picked up the phone to call his boss.

The phone next to Roman's bed rang at 3:15 am. A very tired and surprised man answered the phone, "Major Roman."

"Dan? This is Amy. I'm in the Quitingil jail. Can you help me?" Amy said in a tired and pleading voice.

"What happened?" he asked.

"We were dancing at the Sunset Bar on the National Highway, when a fight broke out. My friend got away but they got me and I didn't start the fight either."

"OK. I'll come and get you. Have you called Morgan?" Roman asked.

"Ah, no. I was hoping that we could talk about that when you got here. I really don't want her to know, OK?"

"OK, but one question," he said. "You said 'we.' Who was with you?"

"Dan, he is a Navy officer and I don't want him hurt or brought into this whole thing. He has a great future and something like this could end his career."

"OK. I'll be there as soon as I can," Roman said, then hung up the phone. His hand had not moved more than six inches before it rang again. It couldn't be Amy that soon, he thought. "Major Roman," he answered.

"Major Roman, this is Mac. We must talk immediately. There has been another Alaska call," he said.

"Great! Just what I needed right now. Do you know where the police station is at in Quitingil?"

"Sure. One of your team under arrest?" questioned Captain Macario Vallamor.

"Well, sort of. Meet me there in thirty minutes and we can go over your information," Roman said.

"Be right there, sir," Mac said as he hung up.

The Quitingil police station was a typical municipal looking building, stucco over concrete block construction that was bleak despite it being very brightly lit. Roman approached the desk sergeant and said, "I'm here to get Amy Riddell out, sir."

The sergeant looked at Roman carefully and shifted in his chair, then said, "Sorry, Major. I don't think that's possible tonight."

"You can't release her because of a bar fight or drunken behavior?" asked Roman.

The desk sergeant once again studied Roman. "I regret to inform you that Miss Riddell was much more than drunk and disorderly. She didn't start the fight but she did significant damage to the two men who did start the fight. One of the two fighters took a wild swing at the young man that she was with. That's when she hit the man with a barstool. He went down like a stone. Then the other fighter who we have in custody started to attack Riddell when she kicked him in the nuts, then cold cocked him with a Coke bottle. My officer arrived about then and was going to arrest the two drunken fighters and the man she was with. Riddell told her friend to escape. Then she held my officer from pursuing her young friend. When he shook her off to pursue the friend he was football tackled from behind by Miss Riddell. It was then that he arrested her. He has a black eye but he refuses to say if she gave it to him.

"So, Major," the desk sergeant said, "Your friend is in a lot of trouble with the law. There are the assault charges by the two drunks, interference with a police officer pursuing another criminal and possible assault of a police officer, not to mention her drunk and disorderly behavior."

Roman was astounded by the story and the charges against his 5 foot 3 inch future sister-in-law. About that time, Captain Mac walked in. The desk sergeant immediately stood up and saluted. Mac returned his salute and went over and shook the sergeant's hand and greeted him warmly. Then he turned to Roman and asked what the problem was and what could he do to help.

Roman recounted the desk sergeant's story to the humorous amazement of Mac.

Mac went to the desk sergeant and asked that Riddell be brought out for him to see. The sergeant did so quickly. Amy Riddell was brought out in handcuffs looking as rough as an old alley cat.

Mac looked at her then went over to the sergeant and quietly said something to him. The sergeant smirked and then smiled. He ordered the officer escorting her from the jail to take the cuffs off. Then he said loudly to Riddell, "You are released into the custody of one of the Philippine's finest officers, so long as you stay out of Quitingil in the future." Then he smiled at Amy Riddell and said, "If I get into a bar fight, I want you on my side. Now, get out of here."

The three left the police station. As soon as they got outside, Dan thanked Mac as did Amy. Then Roman asked Mac what he said that got the officer to drop the charges.

Mac smiled. "His brother is in my unit and I told him that if he took her before the court and they explained to the judge that that little thing knocked out two big men and tackled his police officer and kept him on the floor until her friend could escape, the police would be the laughingstock in town. He agreed and dropped the charges."

Amy hugged him and thanked him again and again, then turned to Dan. "Can we keep this between us?"

Dan smiled and said, "Keep what between us? I'm here to meet with Captain Villamor on official business. Can I give you a lift to your car?" he asked.

"Thanks, Dan!" exclaimed Amy in appreciation.

"Amy, could you excuse Mac and me for a few minutes? We really do have some important business to discuss," Roman asked. Then he and Mac walked away from her.

"What's the news, Mac?"

Mac recounted the taped conversation between Paula Madison and the unknown man in the Aleutian Islands. Mac finished indicating that there were no expressions of love and affection. Roman began to think, "Was he a boyfriend? No, not likely as he's too old to be a boyfriend, so it has to be an agent or fellow Peace activist."

They discussed the matter for a few minutes, and then parted ways. Roman walked over to Amy, who really looked bad in her dirty, torn clothes and filthy appearance.

"OK, killer, let's get you home," he said, smiling. "Now who the hell is this mysterious friend who you went to jail protecting?"

"Dan, he's a very nice naval officer that didn't need to destroy his naval career in a bar fight that he wasn't involved in," she explained. "Can we leave it at that?"

"OK with me. I hope that Anchor Klanker appreciates what you did for him," Roman lamented.

Chapter 18

KEEP THE FAITH, WE ARE HERE

Until very recently, the abuse to Felderhoff had decreased some in the past month. The Dinks seem to think that the United States was about to capitulate to the Hanoi government any day. They must be thinking of what the world opinion might be if a bunch of starved and tortured souls came limping out at the normal prisoner exchange. The fact that they were feeding them better and not conducting the real vicious torture interrogations recently, gave him hope for survival. If they were planning on not repatriating them, the NVA would not have stopped their blood-lust tortures and would not have wasted food on them. They would just take them out and shoot them and cover up the evidence. But there was something else recently going on that he could not put his finger on. He shook off the unknown factor that was eluding him and got into the endless circle that walked around the compound for daily exercise.

They had been exercising a little over twenty minutes when they had to stop. The guards were carrying the mutilated body of one of the young Air Force lieutenants through the front gate. They had been told to go back to the cave entrance as the guards brought him into the barbed wire compound and dumped him. The guards went outside the front gate and told the POWs to tend to their comrade. They quickly went to him to see if he was even alive. He was, but in real bad shape. He was taken back into the cave to attend to his many wounds. Felderhoff looked on as others worked on him. He could see by the obvious head wounds that if he was lucky he would die soon. The NVA

Intel boys really did a job on him. "But why? The treatment and food had been better than when he first arrived. Well, until two days ago, when the food started getting a little less in quantity and quality. But it always goes in good and bad cycles. Now this," Felderhoff thought. "Had there been a policy change in Hanoi? Had they decided to liquidate them after all?"

He dropped his head and walked outside and away from the opening pondering the situation. He stood there just staring without focus into the dense vegetation that surrounding the cave compound. Something caught his eye. He refocused his eyes to what seemed to be a human just barely visible in the trees. It was a human in a Lao military Scout uniform. He was watching the guards as he tried to signal Felderhoff. Unbeknown to Felderhoff the Scout was Corporal Pao who was recently assigned to SFC Richardson's Recon Team for this mission. Then Pao very slowly raised his open palm upward and then placed it over his heart. He nodded slowly to Felderhoff acknowledging that he was looking at him. He then held up his left hand with fingers extended and open. Then he touched each of the fingers with his right hand index finger in a manner that would indicate a counting procedure. Then he pointed to Felderhoff and the area as a whole. Felderhoff knew that he was asking how many POWs were there. Felderhoff turned slightly to the side so the guards could not see him hold up four fingers then take them down then four fingers again then he held up three fingers. Pao repeated the four, then the four then three, movements. One of the guards looked over and said something to Felderhoff causing him to turn back towards the cave. Pao instantly disappeared from sight and headed back to General Vang Pao's headquarters with the prisoner and cave information requested by Major Roman.

Felderhoff went quietly into the cave a very excited man. He knew that the outside world knew that there were POWs at the Ban Nakay Puem cave. He had a good feeling about the possibility of being rescued. His emotional high was suddenly tempered by the recent change in the NVA attitude towards the prisoners. He wondered if help would get there in time to save them.

Chapter 19

FOR LOVE OF COUNTRY
Monday, 4 December 1972

Roman found it hard to go back to work after such a relaxing weekend in one of the most beautiful beach areas of the world. But there was serious work to be done. Captain Moung from the Laotian Air Force, assigned to Grunt Air as liaison officer and a pilot on Arkangel when it flew over Laos, was due in today. He would be bringing detailed Intelligence on the caves and general situation in the area of northeast Laos, gathered by General Vang Pao's Scouts. They were very reliable and thorough in their Intel gathering. He was due in at 1540 hours. Chief Abeel would meet him and take him to his spook den. Then they would go over the data and prepare for a detailed strike briefing for tomorrow morning. In the meantime, he had to fly out to Baler with Hammer, Best, and Sergeant Major Panfil to see how the renovation of the facilities for the POWs was progressing.

As they landed, Roman saw Captain Mac walking toward the Huey.

"Good morning, Mac," said Roman, as he stepped down from the helicopter. "We just stopped by to see how the preparations were going. I see the perimeter fence is completed as are the guard towers. That's great, and ahead of schedule, too."

"Sir, could I have a word with you?" Mac said as he gently pulled Roman aside by the elbow.

He began, "I know that your project here is highly secret and has a priority greater than god. The specific configuration of the barracks and face lift is designed for very important people. We are not providing security to keep people in but keep people and prying eyes out. That tells me you are going back to Laos for POWs. How am I doing so far?" he said as he continued. "Philippine Intelligence has credible reports that there are three to five captured Filipino soldiers being held POW in the far northeastern portion of Laos. This is your old area of operations. If you're going to that area, I want to go with you. I want to be the Filipino representative to the strike force. Please!" he said with passion.

"You are on dangerous grounds here, Captain," Roman said in a serious tone. "I am not authorized to discuss any part of the mission with you, only the cover story of our joint training exercise in Mindanao."

"Sir," Mac said, "If there are my countrymen in the area, I should be included. I know the dangers and risks of missions like yours. I also know that the experience would be invaluable to my unit's development. Especially with our mission to develop Intelligence on the Mindanao Muslim movement and be ready to take on the Baug Sa Moro Army. I've been training with Grunt Air for months and know the organization and procedures. Please give it serious consideration," he said with a plea in his voice.

Roman said nothing, but looked into Mac's eyes, then smiled and gave him a wink. Then he went over to the others to conduct the facilities inspection.

Upon completion of the facility, Roman flew back to Clark where he went over the maintenance hanger to see his friend Tom Reichert. "Hey, Tom," Roman said as he walked into his office. "How're you coming with your preparations for the mission?"

"What the hell are you doing here, Dan? You know damned well I could go tonight. The only thing that we have not done is install the long range fuel tanks. That will be done tomorrow once the new model tanks arrive on today's courier flight from Pearl. So there," Reichert said in his usual gruff tone. "So, exalted leader, if you are bored, go somewhere else as I have work to do. That means get the fuck out of my hair."

Roman was bursting out in laughter at Reichert's tirade and attitude. Dan dearly appreciated his friendship with Tom and respected his talent in keeping the helicopters flyable.

"Thank you, Captain Reichert, for that illuminating discourse on aviation maintenance and intelligence procedures," Roman said tongue in cheek. "I'm headed over to the Flight line Snack bar for lunch. Would you like to join me?"

"Sure, since you are buying," Reichert replied as he put his hat on and walked by Roman and out the door.

Roman went to his office after lunch and ran into Gunnery Sergeant Roger Thornhill as he was leaving. "Hey, Roger, wait one," Roman said as he pulled Thornhill back into the building. He looked around to see who was around the asked, "What do you think of Captain Villamor? Is he squared away enough to go with us?"

"Sure, if he wants to lower himself to our standards. His troops may be a little green but as a Recon type he's aces with me, sir. What do you have in mind, sir?" Thornhill asked.

"We know there are Philippinos in Moung Soi, and I thought it might be good if we had one of their countrymen with you when you bust them out," Roman said quietly.

"Good idea. Let's make Greiner an alternate and put Captain Mac on my team," Thornhill volunteered.

"OK," Roman said. "Let me think about it some more and perhaps check with General Herbert on this one. I'll let you know by tomorrow. He will need to go through several practices with you before we depart."

At 1530 hours, Roman had an urge to go meet Captain Moung upon his arrival. He was a good guy and Roman had a high respect for him. Roman took a Jeep over to transit operations just as the C-130 pulled to a stop.

Roman joined Abeel as Moung entered the building. There were warm greetings and hand shakes despite the heavy briefcase handcuffed to Moung's left hand.

"Well, it looks like you have some good poop for us," Abeel said as he pointed to the brief case.

"You will be very happy with the Intel that we have collected for you. General Pao sends his best to you, Major Roman. He looks forward to your return to Laos."

"Thanks. Let's head to the office," Abeel said in anticipation of the new Intel.

Chapter 20

MISSION BRIEFING
Tuesday, 6 December 1972

Roman picked up his office phone slightly after 0700 hours, Tuesday morning. He thought for a moment to remember the phone number then dialed.

The phone was answered almost immediately, "Captain Mac, speaking."

"Mac, this is Dan Roman. There is going to be a briefing at 0830 hours in our briefing room. If you are still interested in that proposal you made me at Baler, be there. Sit with Gunny Thornhill," Roman said in a firm but soft voice.

"Roger that, sir!" exclaimed a very excited Captain Mac. "I will be there, and thanks."

Roman put the phone down and smiled. "He thanks me today, but will he thank me when he's up to his ass in NVA fifteen hundred miles from home?"

It was moments before the 0830 briefing. Roman, Abeel, and Captain Moung were about to go into the briefing room when Brigadier General Herbert and Captain Bayouth entered the office. Surprised, Roman called the room to attention.

"Good morning, sir," Roman said to Herbert as he rendered a salute. Then he nodded to Bayouth. "I wasn't expecting you, sir."

"We hitched a ride on a KC-135 tanker headed this way. I wanted to hear Captain Moung's Intel briefing first hand. So if you are ready, let's do it," the general said as he anxiously motioned toward the briefing room door.

Roman turned to Moung. "OK, Captain, its show time."

Moung, followed by the general, Roman, Abeel, and Bayouth entered the room. Moung proceeded to the podium at the front of the room. Abeel went to a chair to the left of the map of Laos. Roman and the general took seats at the front of the room.

"Good morning, gentlemen. For those of you who are new, I'm Captain Moung with the Royal Laotian Air Force. I'm proud to say that I was a part of the Grunt Air Big Casino raid, as were five Laotian Army Scouts who have been officially designated as Lao Team One by General Vang Pao. Lao Team One has completed Operation SANPAN and has the following information for you.

"There have been some major changes since the Big Casino raid.

"Needless to say, there were several senior officers fired and reassigned for their gross negligence. The new commander for prisoners and the main Intelligence office for the NLHS headquarters have been moved to the Ban Nakay Neua District Headquarters. They are to support the new operation developed to protect the POWs from you Yankee Capitalist Pigs (laughter.) They've moved in the Pathet Lao 10th Signal Battalion and have relocated the 16th and 769th anti-aircraft battalions to MRII. They are equipped with the old model 37 millimeter anti-aircraft guns. The units were widely dispersed and should not be a factor given the current plan of attack.

"What will be of major concern to us is the recent deployment of two new model 37 millimeter (Anti-aircraft Artillery) AAA owned and operated by the Peoples' Republic of China troops. Both weapons are in the immediate area of the camps. It looks like they're taking no chances of you gangsters stealing their prisoners again. The American Embassy and your higher headquarters may not be familiar with or respectful of Grunt Air, but your enemy definitely knows who Grunt Air is and what you can do. That's why they put one of the 37 mm guns directly above the cave at Ban Nakay Eune, code name Gardenia, and the other 37 is covering the headquarters complex and the approach from the north and east. These two Chinese gun emplacements replace the old style PL gun that was on top of the cave. They have also closed down most of the other active camps and consolidated the remaining prisoners in MR I and II area to the local four caves and Moung Soi. Two days ago, Ban Hong Long, known as Lilly, was closed down. The prisoners were moved to the Ban Nakay Puem Camp codename Daisy near Gardenia."

The Captain paused to let the groans die down, and then continued, "Yes, I know. Puem or Daisy was never confirmed by headquarters as even existing, but they are there. This actually works for us as it brings all the Ban Nakay sites in close and we don't have that eight mile leg to deal with. The two 37 mm's are a different matter for Major Roman to consider.

"There are two other matters for us to address. First, they've moved in a 200 man Pathet Lao security force to support the existing guards. They're the same sloppy and poorly disciplined bunch you had at Big Casino. They run small patrols out to four or five kilometers during 0200 to 0600 hours, then again at 1400 hours to 1800 hours. They're just going through the motions. You can hear them coming ten minutes before they come tromping through the jungle. They don't get off the trail other than to take a piss. At night only a 25 man guard and patrol force stays in their bivouac area along the river next to Route 6A two klicks north of the NLHS headquarters.

"They've also moved in a reaction force to support the PL security force. The force of a small company or reinforced platoon is a part of the 613th PL Mobile Infantry Battalion stationed in the Mounghian area some 100 klicks west-southwest of the prison complex. Unit morale is very low. Their very popular PL commander Phommahaxai was caught in an adulterous situation and he was demoted from general to major. He was replaced by hard core PL Colonel Mahoseuk. The forces don't do anything until ordered to by the new commander. This policy will slow any reaction to our strike.

"The camp guards are still the same sloppy forces that usually were too old or physically unfit for regular military duty. What is new is the posting of an NVA officer 24 hours a day onsite. That's a result of the Big Casino raid and the fear that the idiot guards might abuse or kill the POWs. During the day, a part time NVA advisor from Hanoi comes to each camp for a very cursory inspection. He'll stand by and supervise regular PL security forces as they take one or two prisoners out into the jungle to get wild jungle food or escort prisoners to headquarters for interrogation. They're putting a premium on new intelligence in the last couple of weeks. To say that the intelligence personnel are inhumane would be a major understatement. However, in recent weeks the prisoners have been provided primitive medical care. The food was increased to 600 grams twice a day for a couple of weeks then went back to the very poor quality and quantity. It's unclean, unseasoned, and of minimum quantity to sustain life. The caves are crowded and sanitation is very poor. This has caused a variety of diseases and sores. If they don't shoot them first, they'll starve to death within four to five months.

"They'll usually let outside to get some sun and exercise on a regular basis, which helps some. All in all, it's a pretty sad life. The good news, there are no near death or severely crippled in the camps, other than one man with a blindfold over his eyes day and night in Dasey. We don't know why. All are ambulatory to some extent. They are being kind so they can get more Intelligence from him. Those that resist are brutalized.

"Let's cover each camp.

"First, we have the main holding cell for the Ban Nakay Neua intelligence holding prison. The main prison is not being used at this time. There's only the headquarters holding cell near the intelligence office for interrogations. It consists of one small cave in a standalone 70 foot karst in a large open area facing the headquarters. It's in full view of the headquarters duty officer 110 meters to the north of the cave and 100 meters west of the main road going to Sam Neua. There's a small dirt road that leads from the main road to the entrance. It's seldom used. The cave is enclosed with a nine foot concertina barbed wire fence which runs from five meters either side of the entrance. The wire enclosure is about 25 meters long and ten meters wide. The gate to the enclosure was at the end on the headquarters side. The cave entrance itself is strong. It consisted of a log and cement wall with a small one meter by two meter doorway. The inside was about eight square meters in area. The door was steel with a small hole to look in on the POWs. As usual it was secured with a pad lock and chain. The cave also had electricity provided by a generator located outside the barbed wire enclosure some twenty meters away from the cave entrance. There are three small thatched roof buildings just outside of the enclosure about twenty meters to the right of the entrance. The one closest to the compound entrance was the living quarters of the guards. There are six PL officers with pistols guarding these high value prisoners. The second building was the mess hall and kitchen. The third building is where the generator is located. There are always two guards on duty. The other four are either asleep or out on the town."

"Ban Nakay Teu," he said as he put up a sketch of the cave and immediate area. "It's the smallest cave and the least guarded. It's so close and in direct sight of the headquarters, it's not considered by the PL or NVA as vulnerable. It has four field grade prisoners, all American. There is a Navy Commander, Navy Lieutenant Commander, Air Force Lieutenant Colonel and one Air Force Major. They're interrogated on a twice weekly schedule. The front of the hill mass faces the northeast. It's about 450 feet from a clearing that Chief Dodson can set down in. The trees will provide some cover so approach from the northeast. There's a bamboo type fence with concertina wire at the inside base, and on top the guard has a hut next to the wooden gate. It's secured with the usual chain and padlock. Like the other guards, they're posted for one hour tours during the day and changed every two hours at night. This is standard at all of the camps. The problem is that they work off of their own time and not synchronized with the others. That may be a problem for the recon teams."

Moung looked out over the faces and noted the stunned expression on Captain Bayouth's face. He paused, and then asked, "Does the Captain have any questions, so far?"

"No, not at all Captain Moung. I was just wondering if the NVA Intelligence knows as much about my love life." There was laughter.

"I wouldn't be surprised, sir. The Intelligence service of the NVA is awesome. They're good, but we're better," Moung proudly stated.

"No question about that," Bayouth said.

The next camp is Moung Soi. It's completely different from the others due to its location and nature of the local population. For the most part, the local PL guards do Hanoi's dirty work because they have to do it or pay a nasty price. There's little love for the NVA, but they're not prepared to follow General Vang Pao either. The camp is your typical log fence with concertina wire from the ground up to the top on the inside. Its 600 feet long and 150 feet wide. There are two guard towers but only one is manned at any time. It's located 150 meters north of the west end of the runway. It's basically in a big clearing that is part of a gentle hill which the camp surrounds. The main building and troop billets are on the hill top which is also surrounded with a bamboo type fence and concertina. One of the two guard towers is on the hill top next to the billets. The second is at the only gate. From this one tower, every inch of the area except the creek can be watched. The good news is the guards often sleep on duty.

"There's a small creek that travels the entire length. It might be adequate cover if you crawl in from the west. Corporal Moana Tong was successful a few nights back going in that way. He cut a hole in the wire leading into the billet and headquarters area. He wants Gunny Thornhill not to worry. He can handle it," Captain Moung said as he looked up for Thornhill, who had raised a thumb up signal. Captain Mac, who sat next to Thornhill, looked like a deer in the headlights, stunned at what he was hearing and the detail the briefer was going into.

"There are thirty prisoners there, mostly Air Force, but there are at least four Navy, two Army, one South Vietnamese Colonel and three Filipinos," Captain Moung continued. "The air field next to the camp is closed at night and there's only one guard and he sleeps in the operations building. He will not be a factor. The one phone line is on the exterior of the building and will be cut prior to the arrival of Captain Coltrane and Chief Alberts.

"Now, let's look at the new camp, Ban Nakay Peum (Dasey). It is just north of the cave at Eune and is along the same fifteen to twenty foot wide stream. It and Eune are situated in a narrow valley just east of Ban Nakay Neua complex. Its almost 1,000 feet long and 800 feet wide. All of the buildings and cells are hidden in the jungle that surrounds the camp. The center is open and cultivated on both sides of the stream. It would be next to impossible to see from the air. Like the others, it has a 15 foot high fence with concertina, except that portion that could be visible from the air. They have a thick barbed wire and concertina fence across the open area. While we didn't see any, we expect that the wire in the pen area is booby trapped and heavily mined."

"Access must be from the tree line on the south side. There are six long buildings in the trees where prisoners are or were kept.

Currently there are only eight Air Force pilots in the camp and they're in the middle building on the west side of the stream. There's only the one guard at night. The prisoners are handcuffed to their beds all night. We were told by a local villager that more prisoners would be sent here in mid December. This camp and Moung Soi would be the only two camps open by the end of December. He sells rice, fish and other food items to the camps in the area. He has a store near the headquarters building in Ban Nakay Neua. The remote nature of this camp and the cave at Eune make the reaction force ineffective. There's only one wide path that leads to this valley," he stated as he pointed to the map.

Looking around the room to insure there were no questions about to be asked Moung continued, "There's a checkpoint on Route 6A just north of the headquarters building. From there you go up a steep hill along the path, turning gently from an easterly direction to a southerly direction. As you get to the bottom of the hill, you will encounter a small village and the stream. The path will take you south on the west side of the stream past the village of Ban Peum to the camp gate. If you want to go on to the Eune cave, you must follow a smaller trail that leads you into the trees and around the camp. You can land in the camp on the vegetable garden."

"There's no direct line of sight to the 37 mm just above the Eune cave. The trees will cover you while you're on the ground, but you'll be a sitting duck going in and coming out. Obviously, the attack plan must accommodate the two 37 mm gun emplacements. The valley is narrow and the area is limited, so Captain Barnes will need to come in from the north and depart back to the north until you clear the valley, then southeast to OASIS."

"The next camp is the most interesting, the cave at Ban Nakay Eune. It has become the focus point of the PL and NVA Intelligence services. Why, we don't know, just that this is where the important prisoners come for detailed interrogation. The cave is man made and was dug directly into a limestone hill mass on the southwest side of the stream. The opening faces the northeast. There're your usual trees and shrubs growing on the hillside and the Lianas type tree on top with rope-like vines hanging down over the face of the hill and cave opening. This prevents observation by even a very low flying aircraft."

"You must pull the vines aside to enter the cave. It's at the top of the hill that the Chinese have dug in the 37 millimeter gun emplacement along with one 12.7 machine gun. The cave goes into the hill some 90 to 100 feet. It is 9 feet tall and 15 feet wide. At the front of the cave there is a concrete wall about 4 inches thick, which is a blast deflector. It's inside the concertina wire compound. There is an iron bar door with a small grilled openings set in the center of the bared iron bar front wall which covers the entire cave opening. The iron door is about is locked on the outside at all times.

"Entry to the cave is controlled by two PL guards stationed outside the cave. The headquarters has directed that the two guards be officers or senior noncommissioned officers. As I mentioned earlier the headquarters is concerned that the junior troops might abuse or kill the prisoners. There is a concertina and bamboo fence from one side of the hill to the other side in a 60 foot arc. In the middle there's a gate and a small shack to keep rain off the guards. This is where the two guards stay usually until they are relieved every hour in the day and every two hours at night. The senior guard goes to the steel door and checks the lock and looks in the cave to check on the prisoners.

"One unusual item is that they've strung an electric line into the cave for light. It's powered by a 220 volt 50 cycle generator in one of the small building just outside the fence. There's also a telephone at the cave which goes directly to the Intelligence office at the NLHS headquarters. The extension number is 220. Sergeant Richardson, please don't call for pizza while you are there. Why lights, telephone, and special guards? We don't know. But soon we will find out," boasted the obviously proud Laotian Captain.

"At the present time there are eight Air Force pilots and three Thai women. The women were outside for sun and exercise a few days ago talking in Thai and wearing camouflaged fatigues. Our contact there said the oriental ladies had been passengers on an Air America C-47 that was shot down. That doesn't sound correct, but we'll follow up. The only point to land is the clearing to the south 100 meters. Keep in mind that this is an area that they run night patrols through. I would expect that we would be in OASIS and beyond before any patrol would get to the area. But keep an eye out just in case.

"Speaking of OASIS, it has been cleared and ready to occupy. There are no military units in the area and the population is essentially neutral. They just want to be left alone. Don't expect that they will assist you, but they won't attack you either. I don't think there are any phones close by to call Hanoi in the immediate area. This is a poor and remote area."

"We'll get another update from our Scouts when we reach LS 59. Are there any questions?" Captain Moung asked as he turned to face the general.

Chapter 21

A CHINESE 37 WITHOUT EGGROLL
Wednesday, 7 December 1972

Roman walked into the operations office where Best, Coltrane and Abeel were drinking coffee and looking at the detailed strike plan map. Abeel started to get up as Roman entered the room, but Roman waved him back into his seat.

"Well, I hope that you had a dynamic revelation last night on how we can adjust the plan to take out that second Chinese 37 mm," he said in frustration.

Coltrane pointed to the map with his ever present unlit cigar and said, "We're too few and too many. We need another recon team or another Lao team to deal with the second gun emplacement. The problem then becomes a weight factor and a loss of flexibility. If we went with a third Lao Team, which would be best, the question is who picks them up? The gun is almost 2 klicks from the main complex. Ditton and Donovan have a full load as it is, but they might be able to handle one each. That assumes that the team can blow the gun and get to the LZ in time - not likely.

"I'm not in favor of having the Scout teams blow the two gun emplacements then try to escape through the jungle back to Long Thien. The NVA will be on the lookout for them and they're far too far behind NVA lines to get through. That would be a slaughter of our friends, and that's unacceptable," Roman said in a serious tone.

"Slightly closer is Daisy. It would be a better pickup point for them and we have room for them, unless more arrive between now and then. The other option is for Major Roman to pick them up at the beginning of the strike mission. There goes our flexibility," Coltrane finished and turned to Roman.

Roman looked at the map then over to Captain Best. "Have any miracles up your flight suit sleeve?" Best just shook his head in frustration.

Abeel chimed in, "Perhaps we should first decide how we are going to take them out. From what we're told, the Chinese stand down at night with only a duty crew and sentry. The PL's also have one or two 12.7mm machine guns protecting the emplacement. They can do some damage, too." Abeel then looked over at Best and threw a wadded up napkin at him.

"Thanks," Best said as he threw the napkin back to Abeel. "What if we used thermite grenades instead of C-4 explosive? In both cases, the Lao teams wait until we hit the release point, then silently take out the guard and set off a thermite grenade in the muzzle and on top of the breech block. There would be no appreciable noise to wake anyone up. Hell, three minutes later the Hueys will do that. If the thermite burns a hole in the block or melts the end of the barrel, they're boat anchors. All it takes is one to do the job. In the case of the 37 at Teu, we can have Pao can climb down the vines to join Anderson and his team. Weight won't be a factor," Best said, looking up at the map. Then he turned to look at Roman and continued, "That leaves the fate of the third Lao team to cover. Sorry Boss, you're the only game in town."

The Grunt Air commander got up from the side of the desk where he was sitting and walked over to the recent U-2 reconnaissance photos and put his stubby finger on the one that showed the hilltop and the 37mm gun. "Look at this," he said with emphasis. "The top is mostly clear, especially on the northeast side. The hilltop has a sharp drop-off here and it's away from the emplacement and the trail. When the shit hits the fan, they'll focus their attention on the camp and skies for helicopters and the trail for our Lao team. If I take the lead, regardless of changes I can pick them up, and then move back into position for support calls."

Best looked over at Coltrane and said, "Sam, looks like you may have a shot at Morgan because Dan here will be fucking dead! Dan, those 12.7s will blow your ass completely out of the sky. At that range they can't miss and you know as well as I what a 12.7 can do to a Huey."

"He's right," Abeel said.

"OK, OK, let's get back to that shot at Morgan," Coltrane retorted in a jovial voice.

Roman didn't respond to the comments. He had taken a map ruler and started taking measurements of the hilltop and emplacement. The room became silent as everyone saw that Roman was serious and deeply evaluating the situation and conditions on the hilltop.

Roman turned to the others and said, "First, I can't live forever and second, Sam you can't afford Morgan on your pay." The room erupted in laughter. "OK, it's only eighty to ninety yards from the emplacement to the edge of the cliff. The two 12.7s are positioned close to the trail forward of the 37. The area where the PL are sleeping is at least fifty yards from their guns. Assume the 37 is no longer a factor. By the time the thermite grenades go off and someone sounds an alarm, it will be at least fifteen to twenty seconds. The Lao team will be in the clear at that point and out of sight in the trees and scrub bushes. The PL has to wake up and orient themselves, then run to the guns, another sixty to eighty seconds, if not longer. I can approach low and fast to the pickup point. They hop on and I drop down behind the north side of the hilltop and out of line of fire."

Roman looked around the room for a reaction, then continued, "I'll be clear, and then able to respond to any situation." He waited for someone to speak.

Best turned to Coltrane, "Sam, I suggest you go to the bank and make a big loan to cover Morgan's high overhead."

Abeel was about to speak when Coltrane interrupted, "Dan, that's damned risky. If the Lao are late or if the PL moves faster than you think, you're dead meat. The concept does, however, look good and should work, but it is high risk."

Best looked at Abeel and asked, "Can we get some timers for C-4 blocks? If we can, the Lao can plant charges under the 37s and 12.7s as a backup to the thermite grenades, set them to go off sixty seconds to allow the Leo Team to get far enough away. Then the guns are neutralized."

"That would do it but the sound of the explosions would alert and motivate the troops, not to mention attract attention in the entire area. That could hurt other teams. Best go with thermite on them as well. Lift the back sight and tape the grenade to it. It'll burn right through the breach mechanism. That we can do," Abeel said. "Now, who do we want to lead the third team? It's got to be someone proven and reliable."

"Corporal Yap is on Krumins team and he's certainly qualified and he did prove himself at Big Casino," Abeel said. "And he can do it by himself. We don't need another team. We just use our existing assets."

Best looked a little uneasy, then said, "Yes, but he isn't as aggressive or as ruthless as Pao or Tong. This job calls for a real mean son of a bitch."

Before anyone could say anything, Roman interjected, "Sam, change the plan to conform to this procedure. Jake, you and Krumins have a serious talk to Yap. If you still think that he needs to be replaced after you talk to him, let me know. OK, then, briefing at 1300 hours, insert recon teams at 1530 hours and extraction mission at 1800 hours. Let's do it."

It was 1845 hours and Arkangel had just given the command to execute the break at Bazel when he looked out and saw all the Hueys had turned toward their assigned LZ. "All's well. The training exercises are sharpening the pilot skills to a fine edge," he thought.

Meanwhile, 7,500 feet below him Grunt Air 11 and 22 had made their turn towards Ban Nakay Neua complex. Lieutenant J.P. Ditton, the Aircraft Commander and lead aircraft, was seated in the left pilot seat of the Huey and his copilot M.F. Waldo, better known as The Great Waldo, was flying the aircraft from the right seat. Normally Waldo was a pilot in command but he wanted on this mission and elected to volunteer to be Ditton's co-pilot. The Great Waldo was a very popular member of Grunt Air as he was always cracking a joke or pulling some stunt when things seemed to be overly serious. He was also one of the very best pilots in Grunt Air. His two tours in Vietnam had honed his skills to perfection. Dorsey might be the bravest or the craziest for flying all the really bad hot LZ extractions, but it was the Great Waldo who was the best skilled pilot with a perfect control stick touch.

Today he was flying the practice mission. He had turned to the southwest, dropping into the valley that would take them to the mock LZ Rose. Skillfully, he kept the Huey at 100 knots airspeed and the skids barely above the trees. He always joked about bringing back enough chlorophyll back to base on his skids to build his own plant. "Today would be no different," he thought.

Suddenly, from out of the trees in front of him, a flock of twenty or so large black birds the size of Texas buzzards flew in front of him. There was no missing the birds. The heavy birds hit the front of the Huey with destructive impact. Birds busted through both pilot windows and chin bubbles. The Plexiglas absorbed the majority of the potentially lethal force. But they still hit both pilots, distracting their critical attention from flying the aircraft. Just the fleeting moments of distraction were enough to allow the speeding aircraft to descend the foot or so into the top of the trees. The sudden reduction of speed caused by the trees threw both pilots and crewmen forward against their seat belts. The front of the Huey was being beaten into scrap the further it descended into the trees.

Waldo was shaken by the birds hitting him in the chest and top of his helmet, but he still had the controls firmly in hand. Everything happened in microseconds but to Waldo, the terrible event suddenly was in slow motion. He knew that the aircraft was going down and no matter how good he was he couldn't change the fate of this flight. He was crashing!

His mind told him to hang on for dear life to the controls. Waldo mentally visualized the usual fire associated with most crashes. His thousands of flight hours told him to shut off the fuel to reduce the chances of fire. In a fleeting moment his left hand reached up and turned the fuel switch to the off position. At that same instant the right skid caught on a large tree branch and snapped the aircraft hard to the right and rolled it over on its left side and back. The main rotor blades hit the trees and broke loose from the mast and flew off into the distance.

The tumbling Huey continued to roll through the trees, rapidly slowing down. Suddenly, the Huey stopped rolling through the trees and came to a stop in an upright position. It was over, and they were still alive. The only noise that could be heard was the sound of the AC inverters. Ditton looked at Waldo wide eyed, then reached up and turned off the inverters and main power switch. Then panic struck them. They had to get out and away from the Huey before the inevitable fire roasted them alive!

"GET OUT!" Ditton screamed, as if he had to say the obvious to the already departing crew.

Both Waldo and Ditton unbuckled their seatbelts and got out. Sergeant England, the crew chief, yelled back that there was a clearing and stream fifty feet to the left front of the destroyed Huey. The four crewmen met and hugged each other as they got into the clearing.

Alberts yelled into his microphone, "We have a bird down! Ditton went down. No fire!"

The words ran a cold chill down the back of everyone listening to the radio. It was a fear that lived with every pilot and crewman. Nobody ever thought it could be him that buys the farm, but down deep they all knew it could happen anytime, just as it was for Grunt Air 11.

Roman transmitted, "Abort exercise! Arkangel, orbit and report the status of downed aircraft. Notify Clark operations. Grunt Air 22, stay with 11. Grunt Air 66, 77, 55 pick up your teams. Barnes, pickup Best, then lead everyone back to Clark. I'll stay with 11 and try to effect recovery. Sam, you start the crash procedures and reporting. Let's get it done," Roman commanded. "Now, what about the crew? Can you see anyone alive?"

"Six, this is Arkangel. I have all four crewmen standing next to the creek waving and there is still no fire. Downed crew is 800 meters southeast of the fish farm."

Roman made a long approach to the flat area next to the stream near the crew. Grunt Air 22 was landing ahead of Roman and to the left of the crew. Sam Coltrane in Grunt Air 33 was making a slow orbit over the downed Huey to start his preliminary crash investigation.

Roman shook his head and thought about how lucky the crew was and the fact that they had not had more serious accidents. "This should bring a little reality to the minds and flying techniques of the other pilots," he thought.

It was almost 11:00 pm before Roman, Hammer, and Coltrane finished the necessary reports. Roman dreaded having to call General Herbert about the crash, but it had to be done. When he did call,

Herbert was more positive about the situation than he expected. He directed Roman to call the Army Aviation Commander of Clark and request the loan of a Huey for training exercises. Roman knew where that request would go. He knew that the General or Captain Bayouth would have to pull some strings to get a good replacement bird.

When everything was completed, they went over to the O Club to join the other pilots who were buying Ditton and Waldo a few post-crash survivors' drinks.

Chapter 22

IT'S WHO YOU KNOW
Thursday, 8 December 1972

It was almost 10:00 am when Roman entered the Grunt Air Headquarters in a very foul mood.

"Morning, Top," he said to the Grunt Air First Sergeant. "Could you get me a commercial overseas line or AUTOVAN line to Pearl? I need to track down General Herbert at CINCPAC Headquarters."

"Hello, sir, Roman here," he said in perfunctory greeting. "I'm afraid I struck out with Colonel Ballard on getting a thirty day loan of a Huey. I tried to explain that we needed the bird for the Joint Philippine exercise in Mindanao. Besides laughing at me, he said that I shouldn't have the birds that I have now. I guess I really did sound pathetic. I would have laughed too, if I were him," Roman lamented. "I would suggest that we get a bird out of Saigon but I'm concerned about the maintenance status of them. I can't afford any last minute breakdown," rambled Roman. "Do you have any suggestions, sir?"

Brigadier General Herbert heard a tired and frustrated man at the other end of the phone. "Ah Dan, you give up too easily. I'm sure that Colonel Ballard will loan you a bird. Give me a couple of hours to soften him up. Just stand by for now." Then in a lighter tone of voice he asked, "What's on today's training schedule?"

"Actually, sir, I stood the unit down for safety conference this morning and maintenance this afternoon. That crash really shook them up. I want to capitalize on the shock factor to drive home the need for safety even in a combat environment," Roman explained. Reichert will finish installing the long range tanks in the birds today. That will give us the over water range needed to go from the Hawk to UBON, refuel at night and on in to LS59 before anyone knows we are in country."

"Good idea. That's most appropriate given the situation. How are Ditton and Waldo?" the general inquired.

Roman responded, "They're a little shook up but ready to go."

"Great, let me see what I can do about a replacement bird for you."

"Thanks," Dan said. "I hope that you have better luck than I did."

"Not to worry, I will," He said with confidence. "If the peace treaty is still in effect, would you and Morgan have supper with Bayouth and me Saturday night? We arrive early Saturday morning for a meeting with some of Phil's colleagues at Subic Bay, if you get my drift."

"Perfect timing, sir. We are having a small birthday party for Amy and your presence would be wonderful. She's turning 20, going on 35," Roman said with a tone of excitement.

"Look forward to it. Goodbye," Herbert said as he hung up the phone.

It was almost noon when the first sergeant tapped on Roman's office door jam. "Sir, it's a Colonel Ballard for you on the main line."

"Major Roman, sir."

"Roman this is Colonel Ballard. It seems that a four star general in the Pentagon thinks that I should give your request for a Huey reconsideration. Since he inferred that I might be retiring next month in snow shoes if I didn't, I figured your joint exercise might be of greater importance than I originally thought. Captain Johnson, my maintenance officer, will be at your office at 1300 with four log books for you to review. Take your pick," the Colonel said with a forced pleasant tone. "Just one thing, Roman: Who are you? It took less than an hour for the office of the Chairman of the Joint Chiefs of Staff to correct the error of my thinking."

"Sir, I am sorry to inconvenience you. There is a great deal of pressure from the White House to make these joint exercises work. It has a lot to do with the state of martial law that was declared in September. Everyone is concerned about the Baugsa Moro Army and the Mindanao Muslim Movement."

"You're kidding? If it was that important why were our units not included?" he asked."

"I'm not certain sir, I'm just a Major. I suspect it's because the type mission that the Light Reaction Company has closely matches our own Crash Site Survey Mission."

"Ok, I don't get it, but the best of luck. Don't screw it up. That much interest from Washington can be really rough if you screw up," he said as he got off the phone.Roman put his finger on the phone button to end the call then dialed Captain Reichert's phone number. "Tom, be in my office at 1300. The Aviation Battalion is offering us four birds to choose from." As he hung up Roman leaned back in his chair and smiled.

Chapter 23

FIREDANCE
Friday, 9 December 1972

"Good morning, gentleman," Captain Coltrane said as he entered the briefing room. "Please take your seats and get your Crayolas out. You'll want to take notes. Is there anyone, and I mean anyone, not here that is scheduled to deploy on ROADSHOW? This class is a mandatory class." He looked around the full room.

"OK, then we'll discuss two aspects of ANVIL which is the actual mission execution part of ROADSHOW," he said as he looked carefully at the group to insure he had their complete and undivided attention. "There are two options that can be taken once the mission starts. First, there's codename Raindance. Raindance is mission abort. If Arkangel or Grunt Air 6 gives the Raindance command, you will abort and return to LS 59. The second is a little more serious. It's codename Firedance," he said with strong emphasis. "That is what you call out if you go down during the mission and have to execute the escape and evasion plan. If you go down, you're on your own. The birds are full and can't come back and extract you. You must follow the E and E plan to the rescue point. You are deep inside a very hostile North Vietnam. Since this will be the second time that we will have successfully fooled them and rescued our POWs, they will not be very nice to you. You can expect very harsh treatment should you be captured. Most of you who were on the Big Casino raid saw first hand what they do to prisoners," Coltrane said in a deep, almost raspy, voice. Then he pointed to Major Roman.

Major Roman stood up in the back of the room and started walking forward. "OK, guys, this is like the line in the sand at the Alamo," Roman said. "This is the last chance to back out of the mission. If you, for any reason, want to excuse yourself from the mission, now is the time. If you feel that you can't fulfill your job obligations on this mission I would appreciate if you would resign from the mission. We can not be anything less than 100% effort at all times. If you have any doubts about the mission, please leave now with my appreciation. There is no shame to back out at this time. This is a very hard and extremely dangerous mission." Roman looked around and gave them the last chance to leave. "OK," he said. "I assume that everyone is across the line in the sand. OK, Sam, continue," Roman said as he sat down.

"If you go down in the cave area, move northeast to a small stream. Just beyond the cave ridge line the stream moves northward and down the valley. On your survival map it is called Huoi Vong. Cross the stream to the east side to lose any scent being followed by dogs. Travel along the east side until you reach a major stream or river that moves eastward; that is the Song Ma or a tributary of the Song Ma. Once in the Song Ma you will float to the Gulf of Tonkin. At the mouth, you will find an area of sand and mud which may be visible at low tide. Stay out of the mud and sand. Stay in the main channel until you get to the sandy beach on the south side. That is Land's End, your pickup point," Coltrane said with emphasis as he looked around the room.

Then he pointed to the map with his unlit cigar. "Let's get to the details on how you're to get to Land's End. You only travel at night. That's very important. Never travel in daytime. Do not use flares or fires even to cook with. It's a cold camp all the way. Travel in groups of four to six, no larger. Airborne Recon assets will be tracking your progress down river to the sea and Land's End. Don't try to signal them. It will only get you captured. They will be able to see you at night on infrared and daytime by conventional photos. At sundown and sunrise, be off the river and in your Lay Dog position and configure yourselves in a "T" in the morning between actual sunrise plus thirty minutes. At actual sunset plus thirty minutes, you'll layout in a "V". Everyone is to be in the "T" or "V" so we can keep a headcount.

"Eat your LRRP (Long Range Reconnaissance Patrol) rations at your evening meal. Eat fish and basically live off the land for your other meals. The E & E specialist says that is best for your endurance and health. There are a lot of various fruits, nuts and edible leaves in your area. There're also a lot of fish as well. Just remember to eat them cold and uncooked. Sorry, no fires.

"The water in the Song Ma should be running pretty fast since the rainy season is just finishing. The water will be cool, so watch out for hypothermia. Find a floating log with some leaves and branches to hold on to. It will also give you some cover. This time of the year you can expect the river flow to be two to three knots close to the bank, and four to five knots in the center. If there is any recent rain it might even be more. Take your time and don't try to extend your travel time on the river. The Dinks are usually off the river between 2100 and 0400. That's your window for travel. Be off the river and in your day position by 0400.

"Don't drink the river water without using your purification pills. It may be OK, but the last thing we need is dysentery or typhoid. Another thing is leeches. If you get any leeches on you do NOT try to burn them off. First, your cigarette odor will give you away. Secondly and more important is that you'll cause the little bastards to regurgitate what they've sucked out of you along with their own bacteria, which will make you ill and cause infection. Just take your fingernail or knife blade and slip it under the small end of the leech. What you are doing is breaking the suction. Then flick him off and go on.

"Radio contact procedures: it's simple. Monitor your survival radio during the time you are laying in the "T" and "V." Messages will be transmitted to you then. Otherwise, keep your radio off to save the battery. The only time that you transmit is when the recon bird asks you to confirm. Then only one click for yes and two clicks for no. No other transmissions as the bad guys will be trying to locate you on the 121.5 emergency frequency.

"Don't panic if you go down and have to walk or float out. The route selected should give you a very good chance to get to a point where our assets can pick you up. Follow the plan and survive." Coltrane looked out at the silent faces and asked, "Any questions? Ok, then, Chief Abeel."

"I have little to add, other than there are not a lot of troops or local defense forces in the area. They do run river patrols during the day and until about midnight. They're pretty lax in this area of the interior. You'll pass by the big Bai Thuong fighter base, just after you get on the Song Ma. Towards the end of your pleasure cruise, you'll pass under the bridge north of Thanh Hoa on route 1A. Be careful as there is foot and vehicle traffic all night long. Get past there and you are almost home free. Keep in mind that there is a massive amount of resources being deployed to get you out. You will not be abandoned or left behind. Proof of that is the reason for this mission. We are risking our lives to make sure that every POW gets home alive. Keep calm and follow the plan if you go down. That's all I have," Abeel said as he returned to his seat.

Roman got up and walked to the front of the room slowly, then turned back to the eager faces. "There's nothing else to say. We're prepared and the odds favor our success. The key will be the execution of the plan. If anyone screws up, there are bad consequences for us all. So do it right the first time." Roman looked at Coltrane. "That's all." Sam Coltrane took the stubby unlit cigar out of his mouth and called the room to attention as Grunt Air 6 left the room.

Seventy four hundred nautical miles to the east was the office of U.S. Senator Kerr from Oklahoma. The Chairman of the Joint Chiefs of Staff was a frequent visitor to the House and Senate office buildings. His entry into the reception office of Senator Kerr still brought heart pounding excitement to the Senator's staff as he entered the room.

"I was asked by the Senator to stop by. I don't have an appointment today but I was in the building," said the highly decorated Admiral. "I was hoping that you could fit me in to see the good Senator."

"Not a problem, sir," said the cute young lady who obviously was of Cherokee Indian ancestry, as she jumped up and went to the door leading to the Senator's office. Moments later she and the Senator's staff coordinator appeared.

"Admiral," said the coordinator, "I'm Jack Blane, the Senator's office coordinator. He's on the phone with the Vice President. He wants you to come right in and have a seat. He'll be finished shortly."

The Admiral had no more than taken his seat in one of the two chairs directly in front of the Senator's desk, when the Senator got off the phone. The senior Senator got up and came around his desk and warmly shook the Chairman's hand. "Thanks for stopping by so soon," he said as he took the other chair next to the naval officer. "I just wanted to do a little politicking for one of my long time constituents and family friend," he said. Without losing pace, the Senator continued, "I understand that you're developing a new type of Special Operations aviation unit soon. One of my oldest and best friend's sons is being considered for a staff position in the new unit and I just wanted to put in a good word for him."

The Admiral was confused. There had been no mention outside of a dozen close members of his staff of the unit under development, but the Admiral wasn't about to piss off a very important Senator by telling him that he didn't know what he was talking about.

"Just so I am up to speed with you on the matter, could you be a little more specific?" he asked.

"Certainly," the Senator replied, "the new aviation battalion to be formed at Fort Campbell in the spring. I believe that you were briefed on tactical helicopter operations recently by a Major Dan Roman."

The Chairman felt like he had been slapped in the face. He suddenly realized that Roman had given the Senator a cock-and-bull story about a new unit to cover his trip to Washington. "Not a bad cover story," thought the Admiral. The Senator was a man that was a close supporter and confidant of the President and a good friend to the military. He deserved the truth and he sure wasn't about to divulge a top secret operation that could bring down the administration and get his friend's son killed. "Senator, could you ask your coordinator to post your door for a classified briefing, and not be disturbed for a few minutes?"

"Absolutely," the Senator said as he attended to the request.

It took less than four minutes for the Chairman to explain the POW situation, what was planned and Roman's part in this critical mission. As he finished and stood up to leave, he noticed that the Senator stared straight ahead in utter shock and disbelief. Slowly he regained his composure and rose to shake the Admiral's hand as he departed. He said in a soft and gentle tone, "I've known Dan since he was in grade school. I knew he would be a leader some day but never to this magnitude. He is a rock solid young man," the Senator said regaining his customary composure, "and I think that you have the right man in charge. I just pray that the mission goes well. Please keep me informed and if things turn sour let me know personally so I can be the one to inform Dan's family. They are very close friends. This is a very big mission with a wonderful upside and a potentially catastrophic downside. Best of luck, Admiral," he said with warmth and conviction.

Senator Kerr stood there stunned as he mentally comprehending what he had just been told by the departing Chairman of the Joint Chiefs of Staff.

Chapter 24

AMY'S BIRTHDAY PARTY
Saturday, 10 December 1972

The Clark AFB Officers' club was packed by 2000 hours with the usual young Army and Air Force officers kicking loose on a Saturday night. Add to it the 27 pilots and staff of Grunt Air and it was pandemonium. There was the sound of a finger thumping on the public address microphone. "Attention," the bartender's voice boomed out over the crowd. "All invited guests for the Riddell party please proceed to the banquet room, thank you." The main bar became considerably less crowded as the Grunt Air personnel and assorted wives, girlfriends and Morgan Riddell's associates from Acacia Air Freight went into the banquet room. They were greeted by Morgan and Dan. The guest of honor was absent and that didn't surprise the older sister, but it did piss her off to no end.

Morgan leaned over to Dan and asked, "Are you sure that you can afford this party? Giving an open bar and hors d'oeuvres to this bunch could run pretty damned high."

"Forget it. If I run short I'll ask dad for an advance on my allowance," Roman chuckled.

Most of the guests had arrived and started to significantly reduce the alcohol stock of the bar and devour the snacks like a blight of locusts. When the Brigadier General Herbert and Captain Bayouth arrived, Morgan raised her left hand pledged, "Peace treaty still in place," she said as she extended her right hand to shake Herbert and Bayouth's hand. "Thank you for coming. Please follow me. I have staked out a table away from the drunken riot." Morgan seated them while Roman got a stiff drink for both of them.

"Well, where's the birthday girl?" Bayouth said as he looked around.

"A very good question, sir," Roman replied. "She said that she would be a little late. She has a date with some navy guy who doesn't get off work until 1930 hours."

"Who is the lucky man?" Herbert asked.

"Sir, I have no idea. When it comes to Amy it could be a long haired hippie to a policeman. The one thing that you can count on is that they will be unique or completely off the wall.

"Changing the subject," Herbert said to Morgan, "you still want Dan's next assignment to be something calm in the states?"

"If we are to get married he has to get something stable. I can't give up my job here and live in constant fear of him being shot down and killed in some wild war zone," Morgan answered in a resigned tone.

"Hey, don't I have anything to say about my next assignment?" Roman interjected.

Both Morgan and Bayouth said simultaneously; "No!"

Just then the noise of the room died away to almost silence as Amy came into the room dressed in a chic low cut black dress looking like a beautiful grown woman. Her outstanding figure was accented by the form fitting dress. With her was a Navy Ensign. Amy saw her sister and hurried over to the table with the Ensign in tow.

Dan looked at Morgan and said, "Who is this? It can't be Amy. She doesn't own a dress."

"Hi everyone," Amy said in a joyful voice, "this is Bill Leahy. His father is in the Navy, too."

Bayouth looked at the Ensign and asked, "Is your father Rear Admiral William W. Leahy?"

"Yes, sir, he is," replied the young Ensign.

Bayouth addressed the group at the table, "What young Mr. Leahy isn't telling you is that his father is Deputy Director of the Office of Naval Intelligence, and his grand father was the Chief of Naval Operations just prior to World War II. Yes, he does come from a fine Navy family."

After the appropriate introductions and handshaking, everyone was seated and individual conversations began. Roman looked at Amy and shook his head and said, “Well, you do clean up nicely after a bar fight,” then smiled.

She looked at Dan said, “I finally found my reason.” Then she looked at Bill Leahy then back to Roman. “This is serious, Dan.”

“Looks like a damn good reason to me,” Roman said, then turned to Leahy and asked, “Mr. Leahy, besides practicing Escape and Evasion, what do you do for the war effort?”

The mention of Escape and Evasion took Leahy by surprise and some embarrassment. “Sir, I work in the Subic office of Naval Intelligence.”

Bayouth almost choked on his drink, “Damn, Roman, is there anyone around you that isn’t a damned Spook?”

Roman smiled and said, “Yes, sir, there is one: Morgan.”

Morgan quickly looked directly eye to eye with Bayouth. Neither said anything out loud but there was an exchange of mental messages. Then she quickly turned away.

Herbert and Hammer, who had quietly arrived with Paula, were discussing the growing political problems President Marcos had in Mindanao with the Muslim rebellion. Paula was listening to every word just in case something juicy was said.

“You know Hammer;” the General said casually, “Marcos had better get in control of that Muslim problem before it gets out of control. That upstart Baugsa Moro Army is gaining strength and had better be defeated before it controls most of Mindanao.

“Yes, sir, that’s what we are training Captain Mac’s Light Reaction Company to do. They should be ready to undertake that mission in a month or so. They’re responding very well to our tactics and procedures,” Hammer said as planned. Paula didn’t miss a word even as she was talking to Amy across the table.

As Captain Bayouth sat down with another drink for himself and Morgan, he saw Rear Admiral Thornton Tuthill, Commander of the Subic Bay Naval facility, and Air Force Major General Raymond Kirschner, commander of U.S. Air operations in the Philippines. Bayouth nodded to the Admiral.

Kirchner sarcastically said to Admiral Tuthill, "That's the Army bunch sent here from Vietnam by Coroneos."

Admiral Tuthill looked over to Kirchner and said, "Do you recognize the older man at that table?"

"No, should I?"

"That's Captain Phil Bayouth the Chairman's advisor on Special Operations and head trouble shooter. He reports directly to the Chairman. I think the guy next to him is Mo Herbert. He was Aide de Camp to Coroneos just before he made Brigadier and was assigned to some hush-hush project in J-5.

"God only knows what those two are up to with the Army, but you can bet that you don't want to know or get in the way. One call from Bayouth and the Chairman will bring down hot scalding pee on your head. Let's not join them and opt for a stiff drink instead. How's your food here?"

Chapter 25

THE MADISON PLOT THICKENS
Monday, 12 December 1972

It was almost 0900 hours when Abeel knocked on Roman's office door. "Sir, can we speak to you?"

"Sure, who's with you?"

"Our friends with the black cloak and daggers; Major Singlaube, Captain Mac and Mr. Marcos," Abeel said in a jestful way.

"Gentleman, please come in and have a seat. I assume that we're going to discuss the Madison and the Alaskan Mystery Agent problem."

Mr. Marcos pulled a small tape player out of his briefcase and set it on Roman's desk. "I have two conversations for you to listen to this morning, sir," he said without emotion or facial expression. "The first call was at 0245 hours from Madison's apartment in town to the Sheyma Operations Center switchboard."

Roman listened carefully. The voice had a familiar sound to it that Roman couldn't place. His voice was deliberately being kept soft and altered to make it difficult to identify. Then at the end he remained silent as the Philippine Counter Intelligence agent spoke, "The second call came six hours after the first call. It was from the same Sheyma Command Center on a military AUTOVAN line to the Communications Center here at Clark. The duty NCO patched it through to the American Logistical and Support Officer at Davos Airfield. We are working on identifying the person in Davos, but the tape still doesn't give us a clear voice to identify the man in Alaska. It could be anybody there."

The agent then played the second call. It clearly requested his old friend to assist him in getting even with Roman and Grunt Air for his politically inspired and undeserved assignment in the Aleutian Islands. The conspiracy against the joint mission and malicious intent toward Roman was clear. It is a certainty that they will publicly expose and attempt to sabotage the mission. This did narrow the possibilities as to who it could be. There were over a dozen people that got assigned out of Seventh Air Force for interfering or compromising the Grunt Air mission. It could be any one of the dozen or so transferred.

Roman stared at the recorder when Marcos turned it off. "Well, gentlemen, this is much more than what I had expected. It doesn't leave us much choice," Roman said as he leaned back in his chair and cocked his right elbow over the chair back. "We must have them arrested. Let's do it on a planned schedule so it works for us. Major Sanglaube, get in touch with your man at Shemya and arrange to arrest the man at the same time as Mr. Marcos arrests Madison here. Both must be kept totally isolated until the mission is over. Major, can you do that within the UCMJ?"

"Yes, sir," he said with confidence. We just need to know who to arrest. But we have a trap that we plan to use to find out who the man is. Captain Hammer has agreed to help us just before you leave."

"Mr. Marcos, is that possible under Philippine law?"

"Major Roman, President Marcos ordered martial law back in September. I can hold Miss Madison on treason charges until the Twelfth of Never," he said with a small smile. He was proud to have been able to use a popular old American music classic in his reply.

"That's great, but CBS will put pressure on the government to release her. Just hold her totally isolated until the 20th if you can. That's all the time that I need to complete the classified portion of our exercise."

"Abeel, please call Herbert and give him a detailed briefing on the situation and the action that we are taking," Roman said as he got up and extended his hand to Mr. Marcos. "Great work. You really did deliver the results when we needed it," Roman said in praise. Marcos was visibly proud of the praise.

"OK, gentlemen, we all have our assignments to perform so we can catch this slippery guy."

The daily milk run from Saigon to Clark arrived almost twenty minutes late. As the rear ramp of the C-130 Cargo Aircraft opened, Captain Moung walked to the ramp in preparation to deplane. Roman and Coltrane were there to greet him.

Roman stuck out his hand and welcomed Moung. Coltrane took his ever present unlit cigar out of his mouth long enough to welcome the legendary Laotian combat aviator. Unofficially, he was the direct contact with General Vang Pao, who was the Laotian combat leader in Northern Laos.

"Major Roman, the General extends his warmest regards and looks forward to your having supper with him in Long Thein soon. The General promises to have your favorite fish heads and rice ready when you return." The comment was an intentional cultural slur against the standard Laotian cuisine of the area. The General used the slur as a joke with Roman knowing his intense dislike for fish.

"Oh, joy!" Roman said, "My favorite," then pointed to the briefcase handcuffed to Moung's left hand. "Is there anything in there going to alarm me?"

"Not really, sir. Most of it is for Sam and Alberts. We have some information on the AN-2 Colt and MI-8 that they will be flying. Some details for your Recon Teams, but nothing that changes anything. We did get the fuel tanker from LS-12 up to LS-59. That will make refueling easier. All of the fuel is in place and ready to go. The General made sure of it."

"Great, let's get you with the gang and go over the goodies," Roman said as he climbed into the Jeep.

It was precisely 1800 hours when Roman entered the briefing room, commanding, "Sit down. Sit down. Ok, this is the last full group briefing. Please tell me that everyone is here that is on the ROADSHOW. Good, Captain Moung has a few items for you."

Moung was detailed and short in his briefing. Abeel was next then Coltrane, Best, Hammer, Alberts and finally Roman. "OK," Roman said, "any last questions?"

"Yes, sir," Sergeant Richardson said as he stood up. "Confirm that the pizza is to be delivered to extension 220." The serious nature of the group was broken and laughter rang out through the room.

"Somebody shoot him," Roman said as he left the room laughing.

Roman and Hammer hopped in the Jeep and went over to transit operations just as the KC135 tanker pulled to a stop. As planned, General Herbert and Captain Bayouth climbed down the stairs to meet Roman.

"Welcome, sir," then looked at Bayouth, who obviously didn't like this flight from Pearl anymore than the last one and said "… and the bar is open!"

Chapter 26

LINEBACKER TWO

Senator Kerr entered the Presidential conference room in the West Wing of the White House and was pleased to see he wasn't the only one coming to this highly classified meeting with the President. The first to greet him was the Chairman of the Joint Chief of Staff and Bob Haldeman, the President's Chief of Staff, who were talking as he entered. Also present was the Deputy Director of Central Intelligence and the Secretary of Defense who were seated at the table. Senator Kerr moved around and took a seat at the far end of the table just as the president walked into the room unceremoniously and took a seat. Everyone became silent and focused on the President.

"OK, gentlemen, I am mad as hell and I want to do something about the goddamned North Vietnamese stalling the talks with Henry. Henry just told me that the talks have ended for now and he'll be back here on the 14th. He and Le Duc Tho have agreed to continue discussions but no date was sent for the next meeting. The bastards are stalling! I want to resume the bombing of Hanoi and other key areas until they come back to the table for real. Before I issue that order I want to hear what you have to say about this and another aspect of the POWs. Most of you are not aware of a situation concerning about eighty or more of our boys in Laos. We'll come back to that later. First, let Bob bring you up to speed on the recent Kissinger talks. Then we'll open the floor to discussion concerning the resumption of bombing. Bob, the floor is yours,." the President said in conclusion.

"Thank you Mr. President. Let me first review what has happened during the past 45 or so days in the talks.

"On October 8, 1972, our National Security Advisor Dr. Henry Kissinger and North Vietnamese Le Duc Tho met again secretly in Paris. The purpose was to discuss new proposals advanced by both nations, to reach a mutually agreeable settlement to the Vietnam conflict. Tho presented a new North Vietnamese plan which included proposals for a cease-fire in place, the withdrawal of American forces, and an exchange of prisoners of war. All three Vietnamese combatant governments: North Vietnam, South Vietnam, and the Provisional Revolutionary Government of South Vietnam would remain intact, as would their combat forces. Tho has dropped the demand that the South Vietnamese President be removed from office. We didn't have to cease our aid to the South Vietnam and both sides could continue to resupply their allies or forces. They proposed that no new NVA forces were to be infiltrated from the north if the U.S. agreed to extend post-war reconstruction assistance to North Vietnam. I understand that Henry almost lost it at that point, but kept his cool.

"The new terms also included the establishment of a National Council of National Reconciliation and Concord. It would be a loosely defined administrative structure which would work toward general and local elections. There would be a three party power sharing arrangement between the Thieu government, the PRG, and a third group to be mutually agreed upon by the other two parties. Since it was to work by consensus, nothing could be accomplished by the new council without the agreement of President Thieu.

"On October 17th they met again. There were two main areas of disagreement: the periodic replacement of South Vietnam's American weaponry and the release of political prisoners held by the Saigon government. This was not immediately rejected by Henry as he wanted to see what else Tho had up his sleeve. The North had made significant modifications to their past negotiating position. They appear to be interested in getting an agreement signed before November. Henry believes the North thinks that the President would be more willing to make concessions before, rather than after, the upcoming presidential election. In principal, Kissinger was generally satisfied with the new terms and so notified The Boss, who gave his approval to the settlement.

The finalized agreement was to be signed October 31st in Hanoi. Kissinger then flew on to Saigon on the 18th to discuss the terms with Thieu. Needless to say, Thieu was not happy with either the new agreement or with Kissinger, who he felt had betrayed him. Thieu completely castigated the agreement and proposed 129 textual changes to the document. He was also demanding that the DMZ separating the two Vietnams be recognized as a true international border and not as a "provisional military demarcation line" and that South Vietnam be recognized as a sovereign state. Thieu then publicly released his version of the text that made the South Vietnamese provisions look even worse than they actually were. Hanoi believed that they had been deceived by Kissinger. They responded by broadcasting excerpts of the agreement that gave the impression that the agreement supported Washington and Saigon's objectives. Kissinger held a televised press conference during which he announced 'We believe that peace is at hand.'

"The South Vietnamese presented more revisions and 44 additional changes. Kissinger personally considered them "preposterous." The new demands included that the DMZ be accepted as a true international boundary; that the North would publicly withdraw some troops; that the North Vietnamese agree to an Indochina-wide cease fire; and that a strong international peace-keeping force be created for supervising and enforcing the cease-fire.

"The North Vietnamese read the new demands and immediately began to retract their own concessions and wanted to bargain from the beginning. Kissinger knew then that the North was taking advantage of the unrealistic terms to justify their actions. He knew that they were "stalling." The talks, scheduled to last ten days, ended with both parties agreeing to resume negotiations. Teams of experts from each side are to meet in a couple of days to discuss technicalities and protocols on prisoners and their return. It is clear that the North Vietnamese side is stone-walling and doesn't want to discuss the POW issue at this time. They want to squeeze out more concessions from us. The talks broke down that point and Thieu refused to set a date for the resumption of negotiations.

"Kissinger's 'peace is at hand' statement has raised hopes of a settlement among the American population. Another problem that the president has to be concerned with is the fact that the new Ninety-third

Congress would go into session on January 3rd. The damned Democratic Congress will preempt his pledge of 'peace with honor' by legislating an end to the conflict. Such action would kill any chances of getting our POWs back on a timely basis.

"Now to the plan of action for getting the little bastards back to the table quickly. The President wants some form of rapid offensive action. He wants to resume the unrestricted bombing of the North. This has numerous consequences. First, the political reaction among the American people and, of course, Congress. Then there is the cost of the force mobilization the additional aircraft and personnel assigned to Southeast Asia for the proposed Linebacker Two. The operation would strain the Pentagon's budget. The Secretary of Defense believes he can handle the initial cost but will need additional funds if the operation lasts beyond the end of the year. Beyond that, the President would have to request a supplementary defense appropriation from Congress to pay for it. We are convinced that the legislative branch would seize the opportunity to simply write the United States out of the war. So, our initial bombing would need to be devastating to the point that the North would have to come back to the table.

"After returning from Paris tonight, Henry will fire off an ultimatum to Hanoi. It basically will be threatening 'grave consequences' if North Vietnam does not return to the negotiating table within 72 hours. If they fail to return, the President will direct the Air Force to begin the planned Linebacker Two bombing campaign. It will be a three-day 'maximum effort,' starting the morning of December 18th. Simultaneously, a small clandestine force will raid the Cave area of Northeastern Laos to recover our POWs that are scheduled to be executed within the next few days." There was sudden shock and comments by some of those at the table.

"Mr. President!" responded the National Security Advisor. I was under the impression that none of the military branches could respond in time with a competent force. What has changed to allow such a shift in policy? Won't such a raid interfere with Kissinger's efforts?"

The Chairman raised his hand and said in reply, "I have identified a suitable force to undertake this action. I have deployed the force on my own authority and without Presidential involvement. I take full and total responsibility for this operation. Further, the operation details will be limited to only those who have a need to know. If it goes sour, you and the others have complete deniability. The President and Congress will hold me totally responsible. It is my judgment that we have a competent force capable of pulling this mission off successfully given the time constraints and evolving situation with the negotiations and Linebacker Two. In fact, Linebacker Two will act as a distraction to the enemy so our forces can execute the mission successfully."

The President turned to the Deputy Director of Central Intelligence and said, "I have discussed the operation with Henry and he has actually, to my surprise, blessed the plan. I expect those of you who have not been included in the planning to accept the plan and keep its very existence TOP SECRET. Only those of you in this room are to know. Since the element of surprise is critical to the plan I will have the Attorney General initiate legal action against anyone leaking the operation. Now the rescue plan is not up for discussion. What is up for discussion at this point is the initiation of Linebacker Two. What are your thoughts?"

Chapter 27

CALLING ET
Tuesday, 13 December 1972

Roman, Herbert, and Bayouth had met at the Subic Bay O Club for an early breakfast before they went over to the office of Naval Intelligence. The duty officer was surprised to see a Navy Captain and an Army Brigadier General and some Major walk into the office before 0600 hours. As he rose to attention he greeted the group, "Good morning, General. Can I help you?"

"Yes. Captain Bayouth has a top secret message that needs to go out in exactly eight minutes," Herbert said in an official tone.

"Very well, sir. I will need to see the Captain's ID card first," the duty officer said as a matter of procedure.

Bayouth handed him his ID card and a card identifying him as a special representative of the Chairman of the Joint Chiefs of Staff. The duty officer's eyes widened slightly as he was impressed with the early morning visitor,. "Yes, sir. That is acceptable. Who is the message to?" he asked.

"It's to the Chairman JCS at this TWIX address. It is TOP SECRET SI. You will not retain copy of this or the reply. Just log the two messages only." The duty officer was suddenly nervous at such a procedure. He knew this must be of great importance. Bayouth handed him a sheet of typed paper with the transmission instructions and the usual security markings.

The duty officer called the Yeoman over and handed it to him for entry into the crypto machine which decoded and transmitted the simple message. The message read: "LAST CALL FOR ALCOHOL." After sending the message he noted the military date, time, group on the bottom of the page and handed it back to Bayouth. Less than five minutes expired before the crypto machine began typing out the reply: "CALL ME A GREEN TAXI."

Bayouth looked at the message then handed it to Herbert. He looked at Dan Roman and nodded. Roman smiled. The ROADSHOW was going to start for real in 17 hours. The group silently left the office.

At 0800 hours, Herbert, Bayouth and Roman entered the briefing room. Assembled were the Key Grunt Air staff, pilots and senior NCO's.

"Ok gentlemen," Herbert said as he held up the TWIX from the Chairman, "your mission is on for 2300 tonight. Don't fuck it up." Then he and Bayouth left the room leaving Roman to go over the last minute details.

"As of now, all communications with the outside are cut. Nobody goes off post, or for that matter out of the company area. Look casual to outsiders. You know what to do, so get going." Roman said in an authoritative voice.

At that same moment that Philippine authorities were arresting Paula Madison in her off-base apartment, the Air Force provost martial from Elmendorf AFB was landing at Shemya to arrest the mystery agent that only hours before had been finally identified by the undercover Counter Intelligence agent with the help of Hammer.

The ROADSHOW was now in progress and the many parts and players were in irrevocable motion.

At 2245, Roman drove out to the flight line to see Arkangel and the advance party, codename: STARBURST, depart for LS59 via DaNang.

Roman walked up to Sam Coltrane who called the advance party to attention. Roman quickly returned his salute. "OK, Sam, everyone and everything here?"

"Yes, sir, all present and ready to go."

Roman looked at the list of passengers on Sam's clipboard.

Arkangel: Jenner, Kellogg, the Crew Chief Sgt. Burke, and SSG Blanton the radio operator and interpreter.

Captain Moung, Laotian Liaison and back-up Arkangel pilot

Recon Teams: Captain Best and 14 team members, including Captain Mac.

Chief Abeel: Intelligence

SSG Nelson: Communications

Captain Coltrane and Captain Dorsey MI-8 pilots

Chief Doug Alberts the AN-2 Colt pilot

Roman nodded and went down the line shaking every man's hand. There was pride and excitement obvious in every man in the advance party.

Roman looked at Lieutenant Jenner who would be the command pilot along with Lieutenant Kellogg who would fly Arkangel the Command and Control aircraft on the mission, "OK, crank it up."

The team loaded on board and prepared for the long flight ahead. The aircraft was at max weight with fuel and passengers. It barely had enough fuel to reach DaNang. Planning for this critical part of the mission was down to gallons of fuel or a passenger. Two members of the advance party had to be dropped so enough fuel could be put on board for the long flight from Clark to DaNang. In reality, Alberts knew the plane was over its authorized gross weight for take off. But Alberts knew this aircraft had been flying over-grossed missions since World War II. He had done it himself more times than he liked to think about. Tonight they were heavy, but not as heavy as other times.

It was 731 nautical miles to DaNang. Then, after a fast and hopefully unnoticed refuel, they would fly the next 447 mile leg to LS59. They would arrive a little after 0700 hours on Wednesday, 14 December 1972. The passengers would sleep as best they could in the uncomfortable space of the old World War II C-47. The rest was essential as flight operations would be started within hours of arrival. The five recon teams and the Laotian Scouts that would meet them at LS59 would be inserted deep in enemy territory before the sun set on that day.

The C-47 was cranked up and ready to go. Jenner looked out of the pilot window gave a salute to Roman, and then moved the lumbering aircraft towards the runway for take off.

Chapter 28

I HAVE WAYS …

Darkness had set in at the "Interview Room" of the Pathet Lao Intelligence Office at Ban Nakay Laos. Major Nguyen Thong Tan from the Hanoi headquarters of the Enemy Proselytizing Section of the Political Warfare Office in the Ministry of National Defense looked at his watch and became visibly irritated. He looked down at an Air Force Major Rex Marquardt trying to move in his semi-conscious condition. Major Nguyen was one of the very best interrogators in the Hanoi office. He had a record of breaking every prisoner he ever interrogated. His brutal techniques always resulted in the prisoner breaking down and abandoning his code of conduct and keeping the faith with his fellow POWs. While his techniques always worked, the life of the POW was always generally very short. He really didn't care. The life of another American pig was of no concern of his. He only wanted results.

The subject today was slowly getting up off the floor. This man, the NVA Major thought, "was a tough one to crack." Not nearly as hard as his cell mate, Lieutenant Colonel Anthony Hoover. Hoover was the hardest yet. But to get to Hoover, he must break Major Marquardt down. He looked at his watch. They had been at it for over two hours. Nguyen felt a sense of urgency as time was running out. In just a few days, those prisoners not found to be of value to the State would be executed. He knew that Marquardt was a "Wild Weasel" pilot which made him of some value, but not a lot. But Lieutenant Colonel Hoover might be different. His experience told him that there was a lot more to Hoover than a co-pilot on RB-66 missions. That story was just too simple. In his previous interview with Hoover, he recognized a leader and a high degree of self control. He was no ordinary pilot. But what was he? Marquardt knew and he would give him the key information to break Hoover.

"Enough!" yelled Nguyen. "You refuse to tell me what I want to know. Your silence may be honorable and you have kept the faith with Colonel Hoover up to now. But now it is time for you to give in and tell me the truth. If you keep your faith or silence, it will be at a great personal price to you. Do you understand what I am saying, Major Marquardt?"

Marquardt slowly sits back down in the wooden chair that he has been knocked out of only minutes ago by the guard they call "The Goose." He got his name from the POWs because of his awkward way of walking. He walked like a goose. He also was quite dumb and seemed to be unaware of most things around him. The exception was when he was involved in interrogations. He was mean and sadistic. Tonight was no different. He had hit Marquardt in the head four times with a sand-filled rubber hose. Each time the blow almost knocked him unconscious. His bloody head was screaming with pain.

"I understand," was all that Marquardt said in response.

"Very well then, Major. Perhaps now you can tell me more about Lieutenant Colonel Hoover. What was his job on the RB-66?"

Slowly Marquardt sat up and looked at the NVA Major. 'He was a co-pilot on a RB-66 flying weather recon mission ahead of the planned strike mission on the power plant north of Hanoi," he said as convincingly as he could under the painful conditions.

"You lie!" screamed the NVA interrogator. That lie will require a nasty price, to be paid by you." He then nodded to The Goose and pointed to the roof support bean.

The Goose moved the other wooden chair under the selected beam and attached a pulley and rope to it. He got down in a clumsy manner, as befitting his name. The guard then tied the rope to Marquardt's wrists behind his back. He pulled him up until his toes barely touched the floor. He walked up to the front of the hanging body and carefully buttoned his shirt while smiling in a sinister manner. He straightened his shirt then went to the corner and picked up a four foot metal rod. It looked like rebar used in concrete floors. He then took chalk and liberally wiped it on the bar.

Major Nguyen walked over to the guard and then turned to the prisoner. "Are you curious as to why we put chalk on the rod, Major?" There was no reply from Marquardt. The NVA moved aside and nodded to the guard who swung the bar like a bat hitting the left rib cage. The prisoner screamed loudly as he jerked his legs in an attempt to ward off pain and a second blow.

"Now, Major Marquardt, if you could see from our perspective, you would be able to see that the chalk left a nice clear mark on your shirt where you were hit. This helps the Sergeant here from hitting you in the same place again. Once your rib is broken, there is little to be gained from hitting you there again." Then he nodded to the guard who swung the rod once more hitting the right side. Again, there was a loud scream of pain. The guard smiled as he put more chalk on the rod. Then he hit Marquardt on the left side again. Marquardt was just barely conscious. When the big guard hit him again on the right side, the scream of pain was short.

Marquardt had passed out from the pain. This made Major Nguyen mad. He wanted Marquardt awake and in pain. This had to be corrected immediately. He signaled the guard to throw water in his face. The water did not revive Marquardt, so he took smelling salts out and forced him into regaining consciousness. Once back to consciousness, he yelled and screamed.

Nguyen noticed a small trickle of blood coming from his left ear. That was probably the result of the blows to his head with the hose. The NVA interrogator also knew there could be some internal bleeding and should stop hitting him with the rod or take the chance of killing him before he got the information he needed. He looked at his Sergeant and told him to lower the body until the feet were flat on the floor.

Marquardt's head was exploding with pain as was his lower rib cage, and his shoulders had become dislocated. He could barely keep his mind clear and keep from losing consciousness. He knew that his limit was near, but he had to keep the faith with Hoover.

Marquardt could feel his arms slowly pulling against its shoulder sockets. The pain was increasing there as well. He could feel his feet hit the floor, which took some of the strain on his arm sockets. The time since the last blow to the ribs had given him the opportunity to regain some of his senses and mental control.

The guard again went to the corner. This time he returned with a large hammer. He stood back from the prisoner so he could not see what he had in his hands. In one hand he had the hammer, in the other, he had the hose.

The NVA Major moved back in front of the POW and looked at him for a moment. Then he asked, "Are you ready to tell me about Colonel Hoover?"

"I have told you everything that I know," Marquardt said.

Nguyen just looked at the guard and nodded upward towards the prisoner's head. Swiftly and very hard came the painful blow to Marquardt's head with the hose. The pain was blinding, he could not continue. It had to stop. He prayed that the next blow would kill him. At least the pain would stop, he thought.

Then the Major pointed downward to the guard. A grin came over the guard's face as he got down on his right knee and slammed the hammer on Marquardt's big toe and joint.

Marquardt went wild with pain. He yelled and screamed louder than before. It was uncontrollable. With tear welling up in his eyes, he said. "Enough."

Major Nguyen smiled. He had won again. He motioned for the guard to get the prisoner down and into the chair. Marquardt was delirious with pain and barely conscious.

"Now then, Major Marquardt, what do you have to tell me that will stop the continued pain?"

Gasping for breath and for his vision to clear so he could see the interrogator, Marquardt was trying to talk.

He knew that he was about to commit the cardinal sin of breaking the faith, and it hurt him emotionally more than his head, ribs and toe combined. Slowly he was able to talk. "He was the electronic warfare officer for the EB-66 Squadron flying out of Takhli that was jamming your radars."

"My god," thought Major Nguyen, "The E version of the highly effective electronic warfare aircraft. This was a real prize indeed." He was smiling from ear to ear as he pulled a hypodermic syringe out and gave Marquardt an injection that immediately knocked him out.

"Sergeant," he commanded, "take him back to the cave. Don't let Hoover or the other two see him before you bring Hoover to me."

Chapter 29

WELCOME TO THE OUTHOUSE
Wednesday, 14 December 1972

Jenner could barely see the landing strip at LS59, codename "Outhouse." It was hazy and there were clouds masking the high hills and mountains surrounding the short landing strip. He leaned back to Staff Sergeant Ray Blanton who was working the radios on the right side of the aircraft just behind the co pilot. "Ray," he said loudly to be heard over the noise of the two big engines, "let them know that we're going to be on the ground at 0805 hours."

Blanton turned to the single sideband radio and transmitted "Outhouse 0805" back to Grunt Air headquarters at Clark AFB. The radio operator back at Grunt Air Headquarters immediately notified Roman. Blanton turned to Jenner and nodded that it had been done.

Jenner reduced power and started a long slow approach to Outhouse. There was no wind so he had to make sure his wheels hit at the very end of the runway so he could stop before he hit the other end of this very rough gravel and dirt strip. He reduced his speed to just above stall speed.

He side slipped the big bird just a little to lose some altitude quickly. Then he straightened the bird up just before he flew over the grassy overrun part of the field. He chopped his power as the main landing gear struck the ground. Then he lowered his tail and started to slow the speed with brakes. The aircraft quickly came to a stop far short of the end of the runway and almost directly in front of the old building that served as the airfield operations shack.

He pulled the bird over to the side away from the main access to the back portion of the field where General Vang Pao hid the two old Russian-built aircraft taken from the North Vietnamese over a year ago. There was an old AN-2 Colt biplane that could carry heavy loads and operate at slow speeds. It was a perfect aircraft for Special Operations in a remote area like this. Also taken at gunpoint was a Russian helicopter that resembled a Greyhound bus with a rotor. This was the MI-8 HIP which was a multi role transport helicopter that could carry heavy loads of Cargo or troops.

Today, both aircraft would be flown by American pilots over enemy held land and insert US and Laotian reconnaissance troops in the area of the caves and near the large prison camp at Moung Soi. They would also preposition jet fuel for the Hueys at the refuel point known as OASIS. This was being done in daylight and in front of 60,000 North Vietnamese and Pathet Lao troops.

Jenner shut the big engines down and got up out of the seat to go to the rear cargo door. He was the last out of the bird. On the ground waiting was one of Vang Pao's wives. This lady was almost as tough as the General himself, but he looked a lot better. She was responsible for this district and the direct support that Vang Pao was providing Grunt Air on a clandestine basis. Roman and the General had become respected friends during the Big Casino mission. Once on the ground, Jenner shook her hand and gave her a small wooden crate. She looked at the crate and then to Doug Alberts who was the first off the aircraft. Alberts smiled and raised four fingers, indicating that there were four quarts of Jack Daniels in the crate.

She grinned and grabbed his arm and squeezed it in appreciation of the present. It was her favorite liquor. Alberts had learned of her love of the American booze when he frequently flew in here when Grunt Air was operating out of Udorn Airbase in Thailand.

Alberts could see that everyone including the dozen or so Lao guards were unloading the cargo and getting the camp operational. The Lao troops had already set up the tents and other equipment pre-positioned during the WHIPLASH portion of the ROADSHOW operation. He noticed that they had brought a fuel tanker in from one of the other fields that were overrun during the NVA dry season offensive back in the early part of the year. That would make fueling operations much more efficient.

He went behind the left main landing gear to take a long overdue piss. Then he saw Coltrane and Dorsey head towards the two NVA aircraft with the Lao mechanics. Both aircraft would be in the air within a few hours. Sam Coltrane and Captain Dorsey followed the Lao aircraft mechanic into the Cavernous Cargo Bay of the MI-8 HIP.

Dorsey looked around and said to Coltrane, "Can this monster really fly?"

"You bet it can, and with 6,600 pounds of cargo. The E model can carry over 8,000 pounds of cargo. I got to fly this thing when I was an advisor down in Indonesia a couple of years ago. It flies pretty damned good for a tank," Sam said as he crawled into the pilot's seat. "The controls are sluggish compared to the Huey and you have to make your cyclic adjustments sooner than a Huey. You always be ahead of what you want to do on both cyclic and collective pitch inputs or you can get into trouble quickly," he said as he chomped down on his ever present unlit cigar.

Dorsey got into the copilot's seat and looked in amazement at the instrument panel. He had spent hours going over the translated version of the operating manual and photos of the entire cockpit acquired from Vang Pao. But to see it in real life was another thing. They would spend the next hour going over the procedures and various gauges and switches. Finally they looked at the mechanic and gave him a signal that they were ready to crank up the two turbo shaft engines.

The mechanic smiled and gave a thumb up. The Dynamic Duo, as Roman had nicknamed them, went through the start procedures. Once everything was up and running, Coltrane gently brought the flying monster to a three foot hover. They checked all the instruments for any sign of eminent failures. Satisfied, they moved forward and took off down the Southeast end of the runway.

"Hey this is great," Sam said, as he banked the helicopter to the left to circle around for a landing. After a few approach to landings Sam turned the flying over to Dorsey who handled the HIP like he had been flying it for years. Once both pilots felt comfortable with the aircraft and their ability to safely fly it, they landed and had it refueled for the afternoon insertion mission.

The two very happy pilots took the mechanic over to Vang Paos' wife and gave him two thumbs up signal. The mechanic beamed with pride.

Alberts wasn't quite as comfortable in the AN-2 Colt. He had flown one a couple of times back in 1962 in the Dominican Republic but this one was an older model and he was not totally as familiar with it as he was with the other aircraft. The operations manual for the Colt that Roman got for him was for the newer model. Finally Alberts said to himself, "Hell, its got wings and an engine. I can fly the son of a bitch."

He started it up and taxied it to the end of the runway and went through the pre-take off checks. He had seen Coltrane fly out and land a few minutes ago. Now it was his time to take a chance. He advanced the throttle and the plane started moving immediately. It hadn't gone 600 feet before it came off the ground. He climbed to a thousand feet above the ground and maneuvered the plane from left to right, up and down to get a good feel for it before he flew the pilots over the cave area later today.

He was apprehensive about the flight. He might be in a NVA airplane, but they might know it was captured. But then again that would make the entire fleet of Colts vulnerable. It was just a chance he had to take. He thought Roman had really been creative this time, to use an enemy aircraft to over-fly the route of flight and the specific landing zones the pilots would have to land in with only partial moonlight available. Only Roman would think about something this crazy. But it would really help make the mission more likely to succeed. He checked to his left for other aircraft, and then he turned to land. "This bird is ready to go," thought Alberts. He landed and parked the bird. He smiled and went to get some sleep.

Alberts had been asleep for a little over three hours when Abeel came over and woke him up. "Time to fly the friendly skies of Laos," he said.

Alberts got up and went back to the Colt. He would take off and fly with the HIP. Seeing the two NVA aircraft in daylight together would help to keep the suspicious attention of the Pathet Lao to a minimum.

Meanwhile, the HIP took off and started Operation SIDECAR which flew a straight route like it was headed for Hanoi, and then descended quickly long enough to land and insert the teams. On board were the Grunt Air Recon Teams that would be inserted in a valley three to four miles away from any enemy troop units or the eyes of the guards at the caves. After insertion, the teams would proceed by different routes to positions close enough to the individual POW camps and caves to become familiar with the terrain and daily activities of the camp. Knowledge gained would adjust the strike plan if necessary. After dropping off the teams assigned to the cave area, Coltrane flew to a site three miles from Moung Soi and let off Gunny Thornhill's team, then on to OASIS to drop off Lao Scouts assigned to the OASIS refuel site and sixteen barrels of jet fuel for the Hueys. The mission refuel point was secure and operational. With the SIDECAR mission completed, Coltrane and Dorsey turned back to the west and flew as the Colt did toward the NVA area in the Plain of Jars before descending and turning to land at LS95.

After the HIP and Colt safely returned, Sergeant Nelson sent a message to Roman in the Philippines advising him that both SIDECARS had been completed without incident.

Roman was in his office when the message was received. He left the headquarters and went to the Officer's Club where Herbert and Bayouth were waiting for him in the bar. As he entered the bar he looked at them and gave two thumbs up. They smiled and ordered Roman a drink. "Well, Dan," Herbert said, "So far so good. Are you spending the evening with Morgan?"

"Yes, sir, she's due here anytime," Roman said quietly. "Fact is, here she comes right now."

"Evening Morgan," Herbert said. "Are you here to see Phil and I off, or Dan?"

"You, of course, General. Dan will be back in a week and with any luck you won't return before Dan's transfer orders get here," she said trying to hold back a laugh.

"Right, I should have known," Herbert replied. "Don't worry, I'm sure that Dan will get an assignment to your satisfaction. This exercise is little more than a SUNDAY STROLL," he said playing on words. "Phil and I depart in the morning and are not scheduled back here anytime soon. So you won't have us to kick around anymore," Herbert said, continuing without breaking out in laughter.

"Well, you're welcome anytime. I don't care as long as you don't steal Dan for some Special Operations job."

"I can see it's time for me to go get another drink for everyone, especially me," Roman said faking fear of a fight between Morgan and Herbert.

Bayouth looked over to make sure Roman was still at the bar then turned to Morgan." I know who you actually work for Morgan," Bayouth said. "When are you going to tell him?"

"If he gets a decent job and I can be certain that we will get married, I'll tell him. Until then, he doesn't have a need to know," Morgan said in a business like manner.

Bayouth smiled and said, "You're a hard woman on this point aren't you?"

"Yes, sir, I am, and for good reason," she replied.

"Yes, I guess you are right about that. Have you discussed the situation with the Agency?" Bayouth asked.

"Yes, they have a slot for me at Langley if I choose to transfer there or Fort Campbell."

"Good. I think you can plan on one or the other very, very soon," Bayouth said as Roman returned with the drinks. "Then we'll say 'goodbye' now and let you two have a quiet supper. Good luck, Dan, on your exercise tomorrow," Herbert said as he and Bayouth left.

"Now, Major Roman, do you want to eat here, or at my place?" she said with a sexy voice. "The dessert is much better there."

Chapter 30

SNOOP AND POOP
15 December 1972

During the night, Captain Best, like the other four teams, crossed the very mountainous terrain from the insertion LZ to the daytime Lay Dog position selected for them by their long time Laotian Scout, Corporal Moung Ky. As always, he had done very well in his selection. The position was about 900 feet away from the cave entrance. The position was about fifty feet higher than the cave and the valley it was situated in, the cave entrance was on the west side of the hill mass that separated the Ban Nakay Neua area and the valley that contained both the Daisy camp and Gardenia cave. From this point, they could not only watch the entrance to the cave but the main market to the left the local headquarters, and the main road that went through the village and of Ban Nakay Valley.

Since they had taken up the position, they had seen nothing that was different than briefed. When it got dark and the locals went to sleep, they would leave the position and go down and check the area around the cave and its guards very closely.

Eighty two hundred feet to the southeast of Captain Bests' Alpha Team position was Foxtrot Team that had been assigned to recon the Tulip cave at Ban Nakay Teu. They had found a good point to observe the cave some 700 feet to the east. They had climbed up on a 200 foot limestone karst. It was unlikely that any patrol would discover them in this unusual vantage point.

Shortly after 0100 hours, a small military one ton truck drove up and took an unconscious prisoner into the cave, and then removed another prisoner. The prisoner walked out under his own power to the vehicle. The truck returned shortly after 0400 hours and the prisoner had to be carried to the cell door. His legs and feet were not moving. He was shoved in and the door locked. The guard outside looked inside the barred window then went to his post and went to sleep. Sergeant Anderson knew that they would have to get to the door and confirm the number and condition of the prisoners before the strike, which was now less than 48 hours away. That should be no problem if the guard went to sleep again tomorrow night like he did tonight. Perhaps they would let the prisoners out during the day tomorrow for exercise. That would help them on some of their collection of the Essential Elements of Information or EEI that each team had to collect and pass on to Arkangel. For now the team could rest and observe.

Just over the mountain ridge that separate the Ban Na Tau and Neua caves from the cave at Ban Nakay Eune (Gardenia) and Ban Puem (Daisy) prison facilities, Sergeant Richardson was observing his Lao Scout Corporal Pao climb up on the karst that the Chinese 37 millimeter antiaircraft gun was emplaced. Pao was good at his job and it was very hard for Richardson to keep him in view even with the high powered binoculars. Then he lost him just before the crest of the hill. Richardson knew that it was unlikely that he would see him as he infiltrated the gun emplacement and nearby security force camp site.

Pao was the consummate professional who had over sixty confirmed combat kills with a knife. He had a deep hatred for communists, any kind of communists, no matter where they were from. To him Pathet Lao, Chinese or North Vietnamese communists were all the same, and it was his obligation to kill as many as he could. Richardson kept searching for Pao without success for over two hours. He was becoming concerned as daybreak was less than an hour away. He put the binoculars to his eyes one more time. Just then he felt a hand gently grab his right shoulder. It was Pao!

Just up the Valley from the cave known as Gardenia, Sergeant Krumin's Delta Team had started its visual observation of the large camp known as Daisy. Corporal Yap had climbed the side of the ridge to recon the other Chinese 37 mm gun emplacement and security force two 12.7

gun emplacements on either side of the gun. He moved around to the side of the gun and took careful note of the amount of ammunition and how close it was to the gun. It occurred to Yap that it might be too far away for efficient use. He verified that there were no covers or anything preventing him from quickly attaching the thermite grenades to the 37 mm gun or two 12.7 machine guns. Then he addressed the problem of the security forces and gun crews getting from their tents to the guns. He was convinced that he could set Claymore anti-personnel mines along the path to the guns. That could buy him the needed time to move to the pick up point. Yap knew that he had to delay them or he and his pick up bird would be very vulnerable to the hostile troops. Upon completion of his recon of the tents, he knew that he had to deal with eight Chinese and eighteen or so Pathet Lao security guards. In his mind he knew that he could do this job for Major Roman.

While Yap was doing his recon on the hill, Sergeant Krumins and Sergeant Priest moved quietly inside the walled compound known as Daisy. They got close enough to look inside the building containing the eight POWs. Priest saw that they had been handcuffed to the floor and ankle clamps and chains attached the legs to the floor as well. Priest was impressed that the head count and situation reported by General Vang Pao's Scouts was very accurate. He moved back toward the breach in the fence where he met up with Krumins. Both crawled through the breach and carefully replaced the fence posts so the breach would not be discovered, Krumins hoped! Then they turned west to go down the gentler slope of this side of the ridge when they heard the noise of an approaching patrol. Kramins looked at his watch. It was just past 0500 hours. The recon had taken too long. They should have been back to their observation position just across the cut in the ridge. The main path between Gardenia and Daisy to Ban Nakay went through this cut. Both men dropped to the ground silently and pulled vegetation and limbs on top of themselves. The patrol was not seriously looking for the enemy. They were going through the motions required for this useless patrol. Another stupid requirement made upon them by those fools in Hanoi was the general opinion of the patrol members. One of the members of the patrol stopped and took a piss. The stream fell less than two feet from Sergeant Priest. When he was finished, he hastened to catch up with his comrades without any consideration for the noise that he made. With the patrol gone, the two recon team members continued back to the observation position without any problems. There waiting was Sergeant Boynton and Corporal Yap. They collectively gave Krumins their data and thoughts on the area and situation. Daylight was coming over the mountain to the east. It was time to sleep.

Some twenty-plus miles to the southeast were Sergeant Thornhill and his Bravo Team and his Lao Scout. Captain Mac was trying his best to fit in with these professionals. Mac had always considered himself as a reconnaissance expert. He had quickly learned during the past few days of training for the Moung Soi recon that he was an amateur next to these guys. He hoped that he wouldn't screw up and get someone killed including himself. He sat with his back to the team watching the crude trail that they had used to get to their daytime defensive and observation position. Thornhill discussed what they had learned on their first recon of the camp. No surprises here, was the general opinion of the team, but that could change when they went into the camp tonight to confirm the plan and get a firm headcount for Arkangel. Now it was time to sleep. Mac had the first watch. He would be relieved in two hours by SP5 Brindle.

Chapter 31

TIME FOR A ROWBOAT
15 December 1972

The pilot briefing for the flight out to the Kitty Hawk was scheduled for 0600 hours but the briefing room was full at 0530 when Roman go there. All the pilots, crewmen and maintenance teams were in their seats ready to go.

Reichert walked into Romans' office where he was talking to BG Herbert, Captain Bayouth and Hammer. "We just went over all the birds for the last time and we double-checked the long range tanks. I can't do anymore for them, sir."

Roman looked over to Bayouth and quipped, "He and his crew have been out there since 0200 checking everything, not because of their dedication to the mission but for the reason that they will be flying over water in the birds."

The serious tone was broken in the room and Roman said, "Grab a cup of coffee, Tom. We have about thirty minutes before everyone will be in the briefing room."

"Look again, oh great leader! They're all in there now," Reichert said with a slight mock in his voice.

Hammer called the room to attention as General Herbert entered the room with Reichert, Bayouth and Roman close behind.

Herbert went to the podium and had everyone take their seats. "Looking around the room I can see the same faces that I saw almost a year ago. If there was ever a mission-ready operation this it! My only bitch is that none of you got sick or will let me have your seat like last time. I am going to be a nervous wreck on the Kitty Hawk waiting out the mission. Best of luck guys," Herbert said in a warm and confident tone as he left the podium.

Roman took the podium and looked out at the assembled flight crews and said, "Well, this is it. The advance party is in place and the Recon Teams are on site observing the caves and camps. It's our turn to hit the road, or high seas in this case, and join them. Everyone will be in the aircraft ready to go by 0800 hours. Watch for my crank which will be at 0810. There will be no radio call to start. We will take off in trail going to an echelon right after lift off. I will fly south for about twenty miles then drop down to tree top and proceed west to the Kitty Hawk. When you hear me radio, 'ROWBOAT,' form into a long trail formation. The Hawk will turn into the wind then tell me to land. I will turn for a left down wind then a half mile final. They will bring us aboard one at a time.

"The deck is pitching slightly but it's deceiving. Even in calm seas, the front of the deck is pitching up and down at least eight to ten feet. The Landing Safety Officer, the LSO, will be at mid deck with paddles. He'll guide you to a point at mid ship where the pitching is the least. He'll direct you to a four or five foot hover. Don't do anything or try to set down without his direction. He'll be timing the rise and fall of the deck to coincide with you. When he drops and crosses his paddles, you immediately push the bird onto the deck. Yes, it will feel like a hard landing, but it is much better this way than putting down against the rising deck. Now that is a hard landing. Once on the deck, put the collective full down and shut down the engine. Crew chief and door gunners get out quick and get the handling wheels on the skids. The Navy will hook you up to a tug and move you off the deck and take you down to the hanger deck. Stay with the aircraft until I call you.

"They'll get us aboard as fast as they can, then turn towards point Fang off Da Nang. Stay away from the Navy aircraft or try to take a tour of the ship. You'll be given a bunk, assigned a mess hall and latrine. Stay in those areas. Period! Yes, you can come up and work on your bird but I highly suggest that you get as much rest and sleep as you can. Sleep is about to become a precious commodity.

"Now, let's discuss leaving the Hawk. Thirty minutes prior to lift off they'll reposition the birds on deck lined up in staggered twos.

They'll be chained down at the cargo hook. When it's time to depart, we'll crank up at the same time. Watch for the LSO's signal. When you're up and ready, give a thumb up to the deck handler in yellow that will be at the pilot's door. He'll give you the current magnetic heading of the ship. Verify that your compass and gyros are set right. Once everyone is up and ready, the LSO will notify the bridge. They'll turn into the wind. Keep your collective fully down and blade tips tilted down slightly so the wind won't try to lift you off or throw your blade into your tail boom."

"Ok, now for departing the Hawk," Roman said. "When you crank up for departure, have your hover taxi light, navigation lights and rotating beacon on. Once airborne and at cruising altitude, I'll turn the hover taxi light off. You do the same. Just like we did at Big Casino and in night training, stay in a loose "V" formation, slightly high to the bird you are flying formation off of so you can see his navigation light. When we get to 'feet dry' we'll turn off our rotary beacon and go on to Ubon tactical.

"At launch time, the LSO will be watching the movement of the deck. He'll have a man holding the chain release waiting his signal. When the deck is rising, he'll signal for the chain to be released. Then one or two seconds later, he'll signal you to lift off with his raised hand. You immediately pull back on your cyclic and pull up slightly on the collective. I assure you that with thirty to forty knots of wind across the deck, you will instantly become airborne and beyond translational lift. Once you are 15 or 25 feet off the deck, you immediately fly forward and beyond the deck. You must be moving forward relative to the carrier immediately after liftoff or the aircraft behind you which are moving with the carrier will fly into you," Roman said with sobering tone.

"I'll be first off and I'll make a slow racetrack circle around the Hawk, ending up over-flying the centerline. As you take off, you'll form up on me in a V formation. Once up we'll turn west towards Ubon. Altitude will depend on the prevailing winds. No radio traffic except in a real emergency. Arkangel will be up and will have the winds over land. We'll use the Navy's weather data until feet dry. Over water, everyone stay awake and watch out for the other aircraft. The moon will only be of some help as far as seeing the horizon. If there are any clouds you won't have any horizon reference. It'll be very dark out there so stay alert.

"Refuel and a short rest stop at Ubon. They don't know us there so we can take our time. We just can't be seen by anyone who knows us. If you have to piss do it at the edge of the ramp. Once we get to LS59, pilots are to immediately go to the big tent set up next to operations and get some sleep. They'll wake you for your flight over the caves. Are there any questions?" Roman asked as he concluded his briefing. "OK, gang. It's Showtime!"

Roman walked over to Herbert and Bayouth. "For the trip out both of you can ride with me. The others will spread out between the other Hueys."

"What others?" asked Bayouth.

"For the trip from the Hawk to the LS59 we have one spare pilot and three maintenance men flying with us. We put one with each aircraft. Reichert will fly with me, the spare pilot in the second bird and a maintenance man in bird four and eight just in case we have a problem enroute. I guess that's it. Let's go get your gear and head to the flight line," Roman said to the senior officers.

At exactly 0800 Roman turned on the main battery switch, turned the voltage selector switch to "battery," turned on the fuel switch and started the Huey L-13 engine. As if in a chorus line, the other Hueys followed suit.

"Clark Tower, Grunt Air 6. A flight of eight requests take off instructions. Request south departure," Roman said over the VHF radio.

"Roger, Grunt Air 6. Wind 175 degrees at 10, altimeter 29.92. You are cleared from present position for south departure. Remain west of active runway. Cleared for takeoff!" came the metallic voice of the control tower.

Roman brought his bird to a three foot hover as the others did in succession. Then he took off to the south, climbing to one thousand five hundred feet. The other aircraft quickly followed suit and formed up on Roman's right side. After almost ten miles, Roman descended rapidly to 50 feet off the ground then turned to 285 degrees heading. Within five minutes, they had crossed the beach and were over water. Roman kept the altitude down low until he was certain that they could not be seen form shore or small fishing and sport boats. Then he climbed to a thousand feet so he could spot the carrier easier. He and the flight of eight had been over water for an hour when he heard a radio transmission over his UHF (ultra high frequency) radio. "ROADSHOW this is ROWBOAT, radar contact turn to 295 degrees for intercept. ROWBOAT has you seven miles from touchdown," the Kitty Hawk approach control operator said, pausing then continuing, "ROWBOAT weather 2,700 scattered, visibility eight miles, wind 250 at 15 knots."

"Roger, ROWBOAT," Roman replied then turned to Herbert and Bayouth and pointed towards the carrier that was turning to and into the wind heading of 250.

"ROADSHOW," the controller said, "ROWBOAT has visual. Contact Air Operations on three eight zero decimal nine, good day."

"ROADSHOW, going up three eight zero decimal nine, thanks," Roman replied then turned his UHF radio dial to the frequency given then called, "ROWBOAT, this is ROADSHOW with a party of eight on 295 degree vector for landing."

ROADSHOW, enter a left downwind and cleared for approach. Roman turned to head straight for the carrier. When he was a half mile away he turned to the right in a parallel but opposing course. After another half mile, he made two left hand ninety degree turns that placed him directly behind the carrier. He could see the LSO with orange paddles at the left center of the carrier. He followed the LSO instructions to the point selected for him to set down. Roman quickly looked at his airspeed indicator and noticed it was showing slightly more than forty knots but yet he was at a stationary hover above the Kitty Hawk.

The LSO watched the heaving deck and the helicopter carefully so as to time the landing so it would not be too hard. Suddenly, he gave Roman the signal to set down. The helicopter came down with a jolt. He was down. Roman quickly dipped the rotor slightly down in the front and put the collective full down. He went through the quick shut down procedures. The Navy deck personnel were like ants attacking a cherry at a picnic. Before Roman could finish and get out of his seat the Huey was being moved towards the aircraft elevator on the side of the carrier. He got out and stood at the elevator edge and watched his bird go down to the carrier hanger deck below.

He felt a hand grab his arm. It was Bayouth signaling him to follow him to the door leading into the carrier superstructure. They stopped and watched as the other Grunt Air Hueys came in and landed without incident. All of the lands were better than he expected, since this was one of the few events that they could not train for.

Chapter 32

UNFRIENDLY PERSUASION

It was just after 1:00 a.m. when the guards returned with Lieutenant Hoover. Hoover walked in under his own power with an air of authority and confidence. That angered Major Nguyen, he thought, without showing any outside of emotion. This man was not afraid. That would make his job harder. He only had one or two days before the order would come down to execute the prisoners who were not classified as potentially valuable to this government or the Chinese or Russian military. But he knew that he had an advantage given to him by Major Marquardt. It was only a matter of time to break this man down.

"Good morning, Colonel Hoover," said the NVA Major with a sly and evil looking smile. "Please take a seat. I would like to discuss your job as the Squadron Electronic Warfare officer at Takhli," said the Major watching Hoover's reaction to what he had just said.

Hoover made almost no reaction to the new revelation. He just looked up at Nguyen and said, "Don't insult the Major. I was a pilot, not some high priced ratio operator in back."

The Major was suddenly taken back by such an arrogant response. He condemned his own position as an Electronic Warfare Officer very skillfully and with an air that reflected truth. Major Nguyen thought to himself, "Was I tricked by Major Marquardt, or is this man a very skilled and intelligent man?" As he thought, he became angry; angry at himself for possibly being duped by one or both of these Americans. He felt like his competence had been put into question by these two criminals. He looked over at The Goose and nodded in a sideway manner. The big

Sergeant swung the hose hard against the American's head. The force knocked him off the chair and almost rendered him unconscious. Blood came out of a deep, four inch gash in his scalp. The flow was significant. Nguyen's anger had not been satisfied by the results of the first blow. He nodded again as Hoover got almost back onto the chair. This time he didn't get up. His eyes were open, but not moving. One of his pupils was dilated, the other was not. Nguyen knew that the Colonel had suffered a concussion or worse.

He had to change his tactics. He waited until he started to move again. Then the NVA Major pointed to the pulley and rope attached to the beam supporting the roof.

Like with Major Marquardt, the Sergeant tied Hoover's hand with the rope and pulled him up until his toes couldn't touch the floor. He straightened the shirt and grabbed the metal rod. He smiled as he put chalk on the rod. When he was ready, he stood behind and to the right of the prisoner awaiting the order to strike.

Major Nguyen put out the cigarette that he had been smoking while the Sergeant pulled the man up off the floor. He walked over and reached up and grabbed his jaw and turned his head so he could see his eyes. They were still unequally dilated, but returning to normal. "Now, Colonel, shall we continue?" he asked. There was no reply, only the blank stare in Hoover's eyes.

"What special training did you get as an Electronics Warfare Officer?" he asked. The prisoner looked at him and smiled, "I am a pilot, you fucking dink."

This time it was Major Nguyen that showed an expression. He was outraged! He looked at The Goose and nodded. The big man could see the anger in his superior's face and knew to swing harder than usual. When the bar hit Hoover's side, the sound of rib bone breaking could be heard. The expected screams and contortions came to the delight of Major Nguyen. Hoover had not fully extended his legs when the nod was again and again given. On the fourth blow, a slight pink cloud of blood came out of Hoover's mouth and nose. Nguyen knew that the bar had done some internal damage and the Colonel might not survive any more abuse with the bar. He was near unconsciousness as it was. Time was now a factor. He had to get enough information to qualify for a trip to Hanoi and Moscow or die.

"Colonel Hoover, that was a foolish reply. Let's review the facts. First, you are the head of Electronic Warfare for your Squadron at Takhli. You are not a pilot. You need medical help if you are to live more than thirty minutes. If you want to live, you will answer my next question," Major Nguyen said in a loud and ominous voice. He motioned to The Goose to get him down.

"Your question is simply," was your Squadron equipped with either the ALQ-71 or ALQ-125?"

The Colonel was laying flat on the floor, barely moving. Movement was probably involuntary reaction to internal and cranial pain from the sever damage inflicted by The Goose. He didn't seem to be coherent and mostly on the edge of unconsciousness. Major Nguyen observed his condition and became concerned that he might be beyond answering his question. He also thought that this man might be tricking him again. He was rather convincing in his attempt of deception. He would try once more. Nguyen pointed to the two pieces of lumber in the corner. Sergeant Goose went over and picked up the two four foot length of 4 x 4 lumber joints. He placed one underneath his legs, just above the knees and the second 4 x 4 just below his hip joint. This left a gap between the 4x4 of about twelve to fourteen inches. Once in place, the Sergeant stood back.

Major Nguyen walked over to the prone American and said, "OK, Colonel, we shall try again. Was your Squadron equipped with either the ALZ-71 or ALQ-125 jamming pods?"

Colonel Hoover looked up at the NVA Major and tried to focus on his face, but couldn't. He tried to say something three times before he was able to utter anything through the pain in his head and body. He knew that he might not survive the next few days. Finally, he did get works to come out of his mouth. "Fuck you, gook."

Enraged, Nguyen held up two fingers at the Sergeant, the pointed them downward towards the legs.

The Sergeant then jumped up as high as he could and landed with his big feet on the open leg area between the 4x4. This broke both legs in two places on each leg. The scream only lasted a few seconds before he became totally unconscious. The multiple breaks would make healing without skilled medical attention impossible.

The angered Major looked at Hoover and kicked him in the side. There was no movement or sound from Hoover.

"Take him back to his cell. I will deal with him tomorrow, if he is still alive," commanded the Major as he left the interview room.

Rex Marquardt was about to have an emotional breakdown despite his considerable pain. He could not bear the thought of Hoover being tortured because he didn't keep the faith. He wanted to die. Suddenly, the cell door opens and two guards dragged a lifeless Anthony Hoover into the cell and drop him like a sack of potatoes. His legs were broken and extended in abnormal angles. His head was badly cut and his face was barely visible through the dried blood. Rex could see the chalk marks on both sides of his shirt. Marquardt started to cry and beg for forgiveness, but Hoover was still unconscious. Marquardt took a dirty rag and we it so he could remove the blood from his face. He checked his pulse. He was still alive, but in very bad condition. Again and again he pleaded for forgiveness. Then he went into a dark corner to hide in shame. The two Navy officers came up to Hoover and tried to comfort and assist him as best they could.

Chapter 33

INTO THE ABYSS
16 December 1972

At 0700 hours, Arkangel took off from LS59 and flew an easterly route of flight some fifteen miles south of the caves at 11,500 feet so as to be almost invisible to enemy ground troops but within good radio range of the five recon teams. Each in specific order gave a detailed encoded report on their status and any important information concerning the POWs and the strike mission. This would be repeated at 1600 hours when Arkangel flew to Ubon to refuel and to be on position near Da Nang to act as its usual mission of flying command post for the Hueys flying from the Kitty Hawk to Ubon. Any problem or emergency would be reported to Arkangel who would take appropriate action or contact Navy Sea-Air Rescue in the case of a downed bird. With a relatively short report from the teams Arkangel returned to LS59 to pass on the information to Chief Abeel. They refueled the C-47 and did daily maintenance before getting some sleep. They would be up and flying all night.

Somewhere to the east on the Tonkin Gulf, the Grunt Air personnel were awakened and directed by the ship public address system to proceed to the mess hall for a final meal before their departure at 2000 hours. The Army had looked forward to meal times. The Navy really knew how to cook. The meals were special to them as they joked that Army chow was only slightly better than that given to PCWs. After gorging themselves they went to the hanger deck to go over their birds for what must be the fourth time since they came aboard the Kitty Hawk thirty hours ago.

They were all nervous and anxious to get the mission underway. Most were fine with the dangers of the execution of the mission deep in enemy held Laos. It was the night flight off of the carrier and over the ocean. An engine failure over water is generally a fatal experience. The sea conditions were bad enough once you could get out. You couldn't jump before the pilot stopped the main rotor blade or you'd become hamburger meat. If you were lucky enough to get out before the bird sank, you had the cold water and sharks to deal with. You knew that you would have to float in your life vest until Sea Air Rescue got to you. Hopefully, that would happen before the sharks selected you for a snack, like they did to the crew of the ill fated Navy cruiser Indianapolis during the last days of World War II. The Huey usually went down on its side after the blades stopped which precluded getting the life boat out in time.

The crews were crawling all over their birds at 1900 hours when the PA system announced, "Prepare to position Army Hilos on deck." Suddenly the Navy personnel came from nowhere and covered the eight Hueys like ants. The birds were taken up the aircraft elevator and positioned at the center of the deck area and chained down. Time to launch was now less than thirty minutes.

Dan Roman was in the ward room with General Herbert and Captain Bayouth. Roman looked up from his cup of coffee and said, "We're as ready as we can be and the recon teams report that the ground situation is static. I just don't know what else that there is to say, sir. I expect to see you in 33 hours with a bunch of smiling faces!" Roman concluded.

Bayouth interjected, "I understand that some of your people are concerned that the Kitty Hawk will not be at Crapshoot to pick you up. Rest assured the Navy will be there, promise."

Herbert was about to say something when the PA said, "Army pilots, man your planes."

Bayouth said, "How appropriate. That's exactly what was said to the Doolittle Raiders in 1942. You're in good company, Dan."

"Yes, sir," Roman said as he shook their hands and went out the door and up to the flight deck with a face full of concern.

A warm moist breeze hit Roman in the face as he went out of the island door onto the flight deck. He quickly went to his Huey and strapped in. Lieutenant Gillespie had already gone through the preflight checklist and reported everything a go. Roman turned and looked at his crew chief Sergeant Keller, who knew from experience what Roman wanted to know and gave him a thumbs up. Keller was standing next to the right side inspection panel with a fire extinguisher in case of fire on crank up.

"Army pilots prepare to start engines," bellowed the PA system.

Roman turned the voltage selector switch to the battery position to check his voltage, then turned on the main battery switch and saw he had a good power source. He then turned on the main fuel switch and primed the turbine engine cavity with some start fuel. He was ready.

"Army pilots, start your engines," the PA system commanded.

The eight Grunt Air Hueys all started their aircraft engines and prepared for launch. Roman and Gillespie went through a check of the aircraft systems to verify it would perform properly. It was good across the board. The Crew Chief Keller had gotten into the bird after it started and stuck his head between the two pilots to verify a good start and a flyable bird. Then he went to his seat and buckled up. He looked over at the inflatable lifeboat and hoped that it never had to be used.

A knock on the Plexiglas window in front of Roman startled him. It was the LSO. He was checking to verify that Roman was ready. Roman nodded as he brought his engine and rotor speed to normal operating level. A quick check verified he was a go! He then looked at the LSO and gave him a thumb up.

The LSO nodded then pointed his two paddles toward the Air Operations Center high above the deck in the island.

"Launch Army Hilos," bellowed the PA system.

Roman was ready! Blade tips slightly down and hand on the collective. He looked at the LSO and gave the traditional salute indicating he was prepared to depart the ship.

The LSO looked down the deck to get a feel for the pitching deck which was significantly more than when they had arrived in calm seas. His hands no longer had the oranges paddles. One hand was pointing up making little circles indicating to Roman he was about to go. The second hand pointed to the deck hand holding the chain quick release that held the Huey to the deck in the very windy condition.

The LSO was carefully watching and timing the deck so as to be at the top of the pitch cycle. His finger was going faster as he looked at Roman and pulled his lowered hand for chain release. Roman felt the Huey become light on the skids. The LSO quickly pointed his hand toward the bow of the ship indicating launch. Roman pulled back slightly on the cyclic to get airflow and lift under the rotating blades and pulled up slightly on the collective. He was instantly airborne. He immediately pushed the cyclic forward to fly away from the other waiting Hueys and off the end of the deck. After clearing the deck, he made a left turn to start a slow race track pattern so each launching Huey could catch up and get into formation. The launching birds quickly got into formation just as Roman made another left turn far astern of the massive carrier and headed back directly over it. This was done so each aircraft could verify that his gyro compass was properly set. They knew that the Kitty Hawk had turned into the wind on a heading of 185 degrees.

After crossing over the Kitty Hawk, Roman turned to a heading of 255 degrees and climbed to an altitude of 8,500 feet. The reported winds aloft indicated that 8,500 feet would be the most favorable cruise altitude Roman looked out both sides to verify that everyone was in their appropriate position in the "V" and was high enough to see the navigation red and green lights of the aircraft they were following in formation. Satisfied, he turned off the taxi light as did the others. The night became black. The pilots could only see the lights of the other aircraft as the moon was obscured by high clouds. Nobody could see the horizon. There was no point where you could see the end of the sky and the beginning of the sea. This made vertigo or spatial disorientation a factor with the pilots. High tension and a quiver of fear ran through every pilot on the controls that night. This was very difficult flying and there wasn't a dry pair of gloves that night.

Roman turned over the flying to Gillespie and got out his old stainless steel thermos for some coffee. He poured some coffee out of his all metal Uno-Vac thermos and set the standard Army coffee cup he had stolen from the mess hall on the console. As he poured out the last drops, he turned the thermos over to read the imprint on the bottom.

"Union Manufacturing Company, New Britain, Conn. USA." His Uno-Vac carried serial number T270SE1. Dan's late wife, Cindy, had given the thermos bottles to Dan and Toothman as they left for their first tour in Vietnam in late 1967. Roman smiled as he thought about the time he had gotten himself shot down and was picked up by a flight of Navy Sea Wolf in the Mekong Delta. He had run halfway to the rescue copter when he turned around and dashed back to his burning Huey to rescue his stainless steel Uno-Vac. He wasn't going to lose it to those bastards, even though he couldn't find the cap in all the smoke and fire. Now, many years later, he still had Uno-Vac less the cap. He became somewhat somber when he thought of his best friend getting killed on the Big Casino raid. Now he was on another high-risk Special Operation into the heart of the NVA rear area. Roman looked up through the Plexiglas above him at the black sky and silently prayed that he didn't get anyone killed on this mission. He mentally shook his head and forced his mind to refocus on the current mission.

Then he sat back and watched the formation and then looked out into the darkness and began to think of the many details of the mission ahead. They broke out of the clouds and could see lights on the Vietnam shoreline in the distance. The Administration and press may refer to it as pacified but to those who were fighting there it was Indian Country!

About twenty minutes later, Roman's concentration was broken when he heard the voice of Doug Alberts, Arkangel himself, was heard over his earphones. "Sundance, this is Arkangel with you at eleven five. I have a visual. You are six miles to feet dry; go tactical."

Roman smiled. They were exactly where they were supposed to be and on time. Roman hit his mike button twice to send a clicking sound to Arkangel in acknowledgement. Then he reached up and turned his rotating beacon off. This made flying more difficult but they now had lights on the ground to help them remain oriented in the formation. It also made it impossible for enemy agents to see or able to count the number of Hueys flying into the Da Nang area. Roman could see the lights of Da Nang to his right some ten miles away. He knew that every one in the eight Hueys had sighed a breath of relief now they were back over land and could take off their life preservers.

Roman was looking at his map and estimated that they were about ten miles from Ubon. He reached up and turned on his rotating beacon which would be required as they landed at Ubon. Then he changed the frequency on his UHF radio to the Ubon tower frequency. "Ubon Tower, this is Sundance flight eight miles south for landing," Roman said over the radio.

"Roger, Sundance, you are cleared for a direct approach to the south parking area. Stay east of active runway. Wind two eight five degrees at one zero, altimeter two niner decimal eight visibility eight miles. Be aware of numerous jets in the traffic pattern," the Ubon tower operator said.

Roman turned his Huey toward the airbase which was situated just across the Mekong River from southern Laos. He turned on his hover taxi light and landing light as did the others as they changed from a "V" formation to two lines of four aircraft. Roman looked at the parking area ahead, and he saw Arkangel parking on the north side of the area assigned to Roman's aircraft.

After they landed and shut down, all the pilots came over to Roman and Alberts who were next to the C-47. Alberts started briefing Roman on the events in the field and observations after two nights and one day. Generally speaking, there was nothing new to report. Alberts did present a problem to Roman of an immediate nature.

"The weather conditions in the mountains around LS59 are problematic. As soon as the sun comes up, we have fog," Alberts reported. "The mountains on either side are normally in the clouds in the morning but the conditions of ground fog in the valley present a problem for our scheduled arrival time. I recommend," Alberts continued, "that you take on a fuel and fly direct to LS59 as soon as possible. We would arrive before the fog forms if we leave very soon," he concluded.

"Fine, we crank in 45 minutes. That should be enough time to refuel and take a piss," Roman said with a smile. "My logic was to load up on fuel so we could have plenty on site. Since the General got us a fuel tanker we don't need to bring in extra fuel." Roman turned to the other pilots, "Ok, let's make this a quick pit stop."

Three hundred twenty five miles north of Roman, the recon teams and Lao Scouts were making a final reconnaissance of their assigned camp and the LZ that they would depart from. Nothing was to be taken lightly or overlooked. A lot of lives would depend on it.

Both Yap and Pao took the thermite grenades and claymore anti-personnel mines up to the top of the hill mass containing the Chinese anti-aircraft guns. They were hidden from sight but were easily accessible when time came in 24 hours. Twenty miles to the east, Thornhill and Mona Tong, his Scout, put out a series of Claymore mines that would create a deadly ambush if security forces chased after them. The first set of mines would hit the force from the front and both sides. Any survivors would naturally retreat back in the direction they had come from. A second set of Claymores would be detonated in such a way as to ensure no survivors.

Best was laying back and going over in his mind the last report from his other teams conveyed to him by Arkangel. Everything was going very well, just like it was planned. That was what worried him. The Big Casino raid had been going just like planned until someone overlooked a telephone receiver that had been knocked over and not replaced. That one item set off an alarm at the nearby security force headquarters. That mistake cost the team its Operations Officer Jan Toothman and one Huey. "It could have been worse," he thought, "but it shouldn't have happened." Since then he had stressed to his men the importance of 'attention to detail.' "Oh well, there's always something that screws up even the best of plans ... even this one."

It was an hour before first light and Roman could see the first traces of fog being generated in the low spots of the valley below. Alberts was right as usual. If they waited, they would have to divert to LS20A until noon. That could affect the carefully timed plan. He was glad they took the action they had. Now they would be in place, the long range tanks could be removed, the pilots could get some sleep and, in the afternoon, fly with Alberts over the areas and LZ they would go to tonight.

Alberts radioed Roman that he would fly into LS59 first and that they would follow. Clouds and fog were already becoming a factor in the higher elevations ahead of them. Roman acknowledged with two clicks on his radio transmitter. The other Hueys formed a single line known as a "trail formation" and followed Roman and Arkangel down through the scattered clouds to LS59.

Once on the ground, the birds were shut down just off the short runway on the west side of open area. The fuel tanker came by each Huey and offloaded all of the fuel in the long range tank, which would be removed. The tanks took up too much room and reduced the useable weight needed for POWs and recon teams. The mechanics first went to the tent with the pilots and got three hours of sleep before removing the tanks and going over the birds in preparation for the raid that night. This was a big-time mission and they had an awesome responsibility to make sure that every bird could do its job.

Before he went to sleep, Roman went into the operations building and checked in with Abeel and the others. He was mentally prepared for some last minute problem that could change or cancel the mission. There were no reported problems. That worried Roman. This mission was too complex and the NVA too unpredictable for nothing to have changed or gotten screwed up.

Abeel looked at Roman and Alberts and said, "You two look tired. Go get some sleep. I'll get you up at 1300 hours for a quick bite. Then you can take a sight seeing trip over the caves."

Roman nodded his head and headed to the big tent set up for the crews to get some sleep prior to the mission.

It seemed like only seconds before he had laid down when Roman felt Abeel shaking his shoulder. "Time to fly," Abeel said as he got Roman and Alberts up.

Roman asked again if there were any problems, only to find out there were none. The tank removal on the Hueys was almost complete with no mechanical problems. He finished his LRP rations and headed over to the Colt to join Alberts and the other pilots who would be actually flying the mission as the pilots in command. As they walked up to the big ugly biplane, Roman looked at Alberts.

"Hey boss," Alberts said, knowing what was on Romans mind. "It looks ugly, it flies like a cow, but it is as solid as a rock."

"OK" Roman said, "lets go see how much fire it draws from its previous owners."

Already on board were the pilots who would be flying the mission. They would have an opportunity to see the route of flight and see the Landing Zones that they would have to land in possibly under fire. Getting a Birdseye view was a real help. Alberts cranked up the Colt and took off to the south climbing to a safe altitude before turning to the north to fly near the deep valley that curved from the west to the east providing cover for the helicopters as they fly to the caves. It would also prevent the noise of the helicopter from the watchful path Lao and NVA personnel in Sam Neua and the cave area itself. Surprise was essential to the success of the mission.

After flying parallel to the valley, the Colt flew almost over the cave area. The pilots pushed their faces against the windows to get a good look at their individual LZ's. Then Alberts made a slow turn back to the north and then to the west for a second look. After that, the flight path looked like the plane was heading for the NVA captured airfield in the Plain of Jars. After it had established the obvious route, Alberts descended in altitude to hide his turn back to LS59.

After landing, the pilots gathered under the large shadow cast by the AN-2 Colt to discuss what they had seen. The general concern was the same for all the pilots ... tight LZ's. With the exception of Chief Warrant Officer Dodson, who would be going to Ba Nakay Teu, all the LZ's were barely large enough to land both birds at the same time. The task was made even harder by the nighttime aspect and the marginal amount of light from the moon. Flying the approach into the LZ between high karst and mountains added even more difficulty to the mission. If the element of surprise was lost and they came under fire, the probability of success was reduced to almost zero. They had to have complete surprise like they did at the Big Casino.

Roman acknowledged the problems and asked if anyone had any second thoughts. Almost in unison, they shook their heads in the negative. Roman smiled and then gave a new order of flight.

Roman would lead with Dodson behind him. He had the farthest to fly then he had Ditton and Donavan paired to fly to the main complex at Ban Nakay Neau. Waldo and Redding followed them. They had a problem with the narrow valley leading to their LZ. They had to fly in from the north in a high angle descent. They had to lift off without hitting the other bird in the tight LZ, departing back to the north with a very heavy bird. There was no discussion about the two Chinese 37mm guns. If they were not taken out by Corporals Yap and Pao, they were dead meat.

Roman finished the meeting by reminding them that timing was absolutely critical, so don't fall behind. Then each pilot departed and went to his aircraft and cranked it up to make a final systems check. Then they repositioned their birds into proper flight sequence for the mission. Then it was time to get some sleep before the mission. Roman knew that no Op Plan survives the first shot in anger. This plan was no different. Roman was not aware that the first such problem had already occurred. The team setting up for hot refueling at OASIS dropped a fuel barrel on the radio damaging it beyond repair. They only had one radio, which was an oversight in the plan. They could not advise Arkangel of any enemy activity or other problems affecting the mission. They were to become an unknown factor to Roman in this highly complex operation. A failure at OASIS meant massive mission failure.

Chapter 34

ANVIL EXECUTE
17 December 1972

It was a little after 10:00 p.m. on 17 December 1972 when Roman was awakened by Chief Abeel. Roman rubbed the sleep from his eyes and said "Strange, you don't look like Morgan. Abeel laughed and helped him off of the thin foam sleeping mat. "Anything new?" Roman asked, expecting some bad news.

"No," he replied "and that scares me. We got confirmation from OASIS that all there was ready and there's absolutely no sign of enemy activity. Best reported that the usual patrol made its evening sweep along the tract going by the two mountain caves. If they followed their established procedure, they'll go on a north and west route in the morning. That would put them far away. It doesn't matter as we'll be long gone before they even start," Abeel concluded with a big smile.

Roman turned towards Abeel and looked at him with a concerned look. "What about the men for the two anti-aircraft guns?"

Abeel looked at him and said with a cautious tone, "We have the best two Lao Scouts on the job. I only wish that we had two on each gun."

"Yeah," Roman said looking down. "Weight is the factor here. We just can't take more people on the mission. The birds are over grossed on weight as it is. If we lose a bird at one of the sites, I'm the only flexibility we have. I sure don't want to add to the number of prisoners doomed here. I have to get Yap off that hill before I can even respond to any problem. We just can't have any problems. Everyone has to do his job without exception."

Abeel smiled and asked "Want to eat?"

"Yeah. Have you had any maintenance problems come up?"

"Reichert is over there feeding his face. We can see if there is anything new in the last fifteen minutes. That's how long it's been since I bugged him by asking," Abeel said, walking towards the operations building.

Forty nine miles east as the crow flies there was activity at each of the POW sites and Chinese anti-aircraft emplacements. Each team had moved down from their daytime defensive and observation positions to the individual team's pre-strike positions. Each team was in a preplanned position to observe their assigned objectives. They could quickly overpower the guards silently and open the iron cell doors. Lao Scouts Pao and Yap had also climbed the Karst and hills that the 37mm AA guns had been positioned. Each had quietly verified the situation to ensure that there would be no surprises. Both knew how important their part was to the mission. General Vang Pao had sent each of them a personal message congratulating them on being selected by Major Roman for this important mission. The honor of his command and their Hmong Tribe rested on the successful completion of their assignment.

Pao had positioned himself just below the crest of the karst and about ten feet from the guard who was leaning against the sandbag revetment surrounding the anti-aircraft gun. He had set up a series of Claymore mines between the emplacement and the guard camp. The mines would kill most of the advancing guards and delay the others giving him time to escape down the karst.

He would join the others in assisting the POWs to the Hueys. He was satisfied with the situation and the plan. He only had to wait for the sound of the Hueys or unwanted gunfire from the cave entrance below. He looked over to his right at the large hill mass where the second Chinese 37 mm anti-aircraft gun was emplaced. He wondered if his good friend Yap was as equally prepared.

Corporal Yap also reconned the area where the guards were sleeping. He had carefully set out three Claymore traps in a crossfire ambush pattern. He would manually set off eight Claymore mines covering the tent area at the start. Anyone surviving the deadly blast would fall victim to the three other traps. That should give him the time and ability to get to the pickup point where Major Roman would be waiting ... he hoped. "No," he thought, "that is an honorable man and he will be there." I must not let him or the General down." Yap now had to position himself so he could quickly kill the sentry on duty. Then destroy the 37mm gun and two 12.7 automatic weapons. Shortly before 0130 hours, he armed his Claymores and taken his position near the sentry. He was ready to do his duty even if he must die.

Nineteen and one-half nautical miles southeast of Corporal Yap's position, Mona Tong had also made his recon of the Moung Soi POW camp and was in position to kill the dozing guard in the guard tower at precisely 0200 hours. He had no radio so he would use his emergency strobe light with a red filter on the light focus shield to let Gunny Thornhill know that the guard had been sent to meet his ancestors. Thornhill, Captain Mac and the other Bravo Team members would move through the two large holes in the fence made by Tong. Corporal Kong, the new addition to Bravo Team, would proceed directly to the barracks where he and Tong would silence the sleeping guards. Thornhill, Brindle and Captain Mac would be ready to cut the locks and force open the door to the chained POWs. All was in good order. It was a waiting game now.

Less than six feet from the two guards standing outside the door to the Ban Nakay Teu Cave, Sergeant Anderson and Sergeant Hanks had taken up position under a small Chinese Army truck already in the compound area, which had given to the Pathat Lao Army. Sergeant Sims had moved to the far right side of the concertina barbed wire barrier. After cutting a small hole in the wire, he crawled to within twelve feet of the guards. He laid flat on the ground behind several of the vines hanging down. Foxtrot Team was ready.

By 0130 hours, all of the Recon Teams had taken up positions that would permit quick kills and access to the POWs when the execute order was given by Arkangel. All preparations were complete. Only the slow hands of the watch moved now until 0200 hours.

Back at LS59, Roman and the crews moved to their aircraft. One last check of everything was made before strapping themselves into the Huey feet. It was now 0130 hours. Arkangel powered up the two big engines of the C-47 and took off. It climbed to its orbit altitude of

12,500 feet. Precisely at 0145 hours Sergeant Blanton, the Arkangel radio operator, transmitted one word: "ANVIL." Then fifteen seconds later he radioed "Alpha." It was replied by Captain Best with one click on his radio. Alpha was ready. Blanton went down the team list and got the same ready one click from each of the teams. When OASIS failed to respond timely, he became alarmed. He then told the Arkangel pilot, Lieutenant Jenner, that he had a "go report except a no reply from OASIS." Jenner snapped his head toward Blanton and stared at him in disbelief. He then said "ANVIL ready with no reply from OASIS." Blanton turned to his single sideband command radio and made the report. He then turned towards OASIS to see if there was any sign of trouble. The message was received by Roman at LS59. He suddenly had a cold chill come over his body. Without the refueling capability at OASIS, they would not have enough fuel to make it to the carrier offshore. The best they could expect was the shoreline. Roman pondered the situation and his options. He thought, "Should I abort or take a chance it's nothing more than an equipment failure? The PRC-25 radio was normally reliable but if they failed to turn it off after the last report the battery would go down. They could abort until they could find out the situation but that would blow the entire plan and mean certain death for the POWs. There was no time for consultation with higher headquarters or shifting this tough decision to a higher authority. Short of the Pentagon, he was it. If they went forward, they could be flying into an ambush and certain death and destruction. The Chairman would be burned at the political stake by the press, State Department weenies and others like that chicken shit Spike. The President would be under even more problems with the voters and the press. Roman just stood there silent and stared into the far distance without focus. It was commonly known by combat soldiers as the "1,000 yard stare." He looked up at the sky momentarily and then looked over at Coltrane and said, "Looks like a good day to die. Ok Sam, lets go earn our combat pay!"

At the same time, General Herbert and Capital Bayouth aboard the Kitty Hawk carefully monitored the transmission in the ships Command and Control Center. They said nothing. They stood silent and stared at the radio speaker waiting for Roman's decision to scrub the mission or give the command to Arkangel to execute the mission.

During the time Roman deliberated the situation, Arkangel flew near enough to get a visual sighting of OASIS. He could see the barrels laid out and no hostile fire or bodies. That didn't preclude the possibility that the team was dead and the NVA hiding in wait for the arrival of the strike force. If they were there waiting it would be a massacre. But there was no sign to indicate that possibility. He reported this to Roman, who was slightly relieved but not convinced that it was just an unfortunate glitch. Roman had already made his decision and the mission was on.

At 0155 hours Roman cranked up his Huey. The other aircraft in the strike package followed suit without any radio transmission. Abeel stood on the skid of Roman's Huey, next to Roman. Both remained silent as Roman and Gillespie went through the start procedures and readied the bird for flight into harm's way.

Precisely at 0200 hours Lieutenant Jenner pushed the transmit button on his radio and commanded "EXECUTE!" Then he turned to Blanton and said "Send ANVIL executed at 0200 hours to ROWBOAT." Blanton complied.

Aboard the Kitty Hawk, Herbert and Bayouth heard the execute order. Herbert turned to Bayouth and shook his hand and saying to Bayouth: "Time to call home."

Bayouth smiled and went over to the communications duty officer and handed him a prepared "FLASH" message to the Chairman advising him that the operation was underway.

Upon receipt of the execution order, Albert advanced the single throttle of the massive biplane and started down the runway followed by Captain Coltrane and Captain Dorsey in the purloined communist MI-8 HIP helicopter, both of which were destined to Moung SOI.

Roman shook the extended hand of Abeel and the recently arriving Tom Reichert. They got off the skid just as Roman lifted his Huey to a hover then took off to the northeast. The other Hueys followed silently.

On the ground the Recon Team leaders heard the execute order. They in turn gave the various hand and light signals that set the ground phase of the operation into motion. They had 28 minutes to overpower the guards, break into the cells, cut the locks and handcuffs off of the prisoners and move them to the landing zones.

Seventy two hundred miles away·in the Pentagon, the Chairman of the Joint Chiefs of Staff was handed a folder bearing the yellow TOP SECRET cover sheet. The Admiral opened the folder and saw the "Flash Priority" message from Captain Bayouth advising him that Operation ROADSHOW had executed the ANVIL operational portion of the plan. He looked up at his Aide de Camp and said "Pray this is not a major league fuck up." The Aide smiled and departed the office without comment.

Roman was grateful that the moon had silhouetted the Phou Phi Thi mountain also known as Site 85 from which they had launched the Big Casino mission earlier that year. That mission was successful except his best friend, Jan Toothman, had been killed. Toothman's loss still haunted Roman. Roman cleared his mind of Toothman's loss and focused on the mission in progress. He saw the valley that they had taken before. They would fly down the valley again. It provided both visual and sound protection until they got to the release point approximately three miles from all of the caves except one.

Roman pushed the nose of the helicopter over and descended into the valley. He looked at his watch, "Right on time," he thought.

On the ground the operation started smoothly and without problems. Corporal Moana Tong and Corporal Kong reacted like an over coiled springs when they saw the single red flash from Gunnery Sergeant Thornhill and successfully killed the two guards in the guard towers. SFC Gryner had cut a hole in the concertina wire leading into the billet and headquarters area. He led Gunny Thornhill, Captain Mac into the compound with SP5 Brindle following up behind them. Now that the only two guards had been silenced, the Scouts quickly joined Thornhill and the others at the door of the building where the thirty prisoners were chained and handcuffed to the floor and bunks.

When Brindle tried to cut the lock off the chained door, he dropped the bolt cutters making a loud noise. That had to alert the sleeping Sergeant of the Guard in the main admin building. Thornhill pointed to Tong and Kong, then to the admin building. They departed on the run. No use being silent now. Each of them went on opposite sides of the small admin building. The PL sergeant having heard the noise got up just to make sure it was one of guards dropping their rifle or something. He had no anticipation of a raid. He put his boots on and went out the door and turned into the approaching Kong. He became terrified and started to scream. The beginning of his outcry was silenced by the knife of Moan Tong. The airfield next to the camp was closed at night and there was only one guard, and he slept in the operations building. He could not have heard the noise of the bolt cutters or outcry, and therefore could not be a factor. The one phone line was on the exterior of the building and had been cut by Captain Mac just prior to the Execution order.

Thornhill quickly entered the building and advised the POWs that they were going home. They started to cheer but became silent when Thornhill raised his hand for silence. All three team members got out bolt cutters and started releasing the POWs from the restraints. As they got free, Captain Mac directed them to the front door and told them to wait. The two Scouts fanned out to look around for POWs that they had not spotted during their Recon mission. They got surprised at Big Casino by three missionaries they didn't know about. Their search didn't locate any others. They then started towards the airfield to ensure there were no hostile forces heading towards the rescue party.

Thornhill finished releasing his line of POWs and looked around them. He saw Gryner heading towards him, assisting one of the POWs whose foot had been badly mangled during interrogation. He nodded his head towards the door and Mac led the POWs out the door and on to the trail leading to the airfield. The sound of the incoming aircraft was already getting close. Mac looked over the POWs and saw a Filipino Major and two senior sergeants. He saluted an astonished Major as he moved them to the airfield and safety.

"So far so good," thought Thornhill.

Before they had arrived, the sound of the incoming aircraft awoke the sleeping airfield guard. He rolled over and started to get up when he saw a black shape against the dim outside light just as he felt the fatal knife blow to his chest. Mona Tong retracted his knife and cleaned it off on the guard's blanket before leaving.

Captain Coltrane landed the flying bus next to the operations office just as Alberts landed the Colt on the runway. He quickly directed the loading of passengers onto the two aircraft. He saw a beaming Captain Mac with his three countrymen. He yelled out to him and pointer to each of them and then to the Colt. They got onboard quickly as directed. Within a minute, they were all onboard, and they departed, leaving no man behind.

Captain Best and his team at the Ban Nakay Neua interrogation holding cell had carefully positioned Corporal Ky at the door of the guard hut where the two officers were playing a dice and pegboard game to pass the time. Sergeant Walls was on the opposite side waiting for the execution order to be given. Upon the word from Arkangel, Captain Best cut off the generator in the hut next to the kitchen. The two guards immediately got up and went to see what was wrong with the generator. The only thing that saw was their ancestors. Their bodies were shoved back into the hut so nobody from headquarters would see them and sound the alarm. At the same time, Gunny Stone with the skill of a surgeon silently cut the throats of the other guards sleeping in the kitchen hut. Then he went to the perimeter gate and cut the lock off it. Careful attention was paid by the team to not be visible to the headquarters 100 meters away. While it was doubtful that anyone would be looking at them at this hour, there was no reason to take a chance. Once in the compound area, they quickly cut the door lock and chain and opened the door. The sight of the brutalized field grade officers was shocking to them as was the stench of rotting flesh from their many wounds obtained during severe interrogation. As reported by their trusted Scout, Corporal Ky, there was a POW that could not walk. They had created a rope and poncho carrying device back at LS-59 for this very situation. Best led the fifteen ambulatory officers out and quickly around the side of the karst to a point that they could not be seen by anyone from the headquarters area. Gunny Stone and Sergeant Walls put the semi-conscious Major in the carrying device and took him out to join the others.

Captain Best looked at his watch and saw that they were three long minutes ahead of schedule. They would have to wait there out of sight before they could proceed to the LZ for pick up. He heard the sound of the Hueys and proceeded to the LZ using the karst as cover from prying eyes.

The sound of the two Hueys coming for them was muffled at first until they cleared the hills behind them then it was loud. The pickup was almost complete when they heard the shooting in the hills. The seasoned Recon veterans knew right away it was the sound of the 12.7 machineguns. They knew Roman and the four rescue birds were not having as much success as they had. They quickly loaded and departed to Oasis. As they lifted off, they saw the muzzle flashes over at Tulip. Anderson and Dodson were in hot contact. There was nothing for him to do but precede as planned.

SFC Richardson waited for the execution order with great anxiety and impatience. His team was in place and ready to go. He looked at his watch and saw that he had another two minutes to wait. He looked over to see if he could see Corporal Wang Sing Khan, who was to work up behind the guard at the gate leading into the compound and cave entrance. He was so well concealed Richardson couldn't even see him and he knew where he was. He checked his own concealment behind the vines hanging down in front of the karst and cave entrance. Five feet away was Sergeant White, another new Charley Team member who was to open the gate with the bolt cutters. Just outside the concertina wire perimeter was SSG Mason and SSG Ryder, who were to neutralize the two PL officers in the guard shack and the four sleeping in the guard quarters. As he looked for them, he thought of Corporal Yap seventy feet above them preparing to disable the 37mm and 12.7 guns. If he failed, they would not be able to escape as the big bore guns would savagely destroy Waldo and Reddings Hueys as they came in to pull them out. His visual search was interrupted by Arkangel commanding "Execute, Execute." The guard was silenced by Corporal Khan within seconds after Richardson flashed the red light go signal to him and the others. Before Mason could move into the guard shack, the sound of gunfire came from the area of Ban Nakay Teu. "Shit!" Richardson thought. "So much for surprise!" The two officers on guard also heard the gunfire and stood up to go outside and investigate. SSG Mason was forced to go to the alternate plan and shot them. He caught both of them with one quick shot each. SSG Ryder eliminated the other four with two bursts from his CAR-15. The team moved very quickly to the cave to cut the POWs loose from the restraints.

The Great Waldo and Reddings were just crossing the top of the hill and entered the narrow valley that the Daisy and Gardenia objectives were located. Waldo could see the 37 AA gun emplacements off to his right. There was white smoke coming up from the sandbag emplacement which he hoped was the 37's breech burning up under the thermite grenade. Waldo's eye caught some small flashes to the right of the gun. Those must be Yap's Claymores going off. Maybe, just maybe, Yap had succeeded and they would not be shot to pieces by those damned AA guns. He turned his attention to the small clearing some 100 meters south of the smoke as he reduced his airspeed to fifty knots. He shook his head at the very small size of it. It reminded him of some of the confined area practice sites back at Fort Walters during flight training. He continued to slow down until he came to a very high hover directly over the very south part of the clearing and then slowly started down trying to get as close to the trees as possible without hitting them with the blades. Redding was just a few feet behind him and he needed all the room that Waldo could give him. Waldo looked out and saw the blade tips start chopping on the leaves and branches. He backed away just slightly to ensure he didn't damage the blades and not crowd Redding. He lowered the collective slightly more to expedite the landing. His skids hit the ground and he was on the ground. He looked over at Redding who had also made it down safely. "Now where is Richardson?" Waldo said to nobody in particular over the intercom. "Look around and see if you have any contact with them," he said to his crew. He now had to wait for them. Every second on the ground gave the enemy a chance to blow their asses away. As always in combat situations Waldo's hands were sweating in his gloves as well on his forehead from the ever constant fear that goes with combat. "Where the hell are they?" he said in frustration as he looked in vain for them.

The sound of gunfire shocked Felderhoff and the other prisoners. His first thought was that the NVA was starting to execute the whole bunch of them. Then he heard some dark shadow of a man in the cave entrance say, "We're Americans and we're here to take you home." There were cheers, comments, and questions coming fast from the

POWs. Richardson said in a loud commanding voice, "AT EASE! Be quiet and listen to our instructions. We have only a few minutes to get you to the LZ."

As soon as Felderhoff was released, he bolted to the rear of the cave to the three Thai women. "Nimu! We are being rescued." SGT White was first to get to the women. He quickly cut off the cuffs and directed them to the front of the cave. "Go to the front of the cave but don't go outside until instructed," he said. The freed prisoners did as directed. The team prepared to move the POWs to the LZ. "Hopefully it would not be under fire," thought Sergeant Richardson as he looked out of the cave for approaching enemy. He wondered how the other teams were doing.

Richardson could hear other sites under fire. He also heard Waldo and Redding's inbound Hueys already arrive at the LZ. "OK, let's go to the LZ. If someone can't walk give them a hand. We have to hurry." SSG Ryder took the lead and the group followed with each of the Thai women being helped given their abused condition. He went to check the back of the cave just to make sure there was nobody left. He trotted to the guard shack to see if there were any papers or maps that could be of any value to the intelligence section. He picked up a few documents, and then he spotted the phone. He knew that the gunfire had ended the element of surprise so he picked up the phone and listened to see if anyone picked up on the other end. To his surprise he heard,

"Văn Phòng Tình Báo."

When he heard the intelligence office answer, a devilish smile came over his face. He couldn't resist the urge and said, "Hi, this is Sergeant Richardson with Grunt Air and I need eight large pepperoni pizzas delivered ... and hurry. We have a plane to catch."

The duty officer at the other end of the line was so shocked at what he heard he dropped the phone on the floor. For a few seconds, he just stood motionless looking at the phone laying there before he reacted. By this time Richardson had left the shack running to catch up with the group who had almost reached the LZ. The sound of the Hueys was quite loud and he knew the Hueys would be on the ground waiting before they got there. He caught up and started urging them to pick up the pace. Within two minutes all were loaded and the aircraft was airborne enroute to the Oasis. Richardson was pleased that all the POWs were recovered and no casualties.

SFC Krumins had just crossed the stream that traveled down the valley past Ban Nakay Peum (Daisy) and the Ban Nakay Enue (Gardinia) cave, as his Delta Team moved to take the single guard and two officers guarding the eight Air Force officers chained to the floor of the poorly constructed building. They were in the 1,000 foot by 800 foot containment area of the prison. The team had divided earlier in the day into two strike teams. The first team, which Krumins led, was tasked with the neutralizing the two armed officers in the building next to the POWs. The second team, consisting of SSG Priest and their Scout leader the venerable Sergeant Minh, who was to quick kill the guard who was in the same building as the POWs. He was awake and very attentive to his surroundings which made it more difficult to neutralize him. Delta Team had the temporary service of Sergeant Minh, who was the head of all Vang Pao's Scouts. He was Vang Pao's favorite Scout. He volunteered to replace Corporal Yap, who had been selected for the mission critical destruction of the 37 millimeter gun emplacement above the camp. SSG Priest had moved into position at the rear of the building. Minh was just outside the open door to the room holding the POWs and the PL guard. When the guard was almost to the door in his incessant pacing within the room, Priest was to lightly hit the back wall getting the guard to turn his back to the door. On cue, he hit the wall and Minh entered the room and garroted the guard so fast that there was only the noise of his severed head hitting the floor. Minh then stepped back outside and nodded to Krumins and Boynton who quickly entered the officer's room guns drawn, catching the two officers off guard. They raised their hands in hope that they would not be killed.

After cutting the handcuffs and shackles off the eight POWs, they led them to the open area which had been a vegetable garden. Sergeant Minh came and took control of the two officers and took them back to the POW room. They immediately recognized the fearsome Lao Scout and knew that they would soon be killed by this man. The fear was evident on the faces of the two officers as he handcuffed them spread-eagle to the bed. Then he cut his Grunt Air patch off and stuck it on his knife blade as Corporal Pao had done at Big Casino. Minh looked into the scared eyes of the two men. "You and your comrades in Hanoi have killed raped and tortured Laotians and our friends, the Americans, without hesitation or justification. Your viciousness is your pleasure and not your duty. That is the difference between our cultures and beliefs. Yes, today a number of your soldiers have been killed quickly and humanely as an act of war. Their deaths could not have been helped given the military objective. War and acts of war are unfortunate and a fact of life. Right now, you are scared as you expect me to kill you as the others were killed. The difference is that our tribal culture does not permit the unnecessary and wanton killing even the likes of you. You surrendered when we entered the room. Our mission will be completed by the time others arrive and release you, so your deaths at my hand will not serve a military purpose. Therefore, you will live." He said as he threw the knife with the Grunt Air patch sticking it in the wall. "That is to remind you who spared your lives so you can be with your families." He then went to join the others at the pickup point.

On the other side of the hill, the guards had been quickly dispatched to meet their ancestors. With the guards neutralized, SFC Anderson went into the cave at Ban Nakay Teu. He found that one of the Air Force majors had been brutalized the night before and both of his legs had been broken by his interrogators. A makeshift carrier was made up by Sergeant Sims. He and Hanks put the prisoner on the carrier between them and carried him to the Landing Zone. The security force had just arrived at the LZ when a Pathet Lao soldier spotted them and opened fire.

Above them Pao was having the best luck of all of the team assignments. He had detonated eight Claymores that surrounded the sleeping guards when he heard the gunfire below. Those guards would not be a factor now or in the future. He had already killed the guard standing watch next to the 37 AA gun. He pulled the pins on the thermite grenades on the 37 and two 12.7 guns and watched to make sure they stayed on and destroyed the weapons. He then went to the side of the hill and climbed down to help Sergeant Anderson.

Sergeant Anderson could hear the approaching Hueys. Judging from the sound, they must be at or near the Release Point. He grabbed the radio microphone and transmitted, "Six, this is Foxtrot. The dogs are awake and we are under fire at the LZ."

Roman heard the Foxtrot report just as they hit the Release Point. He gave the "Break" command at the Release Point so each Huey could go to its assigned pickup point. Then he said "77, provide fire support until I can get there." Roman then turned toward the hill that was to be the pickup point for Yap.

Yap was not without his own problems. He had just finished taping the thermite grenades to the 37mm and the two 12.7mm guns when the shots from Ban Nakay Teu were heard. This awakened the soldiers. They started to move towards the 37mm and 12.7mm machineguns when Yap squeezed one of the Claymore triggering devices. The deadly blast from the four Claymores cut down most of the advancing soldiers. The others regained their composure and once again started toward the emplacements. The five remaining soldiers cautiously advanced very slowly and in a deep-stooped posture, looking for the enemy. They were in no hurry to join their now departed buddies!

Yap, in the meantime, had pulled the thermite grenade pins on the 37mm gun breach block and one of the 12.7mm, when a soldier sleeping under a tarp got up. Surprisingly Yap had not seen him during his recon. Yap quickly shot the man in the leg. "Bad shot" thought Yap. He had intended to shoot him in the chest but he was off balance when he fired. The PL soldier jumped behind the sandbag revetment around the machine gun. Yap didn't have time to fight it out with him, so he pulled the pin on the last thermite grenade on the 12.7 and started running toward the pickup point. He could hear the inbound Huey. He also heard two successive detonations of the Claymore tripwire traps that he had set. Again, the Claymores killed or slowed the remaining soldiers momentarily. Yap ducked into some trees so the soldiers could not see where he was headed. The sound of Roman's Huey was getting very loud. He was close.

The wounded soldier that Yap had shot had quickly hobbled to the 12.7 and knocked the white hot grenade off the gun with his helmet before it was rendered useless by the molten white hot flame of the grenade. It was too late to save the 37 AA gun. He heard the approaching aircraft. He turned the gun toward the sound and waited for his chance to get even for the carnage the Americans had done to his friends.

Dodson had reached the LZ near Ban Nakay Teu and saw the situation developing. He directed his door gunner to fire on the gathering NVA and Pathet Lao soldiers at the edge of the clearing. The volume of fire forced the enemy troops to seek cover but some of them continued to fire on Foxtrot Team and the four POWs. Dodson keyed his mike "Six, I need some help over here. If you can put some fire on these bastards, I can slip in and get the team out."

Roman was lifting up to the ledge where he would pickup Yap when he got Dodson's call. "Roger that," Roman replied, "I'll be there in zero one."

Just as planned, Yap was there and quickly jumped into the cargo bay of the Huey. Roman lifted off and turned toward Dodson's position which was broadside to the 12.7, which was now manned by the wounded soldier.

The NVA soldier saw the Huey lift up above the brush and trees. When it turned broadside, the NVA opened fire. The first few tracers flew in front and below the helicopter. Then the gunner adjusted his fire putting the half inch thick rounds directly on the Huey.

Roman's door gunner Specialist Five Shack was the first to see the incoming tracers. He immediately turned his M-60 Machinegun on the 12.7 and started to fire. It was too late for some of the incoming fire, but Shack's return fire ripped the NVA apart, stopping the deadly fire.

Roman felt the 12.7 rounds hit his bird like a sledgehammer. The Huey had been badly damaged by the enemy fire, but the damage was not immediately detected by Roman or Gillespie. There were no warning lights or control problems, but the aircraft was starting to shake. Roman assessed the situation to be unknown and the bird flyable in a combat situation. He moved the cyclic control forward easily to head toward Dodson while trying to determine the extent of the damage. He knew that he had a serious problem, but what was it? He didn't know if the damage was in the blades, the mast, or pylon mountings. Only time and a sudden change in the condition would tell. Meanwhile, Dodson needed help. He was over the hill and at Dodson's location in less than one minute.

Roman saw the situation and directed Dodson to get ready for extraction. Roman flew to the south side of the enemy and opened up with his M-60s. This caught them in a crossfire. Dodson started in for the pickup when the NVA and Pathet Lao turned back toward Dodson, which presented an easier target and the bird that was about to steal their precious prisoners.

Roman banked hard left and flew between the enemy fire and the vulnerable Grunt Air 77 just landing for prisoner and Recon Team pickup. The Crew Chief, Sgt. Keller had removed his M-60 from its mount and had crossed over to the hot fire side to aid to the volume of fire. Roman could feel the enemy hits and kept looking for signs of fatal damage. The bird was holding together ... for now. Dodson got the POWs and team onboard then departed to the southeast. Roman wasted no time in getting out of the line of fire. As he departed the area, he could hear the other aircraft report successful extractions to Arkangel. Roman was relieved to hear that they had not lost any aircraft and all the terms were out with the POWs.

"Arkangel, this is Six. What is the count?"

"Six, all birds off and en route OASIS with all teams and sixty eight bugs. You are the only battle damage. What is your condition?" inquired Arkangel.

We took a few 12.7 and AK fire, but we're flying. We have some unknown structural damage which is making it a rough ride. We'll make OASIS if it's not overrun by the NVA. Beyond that, it's not certain. I have no master caution lights. Roman reached up and pushed the "Press to Test" button and did not get any response. He then said "I have no operable warning lights. No telling the extent of damage." Better get a status report to ROWBOAT before they have a coronary."

"Roger, Six" replied Arkangel.

Roman was flying a little higher than planned or considered safe in Laos due to his damage. He wanted a little altitude in case he had to auto rotate safely to the ground if things went bad. He could see the other Hueys flying their independent courses to OASIS. In the distance he could see the HIP and Colt descending to OASIS. They flew around the site before they landed to see if there were any indications of an enemy ambush. Coltrane saw the Laotian team standing by the fuel barrels as planned. It looked normal to Coltrane and he reported to Roman what he saw. He proceeded to land and hoped that his observations and judgment was correct.

By now, Roman could see the refuel point. He would be on the ground safely in less than four minutes. "Then what," he thought. "If we leave this bird on the ground where do we ride? There's absolutely no room for all of us on the other birds. They're badly overweight as it is. Even if they shorted the amount of fuel at OASIS, there still isn't enough lift capacity for all of us." I'm sure not going to become a prisoner, especially after two successful POW raids. It's either flying this bird out to the carrier or a 45 to the head," he decided.

Roman was the last to land. Refueling was started while he and the crew chief got out and started opening Cowlings and inspection doors to assess the extent of the damage. Most was acceptable for the flight from OASIS to the Kitty Hawk, but a sick feeling went through Roman when he saw a severed support frame leading to the transmission mounting pylon. "A real widow maker, he thought, "but so is staying here." "Hell", he said to himself as he climbed down. "It was flying OK when he got here, maybe it will get to or even close to the Hawk."

The other pilots gathered around and looked at the problem themselves. They were essentially silent as they could see the dangerous situation. It was bad and there were no good options.

"What are you going to do, Dan?" asked Coltrane?

"I'm flying it to the Hawk!" he said with determination. " They only got one of them so I could possibly make it. If it starts falling apart, I'll set her down and follow the Escape and Evasion Plan. There's no other choice for me other than a bullet in the head." There isn't room for my crew on your birds, so I have to fly or die. We'll follow the plan except I'll fly on the far left position. Sam will take the lead. If it gets bad, I'll head to the Song Ma and float to the Yellow Sea. You guys go on to the Hawk with the POWs. Just remember to pick me up when I get to Land's End." He concluded with an attempt at humor. "By the way, what happened to the Oasis radio? Why didn't they respond to Arkangel?"

Coltrane held up a crushed radio and responded, "A fuel barrel fell on it when they were positioning the fuel points."

"OK, Roman said. "Let's get out of here." Just then, Richardson, Pao and Thornhill Pushed their way forward.

"Major, we're going with you and Gillespie." Thornhill said, "Captain Coltrane can take Yap, Shack and Keller in our places. If you do go down, you'll need help. To be honest, you and Lieutenant

Gillespie are Boy Scouts out here in the bush. You'll need Recon types to get your asses out alive."

"Thanks, Roger" Roman said. "I appreciate this and I know Shack and Keller will also, especially if we have to set this bird down in the jungle." OK, let's get on the road to the Hawk."

The aircraft took off and quickly joined in a formation with the Communist MI-8 and Colt in the lead in hopes anyone on the ground looking won't get alarmed at the sight of the Hueys. Roman flew on the left side of the formation just in case. At first the Huey flew OK, and then the vibration became steadily worse. It become obvious to Roman that he had to go set down before the bird shook itself apart killing all on board.

"Six to Arkangel. We're off on schedule. Notify ROWBOAT of ETA. Advise that Grunt Air Six is executing RAINDANCE with five souls onboard then return to base," Roman said. "RAINDANCE" being the codename for a crew executing the Escape and Evasion plan.

"Roger Six, good luck," Arkangel replied.

"OK, Sam, take them home. I'm diverting to RAINDANCE," Roman said as he turned left toward a pre-planned position adjacent to the Song Ma River.

"Adios, Amigo" Coltrane replied.

Roman had not flown for more than five minutes before spotting the clearing in the middle of a thick patch of trees. He descended slowly, trying to keep the bird from breaking up before he could get to the clearing. The vibrations and shaking were getting worse rapidly. The vibrations had made reading his instruments impossible. He wondered if he could make the clearing.

The shaking was just about to tear the Huey apart when Roman set the bird down in a small clearing in the hills above the river. He felt comfortable that his arrival in this rural area was not noticed or of concern to the local Vietnamese. They heard military aircraft all the time as the Bai Thuong Airbase was just four miles away. No doubt they had been alerted of the strike force by the NVA at the caves.

Roman quickly shut down the aircraft and pulled out the last radio chassis from the console while Gillespie pulled the transmitter from its enclosure. Thornhill, Pao and Richardson established a hasty security perimeter while the Huey became useless to the NVA when they found it.

Chapter 35

SAM'S FLIGHT TO FREEDOM

Sam Coltrane watched Roman fly off towards the area near the Son Ma River. He felt sad for Roman. He had a perfect mission going, but would not see it to its successful end. He would be the man who would lead the mission back to the Kitty Hawk and freedom for the prisoners. "It's just not right," he thought. It should be Dan who led the group back to the Hawk. Oh well, he had the mission now, and they were a long ways from the Hawk."

He picked up his map and looked at it while his Dorsey flew the flying Greyhound bus. He could see the landmarks and they were exactly on course and on time. He kept the lumbering Russian helicopter as low as he could, but it was still high enough to be observed by trained military personnel on the ground. He hoped that their luck would hold a little longer. He spotted the town of Dang Tau off to his right. All was well, as he could see the lake in front of him. He would turn east towards the Hawk at that point. Sam's hopes were in vain. A NVA Lieutenant spotted the formation and knew that something was wrong when he saw the American Hueys flying with the NVA MI-8 helicopter and their own AN-2 Colt. He raced to the nearest phone to report the irregularity. It took almost ten minutes before he could get a telephone line that went to his headquarters, some 35 kilometers away. After what seemed a long time, he was connected. By the time they were able to get his commander on the phone, over twenty minutes had elapsed. He knew that by this time the enemy formation had reached the coastline, just north of Hoang Zu. The local commander immediately called the base commander at Bai Thuong Airbase and advised him of the reported American Hueys. Fighters were scrambled and sent southeast towards the estimated flight path. Once airborne, it took less than eight minutes to reach the coast. The aircraft were not in sight or on radar. They had to be flying very low. So the MIG leader started downward to find them. He could see the American fighters flying high in support of the B-52 conducting strikes on Hanoi. He wanted to engage the Americans, but his job was defense of the air base. Suddenly, he saw possible radar return some twenty miles offshore. That had to be the American criminals. He turned his flight of four MIG 21s towards the suspicious radar target. He continued to descend to a lower altitude.

The flight of four MIG 21s heading towards the incoming Hueys was not missed by Big Eye. Big Eye was the Air Force Airborne Command Post flying over the area providing radar support, early warning and strike package coordination. A controller spotted the MIGS and contacted the Kitty Hawk. The Operations Officer in the Hawk Command and Control Center (CIC) acknowledged and directed the Kitty Hawk's MIG CAP to engage the enemy and protect the inbound POW strike force.

Sam was feeling better since they had crossed the coastline and were going out over water. He looked back at the other birds in their flight to make sure they were still flying a tight formation for protection. "Looking good," Sam thought. He had turned in the discrete ratio frequency that they had been assigned for contacting the Kitty Hawk. He turned in 6901 in his IFF (Identification Friend or Foe) transceiver. The Hawk would see the specific number and know it was Grunt Air. They could give them headings to the massive aircraft carrier. Coltrane's hand had barely moved away from setting the IFF when he heard over the radio, "ROADSHOW this is ROWBOAT. Radar contact 38 miles from touchdown turn left to 088 degrees."

"Roger, ROWBOAT, 088 degrees for 38 miles," Coltrane said.

ROADSHOW, you have approaching enemy fighters approaching from your, six at 44 miles. MIG CAP engaging," came the unemotional voice of the Kitty Hawk controller.

"MIGS?" yelled Coltrane. "What fucking MIGS?

The crew chief looked about the rear cargo door and saw small black specs in the distance diving for the flight.

"Captain, I see them. They're attacking from the rear. Our goose is fucking cooked," replied the excited crew chief.

Coltrane thought for a minute then said over the radio. "We have MIGS on our ass preparing to strafe us so standby to scatter upon command." There was silence as the pilots prepared to execute evasive maneuvers to avoid being shot down into the cold Yellow Sea below.

The crew chief was watching as the number of MIGS appeared to increase. It looked like the four MIGS were being joined by six others. Then he saw white smoke trails going from the six new aircraft to the four MIGS. Suddenly, the four MIGS exploded and fell towards the ocean.

"Hey, boss, the Navy just splashed all four MIGS. We're in the clear," called out the crew chief. The voice of the controller said calmly "ROADSHOW, enemy traffic no longer a factor."

"Roger, ROWBOAT," said Coltrane as he saw the ships of Task Force 77 ahead of him. "ROWBOAT, this is ROADSHOW, tally ho! We have ROWBOAT in sight. I hope that you have the coffee pot on."

In the back of Grunt Air 77, Rex Marquardt could not take his eyes off Hoover. Hoover was regaining then losing consciousness. When he opened his eyes, Marquardt would lean over and say how sorry that he was for breaking the faith with him. Hoover saw but his mind was not registering what was being said by Rex. When he eyes closed again, a tear fell and the distraught Marquardt said again, "Please forgive me," as he unbuckled his seat belt, grabbed a hand grenade from SFC Anderson's harness and jumped off the aircraft. He pulled the pin and held the grenade next to his heart as he fell. He almost reached the surface of the sea when it went off. The end had been quick. The other pilots saw the body falling but didn't have a chance to make a radio call before it was over. There was silence and shock at what had just happened. The question that everyone had was "Why?"

"ROADSHOW, this is ROWBOAT, turn left to 075 degrees, assume a trail formation for landing on heading 168 degrees, wind is 28 knots with an effective wind over the deck of 58 knots. You are cleared to land. Watch for LSO instructions. Report LSO insight."

The Hueys were first to land, followed by Sam Coltrane in the MI-8 Hip. Lastly, was Doug Alberts flying the AN-2 Colt. It was something to see, Sam thought as he watched Alberts make his approach. He slowly reduced his airspeed to about five knots faster than the aircraft stall speed. When he had literally flown over the deck to his landing point, he eased the power back, letting the Colt descend and bounce on the deck a couple of times as he cut the power. The plane came to a stop in place, just as if it was a Huey.

Coltrane got out and went over to General Herbert and Captain Bayouth, who were anxiously waiting. They went below and Sam recounted the entire series of events.

Bayouth asked if they should send a rescue party after Roman before dark.

"No sir," said Coltrane. "Dan will expect us to follow the plan. Remember, sir, the NVA don't know he is down and behind their lines. Please stay with the plan. Roman will be hell to live with if we don't." Coltrane said in a plea.

Herbert laughed. "Yes, he would be very hard to live with if we don't."

"Now, sir, can we check on the condition of the prisoners?" Coltrane asked.

"Hang on," Bayouth said as he grabbed a phone from the wall mount. "Give me Sick Bay." He had a short conversation then hung up the phone. "Captain Coltrane, the medical officer assures me that all are in satisfactory shape. The Air Force Lieutenant Colonel is in surgery and will be fine in time. They really did a job on him but he'll make it. Now, we'll proceed toward the Philippines to move the prisoners to Baler." Then Bayouth said, in a loud and firm voice, "Just like Roman planned!"

Chapter 36

UP THE SONG MA WITHOUT A PADDLE

Back in the heavy jungle near the Sung Ma River, Roman followed Thornhill into an area that would provide adequate temporary cover and concealment. Thornhill sent Pao ahead as scout to recon the best route to the river. They would remain in the dense jungle until nightfall before moving to the river and downstream. They assembled the extra canteens, batteries and the few LRP rations they had. They would need to live off the land for some of their food needs. They each would have one LRP meal each day, at sundown to provide energy and vitamins. They would eat raw fish, fruit, and assorted jungle vegetation the rest of the time. Each man had a personal emergency radio and four batteries. That should be more than enough battery life for their trip down to the South China Sea. They also had an emergency strobe light when time came to signal any ship or aircraft coming to get them ... they hoped.

Pao came back after two hours. He showed on the survival map the route he found. He explained to the group that he had pulled some old tree trunks and palm fronds to the side of the river so they could get directly into the river without being detected. They would float downstream on two old trees covered with branches. It would look just like other trees and debris floating down river, especially in the dark of night.

Roman looked at Thornhill, then said, "Sixty-one miles on the river will take between sixteen and twenty hours actual float time.

Seven hours max per night at four knots river speed should put us at the Land's End rendezvous after three nights on the river."

"We could get lucky," Thornhill said, "and secure a boat and cut that by 75%. Hell," he continued, "we might be able to capture a small patrol boat."

Roman recoiled at the possibility. "That's risky. Someone will get alarmed if it turns up missing the next morning."

"Under power," Richardson injected, "we are only five or six hours to the sea. We grab it and rum downstream and scuttle it when we get to Land's End. No trace. Oh, hell, not much chance of getting one, but it sounded good."

"Let's get some sleep while we can. Ninety minute shifts. I'll take the first shift, then Thornhill, Richardson, Gillespie, then Pao."

Roman was as cold as he had ever been in his life. They had been floating downstream for over six hours. Hypothermia was setting in rapidly. The river was moving a little faster than he had predicted. By his calculations, they were moving slightly faster than five knots per hour. His confirmation was when they passed the ferry point at Hai Trach. The ferry carrying two vehicles and half dozen bicycles passed just behind them. The wake bounced them around a bit but didn't dislodge any of the leafy branches covering them. It almost knocked loose the fishnet that Richardson had captured seven good sized fish in. He was hungry and even raw fish sounded good.

Thornhill threw a small branch at Richardson hanging on the second log to get his attention. Thornhill pointed to his watch, then to a clump of trees. It was just after 4:00 am and it was time to get off the river and into hiding for the day. That was just fine with Roman, who welcomed the thought of getting warm again. As they pulled their logs to the shoreline, Richardson was signaling to a sandy area that they could leave the logs and they wouldn't float away with the current or be affected by the effects of high tide, which could be seen even this far up river. As they pulled the logs up on the sand, they made sure they looked like any other driftwood going down stream. While they beached the wood, Pao reconned the wooded area. He came back in less than five minutes and gave a thumb up sign. Roman nodded and Pao turned back toward the woods to lead them to their hiding place. Thornhill followed

Pao, then Gillespie and Roman, with Richardson picking up the rear.

Pao had found a good place to lie down in the woods that nobody had ever been to. It was rough, but defensible if discovered. Thornhill placed each person in a position to cover the four main directions plus the almost invisible pathway Pao had found into the small open spot. Pao quickly gutted and cleaned the fish. Raw fish was at best nauseating, but everyone was tired and hungry. There were no scraps when they finished. Pao also gave everyone a big hand full of cashews that grew naturally in that region. Even raw the nuts were great. Since it was almost dawn, they laid down in the center of the clearing in the "T" formation so reconnaissance aircraft could spot them on infrared. They laid there until 7:00 am, and then they returned to their assigned defensive positions and started their guard rotation and sleep period. The on duty guard would listen to the emergency radio for transmissions to them. About 9:00 am, Lt. Gillespie heard, "ROADSHOW, we have you spotted. CAKEWALK completed. All BUGS headed for SAND TRAP for dry cleaning. ROWBOAT is circling for pickup off Land's End." Gillespie was so excited he woke Roman up from a deep sleep to give him the message. Roman smiled and went back to sleep.

It was almost dark when the group ate their daily LRP rations. Roman thought how good these tasted, for once. "They were not always good in the past," he thought. "Then, again, anything is better than raw fish and those bitter roots Pao found. I'll never bitch about Army cooking again."

Once it was totally dark and most Vietnamese had gone inside for the night, the team moved down to the river. The logs were still there. Luck was with them. As they maneuvered toward the center of the river, Thornhill found a fast current. He halted the two groups in the current. This was faster than last night. "Tide could be helping," thought Thornhill.

About 10:00 pm, a patrol boat passed by some hundred meters away. They didn't even have their spotlight on. They weren't really looking for anyone. The NVA command must have thought that all the Yankee criminals had escaped with their precious prisoners.

Roman noted that they were approaching the Kien Trung Bridge. That would mean they were moving well over six knots an hour. The risk was still too great to consider taking over a powered boat since any disturbance or unusual events would change the entire dynamics of things. Nobody was looking for them, so why change that, especially since they were going downstream so quickly. He expressed his concern to the two pros in the field. Both Thornhill and Richardson agreed. They could always take action if forced to.

At this rate they would be at or very near Land's End by the time they would have to get off the river at first light. So they floated along, freezing in the cool water.

It was shortly after midnight when the patrol boat came back, as before, with no search or spot light on. They were in the clear again. Suddenly, the light came on and pointed to the shoreline. Everyone reached for their CAR-15 rifles just in case. Then the boat turned toward the shore and headed toward a dock right below the bridge linking Thanh Hoa and the north. It was docking. Everyone breathed a sigh of relief.

Roman and Thornhill were carefully monitoring their progress. As they neared the town on the north side of the river, named Bot Trung, it became evident that their pace had not only slowed, the tide was turning upstream. They would have to get off the river immediately or start going up country again. Roman could barely make out some marshy islands on the south side. They would go there first. They were only four and a half miles from Land's End - so close, but so far.

So, once again, they beached their logs in a little inlet in one of the marsh islands. There wasn't a great deal of vegetation to hide them on the island. They would have to go over to the mainland area. To do that, they had to cross the main road which was always dangerous, even at four in the morning. "The good news," Roman thought, "is that the mangrove and water is separated only by the narrow road." That was a reasonable risk.

The movement across the road was quite uneventful. Pao quickly found a small area for them to form their "T" and defensive position. As scheduled, they formed their "T" and ate the catch of the night. This time Pao had the fish wrapped in a large leaf with some form of bean sprouts inside the leaf with the fish. "Much better," Roman thought, "but it's still raw fish."

As the day before, the message on the emergency radio came on Lieutenant Gillespie's shift. This time the message was a question.

"Extract 0230 Land's End. Confirm one click." Gillespie had already awakened Roman with a soft kick with his boot. He told him and the now-awake others the question that had been asked. Roman looked at Thornhill for confirmation. Thornhill nodded. Roman smiled and said, "One click, please."

They crossed the road and entered the river a little later than usual. There was a lot of traffic on the road in the early evening. The tide was still outbound and strong.

It was a little before 10:00 am when the ominous sound of the patrol boat was heard. This time the spotlight was on and stayed on. The boat was obviously searching for something or someone as it approached. As they approached floating debris the machinegun on the bow fired a short burst into the debris in hopes of killing or wounding whoever they were looking for. They must have found their Huey. The boat turned towards them and increased speed as though they had seen something unusual. Just before it hit the floating logs and brush, it once again slowed and the machine gunner started to shoot at the debris that had been Gillespie, Roman and Thornhill's. They had dove deep under the water and away from the logs as the bullets hit the logs and water surrounding them. Then the gunner shot at the other log and brush. Roman thought at first that they missed them. They had gone deep and away from their floating ride to the sea. Satisfied that there was nobody there the boat went on downstream to the next clump of debris all the while searching with the searchlight. As the muffled sound of the departing boat was heard underwater, the men slowly surfaced for breath and to determine the situation, all except Gillespie. He had not come up. Thornhill and Richardson sized up the situation and motioned for the others to go back to the logs and continue downstream. They dove underwater and searched for Gillespie. They found his limp body just under the surface about twenty feet from the log. They brought him up and signaled to Roman that he was dead.

Roman lowered his head and almost cried. "Dammit!" Roman thought somberly. "Last time it was Toothman and now I've lost Gillespie. How many men am I going to get killed doing this type of work? Yes, this is high risk operations and there will be casualties, but a really good plan should not have any casualties. Where did my plan go wrong? Should we have done something differently to preclude this tragic loss?"

Thornhill looked over and saw the anguish and despair on Roman's face. He knew what was on his mind. He had seen that gut wrenching emotion many times before on the faces of really good officers that he had served with over the past twenty-nine years of service. He could remember seeing that same expression on Chesty Puller's face when he saw the combat casualties at the Hell Fire Valley in Korea. Puller had been directed to send a relief column from Koto-ri to Hagaru-ri near the Chosin Reservoir. The Chinese ambushed the 900-man relief force with persistent savagery. The losses were substantial and it deeply hurt the legendary Marine leader. Twenty years later he saw the same deep seated hurt and despair on Major Roman's face. He moved over next to Roman and said, "Focus on those that you have saved and will save. There'll always be death in combat. That's just a fact of war. Just make sure that every life lost is not in vain. Now get your mind off Gillespie and on how you are going to get our asses out of here alive."

Roman looked over at Thornhill and smiled as he nodded his head.

Richardson grabbed Gillespie's flying suit from the back. The cloth of the flight suit came up above the water a few inches but the body remained in the water. He then draped the top part of the flight suit over the log and then stuck his knife through the material and into the log. The log would carry the body downstream along with the remaining four crewmen of Grunt Air 6.

They had to work to stay close to the mud cay and shallow sand bars or be swept out to sea. Finally, Thornhill waved his arm to indicate time to go ashore. They released their logs once they got to waist deep water. They struggled through the mud and sand for over 100 meters until they were on solid ground. It was particularly difficult carrying the dead limp body of Gillespie. They had over 2,000 feet to walk to the pickup point. The problem was, it was wide open beach with no cover. Roman could only hope there were no guards, beach lovers, or fishermen. Walking in the very edge of the lapping sea water, they walked ever scanning for the unexpected. Finally, at 1:30 am, they had arrived. Thornhill picked up his radio and quietly said, "Ready for a taxi." They had to wait an hour for the extraction and hope that the bad guys didn't show up.

Roman could hear the sound of a high flying jets going east to west directly above them. That was probably a recon aircraft verifying the location and number of people at the pickup point. Nobody wanted any surprises when they sent in the vulnerable helicopters for the pickup. Then he faintly made out the sound of multiple jets to the southeast on a north-south orbit. He thought that had to be the fighter cap. This gave Roman a feeling that he just might get out of here with his skin yet.

Thornhill had the emergency radio to his left ear and a strobe light Marker in his right hand. He had a beam focus attachment so the flash of light that it emitted could only be seen by pilots that it was pointed directly at. No use advertising their position to the NVA.

Suddenly, Thornhill pointed the device out to sea toward the faint sound of an approaching helicopter. "Here comes the Navy to the rescue," Thornhill said in an excited but hushed tone. It was less than thirty seconds from the time Roman first heard the chopper before it was virtually on top of their position and landing. The bird wasn't on the beach ten seconds before Roman and his very tired and dirty team were safely on board and lifting off enemy soil.

They were feet wet and headed to the waiting carrier and safety.

Chapter 37

MANEUVERING IN A POLITICAL MINEFIELD

A knock on the President's door some 7,263 nautical miles east of Roman got the Commander in Chief's attention. "Come in Admiral," said the President.

The Chairman of the Joint Chiefs of Staff entered the Oval Office and came to attention before the President's desk.

"Stand easy, Admiral, take a seat. What do you have for me?"

"Sir, I just got the word that they got Major Roman and his crew out safely and in good shape about fifty minutes ago. They lost Roman's co-pilot on the trip downstream and one of the POWs killed himself en route to the carrier. It is so bizarre as he said nothing before he jumped to his death. He and Roman's co-pilot were the only losses on the mission. They're safe on the carrier Oriskany. They will proceed on to Clark for two days and then back here as you directed."

The President leaned back in his leather chair and joined his hands behind his head smiling. "That operation was picked cleaner than a Thanksgiving turkey," said the President with pride. "When he gets back here have Coroneos come in with him as well. He obviously had a great idea. I want to congratulate him. I know that he's had a rough time lately since he was relieved. I want to give him due credit for his idea.

"What do you think of this combined forced concept that Coroneos came up with in this Grunt Air unit?" the President asked.

"It's worked twice in critical high risk missions. It's hard to deny its success. The concept has real merit. I'd like to put together a

Battalion sized test unit based upon Grunt Air. It could be of great use in specialized and unconventional high risk situations, especially guerilla or terrorist type conflicts overseas."

"Admiral, I totally agree. Who would you use to head up this unit?" asked the President.

The Admiral quickly responded as he leaned forward in his chair. "With your approval, I'd bring in Brigadier General Mo Herbert and Dan Roman. We'll need to get some black funding from Congress. I don't expect too much trouble, if we can keep it quiet and not let the other branches get involved. You know the turf war problems. Herbert can get the project started but will have to go back to J5 at some point or the Marine Jack Lee will storm ashore on your carpet. By the time he has to go back Roman will have it well in hand and not need him."

The President agreed then quietly discussed the funds that would be needed. He smiled and assured the Admiral that the funds could be sneaked through with the help of Senator Kerr and his cigar-chewing buddy on the House Appropriations Committee. "I concur and authorize the project as proposed. But why wouldn't you just expand the existing Grunt Air unit?" the President asked.

"Sir, it has served its purpose but it has attracted unwanted visibility in the field and here in the Pentagon. It has served its purpose and time for it to move on to another area and another conventional mission. I'm having it redeployed to Fort Clayton in the Panama Canal Zone. There, it can continue to train for jungle operations and be of normal use in the short term. Later, once we've developed the primary mission objective and table of organization of the new unit, then we can use parts of Grunt Air as a test bed until we're prepared to formally organize the Special Operations Aviation Battalion at Fort Campbell."

"I assume," said the President, 'that you'll select Roman to be the initial program manager and ultimately the first commanding officer?"

"Yes, sir, that's my plan," responded the Admiral.

"Good," exclaimed the President. "I fully agree. I just had a thought. You say Grunt Air is on its way to Panama. If we expedited its movement by airlift, it could be used clandestinely to work with our Special Forces units in the Central America region and the tri-border area of Colombia, Ecuador and Venezuela? I've got some real problems down there and experienced air support would be a real help to our

Special Forces and CIA assets in the field." Perhaps Roman can go down and meet the local commanders in both areas and get a feel how best to utilize Grunt Air in support of their covert operations. He could do that independently of Grunt Air as a member of the J5 Staff. He can report his findings back to you and General Lee. Hell, I should send him over to Africa with the CIA team I'm sending to Central and Southwest Africa in late February. The Deputy Director of Central Intelligence and a couple of his staff are going over to access the situation. Then we can decide what we're going to be forced to do in that cesspool. Pick a country, Zaire, Serra Leone, Angola, Burundi, Tanzania … you name it, and it's a trouble spot that has to have some form of support or military advisors. Air support is critical to any plan. Bart Coltrane's Acacia Air Freight is flying some clandestine missions for us there but they are limited as to what they can do. We need our own dedicated assets over there. It's gratifying to see generations of American military heroes come along. Bart distinguished himself in World War II and today is assisting the CIA all over the World with his freight and shipping operations. Now, his son Sam helped plan the operation and lead the strike force with the POWs back to the Kitty Hawk. I see great things from him and Roman in the future." The President looked silently at the Chairman in contemplation, and then went on. "Now that I think about it, I do want Roman on that mission to Africa, Admiral. Make it happen!"

"You've embarrassed me, sir. I should have thought about that type of utilization of our proven Special Ops assets. They're perfect for that job in South America and Roman will undoubtedly work well with the CIA. I'll tend to that matter today," the Chairman said knowing that that was the exact reason he had directed, on his own authority, the Grunt Air expedited move to Panama.

"When are you going to transfer Roman to the Pentagon?"

"Actually, sir, he will be turning over command to his XO in the next 24 hours and could be here almost immediately. Perhaps we should put him on survivors leave until 24 January so he can rest from the mission. Then he can report to the J5. He'll need to go back after his visit here this week to pack up and take care of some personal matters and complete the change of command. He could make the South American evaluation upon return from leave and still make the Africa trip. By the time he gets back from Africa, the funds should be available to start the SOAB project."

The Chairman took a breath as he kept close eye contact with the President, then continued in a softer and more personal tone, "It seems that he's to get married. His bride-to-be is a CIA operative working for Acacia Air and has laid down the law on his next assignment not being in Special Operations. This job will qualify him for marriage under her terms," the Chairman said, laughing. "The real irony is that Roman is a skilled spook and he doesn't know that she works for the CIA under the cover of Acacia Air."

The President broke into laughter as he said, "Marriage to a CIA agent! Hell, he'll be begging for the peace and quiet of combat within six months." The President slowly regained a more normal composure and continued. "Well, Admiral, I'm delighted at what we've accomplished with this visit. Keep this plan going and don't lose momentum. I'll ask Bob Kerr to get busy on your funding. Get the Air Force to move Grunt Air to Panama on a priority basis. This could cure a couple of my political headaches down that way," said the enthusiastic President.

The Admiral stood at attention and said, "Thank you, Mr. President. I'll take care of these matters." Then he departed in a brisk walk.

Chapter 38

LAND'S END IN MY REARVIEW MIRROR

Roman lay on the floor of the Navy Sea King helicopter, completely exhausted. The tactical part of the mission was over and he could relax. He realized just how mentally and physically spent he was when he started to shake. His body didn't care that he had succeeded in saving all those poor devils from certain execution. His body was only concerned with itself and didn't care about the larger picture. The crew chief tried to get Roman up off the floor and into a seat for the short ride to the waiting carrier. His body just wouldn't cooperate. The crew chief got Thornhill to help him lift Roman into the seat and strap on the safety belt. Roman remained silent and detached from everything around him.

The helicopter made a slow bank to the right and he could see the massive aircraft carrier Oriskany through the cargo door. Then it completed its turn and raised its nose to slow down for touchdown on the deck. The helicopter was still shaking from the landing when a flurry of activity started around him. The crew chief jumped up, unfastened Roman's seatbelt, and helped him up and to the open cargo door.

Another crewman and several Navy personnel were helping him and his team out of the aircraft. Much to Roman's surprise, there stood Brigadier General Herbert and Captain Bayouth along with another Navy Captain and what looked like an admiral. As the admiral stepped forward, Roman regained his composure and straightened up to a position of attention.

"Welcome to the Oriskany, Major," the admiral said, extending his hand. "You have done a great job and we are proud to be a part of your recovery. Let's get below deck. We have strike package to launch against Hanoi."

Roman shook Bayouth's and Herbert's hands as they moved quickly to the door at the base of the carrier island. Inside the door, a Marine Corp Gunny Sergeant noted Roman and his team's arrival into the ship's record. "Welcome aboard, sir," the Marine said as he stood at attention.

Herbert asked if anyone needed medical attention before heading down the companion way and on to a small dining room.

"Major," said the admiral, "these people have a lot of questions for you and your team, and I have to let the Chairman know that you are safely aboard and get that strike package launched. So if you will excuse me."

Roman stood up quickly as did the others. "Thank you for the warm welcome, sir. We appreciate your getting us out of the frying pan."

"The pleasure is all ours. Now, please carry on," the admiral said as he left the room.

The admiral hadn't fully left the room before Herbert started talking. "Dan, you really pulled it off, and only one loss. That's incredible! I have so many questions, I don't know where to start, the mission or your trip down river. But first, let's get you cleaned up and let the medical team look you over. You want to get something to eat before we talk?"

"Sir," Roman said in a strong voice, "please, yes sir. Hot shower and some real food would be great. I'm fine and don't need to see the doc unless he has some medicinal whiskey for me. Before any of that, please tell me about my crews and the POWs. What happened after we separated?"

Captain Bayouth went over to the coffee urn and picked up four large navy coffee mugs and put a triple shot of whiskey in them, out of sight of Roman and the others. He returned to the table and handed each man a mug and asked, "Gentlemen, can I offer you some strong coffee?"

"Thank you, sir. This is the best coffee I have ever had," said Roman as he quickly drank the wonderful fluid.

"Dan," said Herbert, "there is just so much to tell you and the team! But, in a nutshell, the mission went just like you planned it. They arrived on the Hawk right on schedule. We did lose one POW en route to the carrier. For some unknown reason he jumped out of the Huey just before it landed. We are at a total loss as to why. At the same time the President resumed the bombings in the north. We're bombing the hell out of Hanoi. The NVA were focused on the bombings in and around Hanoi, which kept attention off you. We have been hitting them hard ever since then. The Hawk sailed directly to a point northwest of Baler. All aircraft and prisoners flew ashore and arrived at Baler at 1705 hours yesterday. There were none who needed better medical care than what could be provided here. They were flown to Baler as planned. Nobody needed to go directly to the Clark hospital, thank god." One prisoner had both legs set on the Hawk. He had some nasty head blows but nothing that couldn't be handled by the Navy surgeons on the Hawk. That was the worse medical problem we had to deal with.

"The Hammer and the medical team were ready and have everything in good order. Our security has not been compromised. It just doesn't get any better that this mission. Now, go get cleaned up and grab a bite to eat. We will meet back here in two hours. We can talk until our departure on the COD at 0700 hours, OK?" said Herbert, finishing almost out of breath.

"Yes, sir," responded Roman in a tired tone of voice as he got up to leave with the Navy escort.

Almost two hours to the minute, Roman returned to the ward room where Captain Bayouth was waiting. "Come in, Dan," he said warmly. "Coffee? Regular Coffee?"

"That would be nice, sir," Roman replied.

Bayouth slid an empty cup over to Roman and pointed to the coffee urn to Roman's right side.

Roman filled the coffee cup and looked at Bayouth and asked, Did they ever find out who the mysterious man was in Sheyma?

"That's right, you were gone before they arrested the man," the Navy Captain said with a shy smile. "As it turns out it was an old friend of yours. It was Lieutenant Colonel Jack Sweeney. He was the 7th Air Force Supply Officer who was interfering with your mission critical supplies last year before General Coroneos got pissed and shipped him to exile on Sheyma."

"I'll be damned! I thought that I heard that taped voice but I couldn't place it. It was very poor quality recording and the voice was obviously trying to disguise it. I can't believe he would still be that malicious as to go against the best interest of the country and the POWs," Roman said in amazement.

"Well, Dan, he won't be hurting anyone anymore." Bayouth said softly, "He'll spend the next twenty years in Leavenworth Prison for what he and his daughter did."

"Madison was his daughter?" Roman exclaimed.

"Yes, Madison was her married name which she used as a cover and professional name," Bayouth responded. Mr. Marcos over at the Philippine National Security Agency (Special Intelligence Department) found out from Captain Mac what the mission was and what she could have done to spoil getting their countrymen back. He became very mad and went to President Marcos and got him to back his plan to publicly try her for treason and espionage against the Philippine nation. They plan to try her and put her away forever. CBS had no effect and the State Department was told to go to hell. They plan to make an example of her. Life as she knows it is over when she gets to a Philippine prison.

Roman shook his head in amazement. "They'll let her go eventually. She'll drive the penal system personnel mad within a month. I bet the State and Justice departments cut a deal to put her away in a U.S. prison for an agreed upon time. I just hope they don't get done for a few years so she can learn to appreciate this country and what it stands for.

He looked at Roman and continued. "I can't tell you how happy everyone from the President on down is with this mission. It has proven your concept of integrated Special Operations aviation units. It has definitely gotten the Chairman's attention. I'm sure he'll want to discuss the matter when you see him," Bayouth stated in a soft voice. Captain Bayouth looked at Roman and studied his face before continuing. "You're going to be reassigned stateside when we get back. Do you have any preference on where you go or what you want to do?"

Roman was silent at first while he considered the question and his answer. He leaned back in his chair and hung his right arm over the chair back and looked directly into the Captain's eyes. "Well, sir, it's going to take me four to six months to evaluate our performance and correct the multitude of mistakes we made. Then ..."

"Stop there, Dan," interrupted the middle aged naval officer. "You are not going back to Grunt Air." Bayouth could see the shock in Roman's face and then he continued. "You've created an exceptional unit and accomplished not just one incredible rescue mission but two. It's time to move on and use your ability and experience in the advancement of the Grunt Air concept. You need to create that Grunt Air battalion or regiment that you talked about to Senator Kerr."

"How did you know about that bullshit lie I told Senator Kerr?" Roman injected.

"Well, it seems that the good Senator took the subject up with the Chairman a couple weeks ago," he said as he poured more coffee. "The Chairman has seen the merit of the Grunt Air concept put into actual practical application. He'll discuss the idea with you and Herbert when we get to Washington."

"Washington?" Roman asked in surprise. "I assumed that we were headed to Baler."

"No, Dan, the COD is taking us to Clark where we're catching a flight to mainland at 1830 hours day after tomorrow to see the Chairman and another of your admirers. When we get to Clark, you'll hand over command of Grunt Air to Captain Hammer."

Bayouth could see deep-seated emotion in the tired eyes and face of Roman. "Dan, I hope you concur with that selection. I think he and Coltrane will follow up with what you've started."

"Yes, sir, he's a good officer and thinks in an unorthodox manner like I do. He's a very good choice, now that I think about it. Why can't I stay here for a little to finish what I've started?"

"Dan, stop! The decision has been made! You could, however, elect to accept that job with the CIA. They've been screaming all the way to the White House for your assignment to them."

"So, that's it. Either play spook in some Eastern Europe shit hole for the CIA or be a Pentagon Warrior. I'm fucked wither way," returned Roman very dejectedly.

"Well, I wouldn't say that being the project manager for the development and activation of a Grunt Air type Special Operations

Aviation Battalion is being fucked. Most Lieutenant Colonels only get to dream about such assignments," the Captain said in a sly voice as he carefully watched Roman's facial expression. "Besides, you would get to work with General Herbert on the project, and I suspect that I'll also be along for the ride from time to time."

Roman leaned back from the table with a frustrated look on his face, the said, "That's fine for Lieutenant Colonels but I am a relatively new major and I've a woman in my life that I have to consider. As you know she's been pushing me to get out of Special Ops and go over to the CIA, or anything else but Special Ops. I don't suppose I could discuss the options with her, could I?"

"No, but I am sure that Morgan will be happy with either choice, don't you?"

"Yes, sir, she will," Roman said smiling. "Will I be stationed in the DC area if I go with door number one?"

"Yes," replied the naval officer. "You'll work in the Pentagon initially until we're ready to activate the Battalion. Then you will relocate to Fort Campbell."

"I knew when I made Major that my time in Special Operations was going to be short. I was destined to be a goddamned staff officer," chortled Roman. "I sure wish that I could stay with Grunt Air."

Bayouth leaned forward and said in a soft fatherly voice, "Besides a waste of talent and experience, the Pentagon doesn't put Lieutenant Colonels in Major slots." Bayouth watched Roman for him to realize the magnitude of what he is being told and react.

"True, but I am a Major and a junior Major at that," he said.

Captain Bayouth smiled widely and said, "You haven't been a Major since midnight. By direction of the President of the United States, you were promoted to Lieutenant Colonel. Congratulations Colonel!"

Roman recoiled in amazement. "You're shitting me, right, sir?"

"No. It's for real. I personally agree with the President's decision, too. If anyone ever deserved a merit promotion, you do," he said with pride. "Now, which door do you want?"

Roman smiled as Brigadier General Herbert came into the ward room with the Admiral.

"That's good timing, General," said Bayouth. "Our new Lieutenant Colonel has chosen to work with us on the new Special Operations Aviation Battalion."

"Congratulations on the promotion, Dan," Herbert said. "It'll be great working with you on the new SOAB unit. Now we need to gather up the others and get up to the flight deck for our flight to Clark. I had Hammer call Morgan to alert her that you would be home today and that we were going to celebrate tonight ... Big time! I was going to throw you a promotion party for you tonight that would go down in history but there seems to be a better reason to celebrate. Amy and young Bill Leahy have announced their engagement. That might be a better excuse and it won't attract as much attention to you and the unit. But we'll not forget the promotion either."

"Yeah," Roman said sarcastically, "celebrate being promoted to Pentagon Warrior!

John R. "Rick" Taylor (OUTLAW 3) is a decorated Vietnam veteran that served in the U.S. Army for ten years. He had overseas assignments in Vietnam, Korea and Germany.

His duty assignments included Aviation, Military Intelligence and Air Defense. His first-hand military experience gives him the background needed to write "The Caves." Today he is an oil and gas executive who has returned to post-war Vietnam to engage in petroleum exploration operations in the Mekong Delta. He has met with many former North Vietnamese combat leaders, including the legendary military architect of the war, General Nguyen Vo Giap. In the early and mid-80s he was an activist for the return and full accountability of POWs and MIAs in the Vietnam War. His job has taken him to central Russia, Chechnya, Turkey, Azerbaijan and Bosnia. He was principal in the early post-war Bosnia war damage assessment and reconstruction planning efforts. Taylor still enjoys his love of flying, as well as sailing and racquetball. He started flying at age 13 and later became an Army Aviator and flew combat missions in Vietnam and Laos. He currently lives in Texas. Rick is the author of A FEW BRAVE MEN and GRUNT AIR.

For sales, editorial information, subsidiary rights information
or a catalog, please write or phone or e-mail

iBooks
1230 Park Avenue
New York, New York 10128, US
Sales: 1-800-68-BRICK
Tel: 212-427-7139
www.BrickTowerPress.com
email: bricktower@aol.com

www.Ingram.com

For sales in the UK and Europe please contact our distributor,
Gazelle Book Services
White Cross Mills
Lancaster, LA1 4XS, UK
Tel: (01524) 68765 Fax: (01524) 63232
email: jacky@gazellebooks.co.uk

www.ingramcontent.com/pod-product-compliance
Lightning Source LLC
Chambersburg PA
CBHW070835020826
48982CB00019B/1252/J
* 9 7 8 1 5 9 6 8 7 9 7 7 5 *